Prophecy

BY

Kathy DeMatteis.

Table of Contents

Dedication

Be proud of your bravery!

This book is dedicated to all the people of the world who dare to be themselves.

Acknowledgments

The list of creative people to thank who have helped us with this project is overwhelming:

I really want to thank each one of you personally, but to do that would require another ten pages!

Thank you, mom and dad, for everything you have done to raise me into the woman I am today. Much of who I am is because of you both and what your backgrounds were.

My children for putting up with me,

My husband, Conrad, for handling me,

My mother-in-law for making me stronger,

Edward Gossett for formatting the book and keeping my head in the game.

Wolfgang von Baumgart for editing and inspiring me to think higher.

Shonta Gibson and Eddie Bell for the inspiration you guys give me to not quit.

Pete D., for everything you have done to help us over the years.

The list is long.

Cast of Characters

- **Young Charlotte Bennett**
- **Young Bob**
- **Tina**- Charlotte's friend
- **Mark**- Bob's friend
- Main character – Celebrity Cannabis **Chef, Charlotte Bennett**
- Supporting Character- Owner of the *Center of Love Club*, **Kennedy McCormick**
- Supporting Character-Tycoon, Co- owner of the *Center of Love Club*, **Clinton Tuckerman**
- **Karissa McCormick**, Co-owner of *Center of Love Club* (Kennedy's wife)
- **Jaxson**, Investor in the *Center of Love Club*
- **Nadia**
- **Eddie Bell** - Played by Himself
- **Olivianna**
- **Chef Shane**
- **Chef Paul**
- **Jerrod** - Spiritual Guru
- **Spike**
- **Betty**
- **Jane**
- **Monique Outerbridge** -Investor, played by herself
- **Imp**
- **Aunt Mabel**

Gratitude Prayer

Oh, My God! We did it! Thank you for seeing me through this project. The ups and downs and twists and turns. Everything you have been working through me for. Thank you. You hold me when I cry; you answer all my prayers with just a simple message. You remind me of the story of Hansel and Gretel with the little crumbs. I know it connects the dots. The stars show us all the time. Thank you for always guiding me.

This is what this meal meant to me. Therefore, I can no longer hide behind the sheets. I have wanted this for as long as I can see. I have wanted to marry people is what is inside of me. Try as I might, my plan did not work, perhaps it is because I was hiding how I worked. I am the Queen of Love, and I did declare that I would have a Dinner and Bed Theme in my dares. I wanted you to remember what you fell in love with. To make love through the nights on the sandy shores.

I wanted you to taste my love on your lips. The only way I can do this is a culinary tryst. You see I am not what I appear to be, but I do hope you will enjoy me. I want you lapping from my cup. What did you think the *Center of Love Club* was about?

In your mind's eye, imagine yourself lying on a bed of rose petals. Imagine flowers, the sounds of a waterfall, the call of the loons. Create your own place to heal you. There is no judgment in what you need for healing. Some pasts are not that pretty. Kathy S

Introduction

In the winter of 1990, my life changed. One minute, life seemed normal, and in an instant, it was turned upside down. By the time the dust had settled, my mom was in the ground, and I was promptly shipped from South Carolina to her best friend's house in Delaware. She had a daughter named Tina, who was my age. Her mom had helped me with college forms, and today, the letter came from Johnson & Whales in Rhode Island. I was going to culinary school!

With her mom away on business, Tina decided to play Cupid, as it was Valentine's Day. She arranged a dinner date for her boyfriend and a guy named Bob, who they knew I would love. Running my fingers over the gold embossed letters of the school, I could see my new life fast approaching. The more I lay on my bed daydreaming, the more I saw the shrimp dancing around in my head.

With my seven o' clock dinner date fast approaching, I ran into the bathroom and put on some makeup. My size four jeans slid up well, though I needed to lay on the bed to get them zippered. I grabbed a large sweater from the shelf that covered me from my neck to my butt. The hot rollers were ready, and I ran the length of my long, dirty blonde hair and secured them with pins.

Then, it was down the stairs and into the kitchen to get cooking. The dining room table was set with her mom's good crystal. As I pulled open the buffet drawers, I found a red set of tapers. Tina came around into the kitchen, running around in just a t-shirt and underwear, with her hair in hot rollers as she applied her mascara. As she rummaged through her mom's liquor cabinet, she pulled out a bottle of champagne and said, "Here, use this".

I found a tin bucket, put the bottle in, covered it with ice, and set it on the buffet stand. I stood there for a few moments as I scanned the table wondering what it needed, when it hit me. Flowers! I looked at the time and saw that it was 5:45 and as much as I wanted to run out that door, I knew if I did, there would be traffic galore.

I shrugged my shoulders and headed back into the kitchen, where a filet of beef was waiting. Wrapping the steak with a piece of hickory smoked bacon, they were ready for the grill. I set my sights on the shrimp I cooked an hour ago and peeled the shells off. I found pretty ice cream sundae glasses and decided to use them. I mixed some ketchup with horseradish and filled the glasses. Along the edges, my shrimp lined the rim, and in the middle, I placed some celery stalks with their fresh leaves protruding out over the top. I was so proud of myself as I placed them back in the fridge.

The eggs sitting on the counter were ready for their debut when I rubbed the large bowl with butter and wrapped some wax paper around the top. I had to improvise with dental floss to secure the collar, as no type of string could be found.

I almost used my shoelaces until I realized that they might catch fire. "Who's going to know?" I thought as I pulled the string out of the box, sniffing its minty fragrance for a minute as I tied it to the rim.

I grated some Parmesan and Swiss cheese, melted some butter, and tossed the flour, milk, cheese, and yolks until I had a nice creamy base. The panic began to set in when I heard a car pulling in. "They're here!" exclaimed Tina as she came running down the steps.

After scrambling to look for the beaters, I began to whip up my whites when a tall, handsome man walked in with a bottle of dry wine and a bouquet of grocery store flowers. His brown, wavy hair caught my attention as he walked straight up to me.

"Hi, my name is Bob," he said, "You must be Charlotte," he continued as he extended his hand. I was beyond excited with the flowers as I grabbed them. Under the sink, I found an old vase and away to the table they went. He must have thought I was crazy when I just grabbed the flowers and ran to the dining room to place them on the table and dim down the lights.

As I headed back to the kitchen, my egg whites needed a good beating. I placed the mixer in the bowl and watched as the egg whites turned into a mountain of white gold. I carefully folded in the two ingredients until I was confident that they were well blended before tossing the mixture into the preheated oven.

I shut the door and turned around as Bob handed me a glass of wine. "Hi, I'm Charlotte," I said, clumsily grabbing his hand once again.

"Drink up," he said as he handed me the glass.

I took the glass in my hand and downed it like it was a root beer when suddenly, the strange taste hit me, and out it came all over him as I yelled, "What the hell is this?" I still remember the splash of wine as it sprayed out my lips, the way he shielded himself from the spray, and my warm spit splattered all over his face. I stood there in utter shock and awe.

"My souffle!" I screamed. Turning to make sure it was still

okay, I sighed a grateful breath of relief and asked him if he was okay. Looking back at me, he laughed as he took off his shirt. I felt like such a fool as I ran for a washcloth, yelling at him to take off his shirt and wash it off.

My fingers trembled as he stood nearby, daring me to look straight into his eyes when Tina and Mark started laughing at me. I looked back at them and wondered what they were talking about when I ran back to the kitchen.

In the reflection of the windowpane, I saw that the curlers were still in my hair! I stood there, frozen in time. "This just can't get any better if I tried," I murmured sarcastically as I frantically dashed upstairs. Into the bathroom I went to pull my curls out.

Catching my breath, I looked at myself in the mirror again, exhaled, and said, "You got this." I made my way back down the steps, where, to my surprise, Bob was outside lighting the grill.

He looked up at me from the back door. "Damn, you sure shine up nice," he said as he poured himself another glass of wine and offered me a sip.

"No thanks, I'll drink a soda instead," I replied. I looked for the icy cold bottles that were in the case on the back porch, popped the lid and took a sip. I looked at the clock and saw that my souffle still needed thirty minutes. I thought for a few moments, and then it hit me that the shrimp cocktail was ready, so I made a bee line for the refrigerator.

I watched as Mark popped the champagne cork and topped off our strawberry-filled flutes. The bubbles tickled my nose as I let it come close, and the taste was not so bad this time as I took little sips.

The *Journey* music playing on the boom box had a very romantic way about it. Mark focused on what his true male intentions were for the night as he led Tina upstairs to celebrate their first year. The moment was beyond awkward as I stared over at Bob. "Let's get these dishes cleaned up," I whelped as I jumped out of my chair. I did not get two feet into the kitchen when he came behind me, carrying the dishes, as he placed them into the sink.

"Come with me," he said as he led me into the living room. His touch was stimulating as we sat upon the love seat with my knees touching his, as the fire glowed steadily.

My hands curled up into a ball as I made small talk while his fingers played with my hair. I felt like a Mexican jumping bean as my legs switched from one side to the other. One minute, I had one leg over the other, then back to the other side, then forcing my hands on my knees, trying to get the chatter to quiet.

As the avid lovemaking was happening above us, I wondered in my head if we were going to do the same thing that the couple upstairs were doing. I did not even know his last name. What if he has no protection, and I get pregnant? My mind was going in over a hundred different directions as my muscles began to spasm.

My body shook as I felt him lean in closer to me. "Oh my God, I just peed myself … I could just die," I thought as I crawled backward, mortified. My smooth Gloria Vanderbilt® jeans were so skintight that I could not get them off, even if I wanted to. I jumped off the love seat like a tigress.

"WAIT!" I hollered out as I pulled myself back around, totally caught off guard by the bulging energy in his jeans. His body pulsed excitedly as it pressed closer to my own.

As the psychological warfare inside my head raged on, I was even more thoroughly confused. "What is his last name?" I asked myself, as I heard another voice that said not to ask questions that I might not want answered. With that, I sighed as the soothing voice of my internal angels of love guided me forward.

Bob told me to relax as he brought me back to life with a kiss that tasted of honey and cinnamon. I felt my whole body open to him as his body eagerly pressed up against mine. His button flew down into my pelvis as he gently lowered me to the floor.

I felt myself spasm once again as I shouted out, "Wait, I have got to pee!" He did not seem to care as my body quaked and trembled under his wavelike heaves.

His mouth feverishly kissed my face as he exploded in his jeans, sending bolts of electric magic throughout me. The images of his chest that I saw less than two hours ago started flooding back in my head, and my mouth exploded in a river of fluid as our bodies spasmed in unison.

Lying there on the carpet, with my body still shaking, he confessed that he would shortly be enlisting in the Navy. A Seaman, he would be. Suddenly, I saw my entire life flash before my eyes: a lonely bride at home in the night. All my fantasies came crashing down, and I could not fall in love with him, at least not now.

The shrimp dinner was still sitting on the table as the unmistakable sounds of lovemaking upstairs lingered on.

I prudently kept my distance and let the night fade. I never even let him kiss me again. As I dreamed of Johnson and Whales in Rhode Island, the lure of Seamen is what scared me. The men in uniform enticed me. The whites and blues, as the men of the ship called out, "Make love to me." I closed my eyes and walked away, a chef I would be.

1
Charlotte's Web

It has been over twenty-five years since that night, working up and down the East Coast, gaining experience in different kitchens. In my pursuit of culinary greatness, I found myself alone at night, waking up in my bed and waiting for the time to pass. Looking over at the other side where a pillow lies, waiting for a head to be on it, I realized that all the years I have spent in the kitchen on the line have taken a toll on my love life.

Every penny I have made, I saved in the hope of one day opening my own inn in the western mountains of Maine. I have no husband or children, as my life has been mainly spent toiling in the kitchen, pouring my love over the stove. Instead of wiping noses and tears, I wiped the plates clean of any drips. I placed orchids on the China and prepared signature dishes that made them look like masterpieces.

I lived for this dream as I sat up late last night with the laptop by my side, working on my third cookbook. The knotted pine walls of the bedroom all seemed to talk to me. Endless miles of woods surrounded my camp on Lake Kezar in Lovell, Maine, which my Aunts Mabel and Anne had willed to me. Maine had just legalized the recreational use of Cannabis, and all sorts of inns and B&Bs have been incorporating the herbs in their operations. The *Moose and Deer Inn* is in Bethel, where my dishes are their secret weapon.

My editor, Siegfried, sitting in the dining hall, told me, "This next one is going to be a winner." I looked around the dining room, where every chair was filled, as people came from miles around just to stay at this newly cannabis-infused inn.

I walked around the dining room and could not help but notice Kennedy McCormick sitting in the corner. Looking out to the grounds, he was sitting in his usual spot with a plate of wings in front of him. Across the table was a tall, dark and handsome man sitting with him. Kennedy caught me staring at them as my jacket became caught on one of the chairs, and I nearly fell into their table, scrambling to get to my feet, as the ebony middle-aged man leaped out at me.

"Are you the chef responsible for these?" he inquired in a

firm voice.

"Yes, they're mine. Are there any problems tonight?" I replied.

"No, no, not at all," he said as he used the cloth napkin to wipe his mouth. He extended his hand, "Hi, my name is Clinton".

My hands began to sweat as nervous laughter came out of my throat, as I shook his hand and said, "Hi, I'm Charlotte." I looked into his eyes long enough to be mesmerized when I realized I was stuck staring. With his hand still in mine, it took a few seconds for my senses to come back. "I need to get back to the kitchen," I said, pulling away.

Back through the double doors, I headed to the stove, where another order showed up on the screen. Curiously, I peeked out the window towards their table and secretly longed to be sitting down with them.

I looked over at the man who owned the joint, Chef Paul, a burly man who I could swear did all the hunting himself with all the wild game on the table and their heads on the walls. After closing that night, I headed out the door and started my old Pontiac Firebird® on the drive home.

The rattle and shakes of the engine told me she did not

have long as I pulled down the driveway and headed back home. Amid the howling of the wind, as it flowed over the lake, the pine shafts fell with the snowflakes. My boots were covered in powdery snow as I made my way through to the back door.

I turned the electric blanket on high with fleece sheets on the bed and ran for the shower. My head was still wet when I jumped into the bed. My down blanket had more rips in it then I could shake a stick at as the feathers flew around the room. Some landed on my nose, and as I blew them off, I wondered when I would catch a break. The tiny light of the laptop brightened up my bedroom, and the allure of the computer virtually called out to me at half past three to write my next recipe. I had spent the morning editing when I looked up and saw that it was a quarter past ten, and I was running late again.

Racing around the back roads of Maine, cooking in the kitchen of a house that overlooked the mountains, with orders coming through the screen, my cannabis-savory dishes were making a lot of green. My herb-infused orange wings with ginger was one of the most popular items.

Each dish was a marriage of different strains of carefully chosen herbs with the intention of taking our guests on a tantalizing range. During the summer months, I am the head chef at a restaurant called *The Lobster Dock*, an old cottage that was converted years ago and sits overlooking the coast.

The beach out front attracted the kids as the parents sat and watched them play. How I longed for those sultry summer nights as I looked out the window and watched the snowfall.

It was after one in the morning when Chef Paul said, "Come on, stay the night with me."

I smiled back at him and said, "Tomorrow's Sunday, and it's my day off. I was going to do some more edits on my book."

"Whatever," he replied as he gave me a little kiss. "This could all be yours, Charlotte, if you just give me an inch," he said.

I looked back at him, with his brown hair all brushed to the side. "I knew it could be," I laughed. "It's just been a long time since I've been with a man," I explained. I sat down and switched my boots out, bundled up my coat and headed on out the back parking lot, where I tried to start the motor. The more I tried to turn the ignition over, the more I knew that my car was going nowhere. I reluctantly headed back and knocked on the door.

Chef Paul's head popped around the corner. Unlocking the door and letting me in, he said, "That piece of shit won't start again."

"She's not a piece of shit. Just you wait. Someday, soon, she will be running with ease," I retorted.

Chef Paul broke into hearty laughter. "Yeah, right," he said, "come with me".

I found our back-and-forth banter rather amusing. "Can I stay the night?" I blurted out.

"How much dessert did you eat?" he asked.

"I could eat a cookie and some ice cream," I replied.

He led me to the main dining room, where the fireplace had died down to low embers. He picked up another log and threw it in the fire as he headed back to the kitchen. He came back a few minutes later with some of our famous cannabis-infused hot chocolate and a can of whipped cream. He plopped down on the couch and stared at me intently. The restaurant was still warm, and I curled up on the one end. Pulling the afghan off the back, I wrapped it around me.

The alarm on the oven went off, and within a minute, Chef Paul was back sitting down next to me with a plate of warm, freshly baked cookies. Between the fireplace and the snow-covered window casings, the room no longer looked like a dining hall. The poinsettias lining the fireplace with the Christmas tree still lit gave the room such a homey feeling even though it was mid-January.

"What are we doing for Valentine's Day?" I asked him.

"Whoa, you're getting way ahead of yourself now, Charlotte," he retorted as he flopped back down on the couch.

I looked back at him and said, "What do you mean? It's January 15th, and we have less than four weeks to plan a Valentine's Day event!"

He looked at me and said, "I know what it looks like to have a woman seduce me. Are you sure you know what you're doing?" he said with an air of detachment.

"Of course, I know what I'm doing," I snorted back. *I thought he was referring to Valentine's Day at first, but then I realized it was not what he meant.* Reluctantly, I looked back at him and said, "No, I don't know what I am doing."

"What ... do you need to be taught?" he asked firmly as he ran his fingers through his hair.

"I don't need to be taught anything; I'm just a bit rusty," I quipped back.

The rush of the cannabis entered his pants, and I no sooner had my hands around his can of whipped cream when as he began to moan. Chef Paul sensed my reluctance and started to pull me closer to him when all I was thinking about was a Valentine's Day menu with a chocolate-covered banana!

I pulled my hair up from around my face as he pulled me closer, took three deep breaths, and closed my eyes as my lips touched the nozzle of his can. My body began to shake as I felt my legs quiver. A deep grunt came out of his throat, as I reached for my hot chocolate, thinking I could flush the taste out of my mouth. I felt my stomach churning, wondering if his cream was sour.

The moment of truth arrived when I started barfing up on him. Running for the bathroom, I put my head into the sink with the water splashing heavily as I regurgitated my last meal, wondering what the hell was I doing with this man. Not knowing what to think, I washed myself off and came back out.

"Impressive … How did you like your lesson?" he asked wryly.

I wiped my mouth again as my stomach did another backflip and murmured, "Apparently, I forgot to put away the cream," I murmured.

He led me into the main house and took me up to his bedroom. It was almost a quarter past three, and I was embarrassed beyond belief. He guided me into his bed, where a set of flannel sheets were crumpled in a heap.

"It's freezing like Siberia in here! Where is your electric blanket?" I complained, as I took my shoes off but left my clothes on.

"Right here, baby," he replied as he rubbed his hairy chest.

I laid down next to his physique, struggling to get warm and snuggled closer to him. The pungent scent of the kitchen infused all over the sheets kept my stomach bubbling. My eyes grew heavy, and I drifted off to sleep.

Later, I was suddenly awakened by the sounds of Chef Paul snoring at almost eight in the morning. Looking out the windows, I saw that another foot of snow had fallen. I heard the plow clearing the parking lot, as I sent my insurance agent a message, "Hey Rick, I need a tow truck," was all I texted.

I walked down the steps to the main kitchen, already feeling that the walk of shame had started, as I heard Jamie, the morning kitchen chef, bitching as she cast her eyes down towards me. I scrambled up some eggs and French Toast and headed back up the stairs to Chef Paul's bed. This was not exactly what I had envisioned when I thought I would have sex with him. I walked the hall back to his room, where I distinctly heard a toilet flush. I stepped back in and saw him standing naked, turned and looked away.

He rubbed his belly and climbed back under the sheets. "What, you never saw a naked man before?" he jibed. "What did you make me?" he asked boyishly.

"I made French Toast and scrambled eggs," I replied, as I handed him the plate with reluctance, cringing as I watched a large piece of egg-soaked bread go into his gaping mouth. "How was I?" I inquired, summoning the courage to ask him the question burning in my mind.

"In what part?" he asked laughingly. "Your French toast, or you are puking up my clotted cream?"

"Well, both, I guess," I muttered softly.

"You need more practice," he said, looking over at me with a grin.

"With what?" I replied, perturbed at his utter coyness.

"Both," he said, halfway snickering.

"BOTH," I responded with disgust. "What's wrong with my French Toast and eggs?" I asked as I sat next to him, not knowing what to do. The snow was obviously a factor, and my car not starting did not make matters any better. I slid back under the sheets and began to take off my clothes as I looked over at Chef Paul.

I felt his firm hand touch me as he made his way up my thighs. I started taking deep breaths as I told myself to imagine what I do in my dreams. The yearning voice of my mind beckoned me to open my legs wide. My inner struggle began as I trembled feverishly in anticipation and began panting God's name.

Chef Paul quickly climbed on top of me as he spat into his hand and rubbed himself. The full, crushing weight of his body made it hard to breathe. He pulled himself all the way out and asked if it was OK to proceed.

I smiled and nodded my head, reassuring him it was okay. It was all over in a couple of pushes when he suddenly pulled himself out and ejaculated into the sheets.

"No babies for me," he uttered curtly. Then, he asked how it was for me.

"How was what?" I asked, somewhat annoyed. "We barely got started," I shot back, looking up at him even more confused as I pulled the covers up over my head. "Is that all there is?" I asked myself in sheer frustration.

Appropriately, in the irony of the moment, I looked at my

phone for a reply from the man who has always been by my side, my insurance agent, Rick. From the time my "bird" hit the tree to my policy changes, he was always good to me. His text inquired as to the location of the vehicle, and I immediately responded with the address.

Within an hour, a tow truck came out from North Turner to take my car to the shop.

"It wasn't the battery," Daryl, the tow truck driver, said coolly. "I think she needs to be laid out to rest," he concluded before winching up my Firebird® on its journey to the back shed.

Pausing and taking a deep breath, I calculated just how much this was going to set me back. I bit the bullet and ordered a ride to Auburn. Shortly thereafter, I drove away in a 2010 Mustang® GT convertible with over a hundred thousand miles on it. "Yeah, I know. What was I thinking?" I mused. All I could think of was the construction project I had started on the house.

The winter months were long and cold as I strummed away on my keyboard when one morning, a blue jay made his first appearance out the window, announcing in inimitable cries that spring was here. The disaster in the bedroom at the *Moose and Deer Inn* was proof positive that my figurative head was on the proverbial chopping block, and I knew that once the season died down, I would be gone too. Then, I took another sous position in Auburn while I waited for my next cookbook to be released.

By late March, I began traveling the East Coast, selling my cannabis-infused recipes, making guest appearances at book signings, coffee houses, radio stations and podcast platforms, cannabis conventions, and any gig I could get my hands on. I was systematically laying the groundwork for my next phase by churning out recipes for my latest book when I made the long drive back home.

The good news was that I was making enough money to finally support myself without having to work three jobs. My internet sales were climbing by over ten percent each week, and I was finally bringing in paychecks that netted over ten thousand dollars a month.

2
Fallen Angel

The spring morning had given way with the snow melting every day as the additional miles on the old Mustang® began to take its toll. I began contemplating purchasing a new car this time and went back and forth between a 2020 Mustang® or the car of my dreams, a Cadillac® 2020 XT5. The icicles that lined my camp (that could kill or severely injure a person if they fell at the right time) were melting, causing a cascade of notes as they hit the wooden walkway.

The broken limbs and pine needles were ever-present as I cleaned my front beach up. Looking across the lake at the compound of camps, I waited for the day when Kennedy McCormick would show up again. I sat down on my back steps, running my coffee mug around my lips. My eyes had now settled on the compound of six, and I wondered how long it was going to be until the McCormick's were back here. I walked back into the kitchen to refill my mug, grabbed my binoculars, and flopped down on the daybed that overlooked the lake. Running the warm cup up over my face, as the whipped cream cascaded over the top, lapping the cream from the base to the rim, I begged God to find me a mate!

Then, it happened on the first of May. I watched the crew open the homes that sit in the cove. A man attempting to fish on the lake caught a yellow sunfish and put it in his pail. My eyes drew back to the woman on the beach, mesmerized by her curvy heart-shaped cheeks, as she bent down, tending to her flower bed. High-pitched, siren-like laughter emanated from her as the wild wind soundly whipped her long red hair.

Suddenly, her dress whirled up, revealing her scanty black lace thong, and I could not help but stare intently. It had been years now since I felt the soft hands of a woman on my skin. I watched intensely her plant, her pansies and herbs. I wondered how long I was going to torture myself with my lustful voyeurism.

The week went by rather quickly when I thought that I heard a rumble in my soul. As I listened more deeply, I felt the vibration increase, not the whine of the cat or the roar of the bear, but the naturally aspirated golden beauty from an era long past. It was the rumbling sound from the three-inch exhaust pipes of a Solar Gold 1979 Trans Am® echoing off the trees as it roared around the bend. After pulling into the long driveway, he parked the car.

My binoculars were glued to the window as I watched him on the steps, and I knew they were back for the season. Their lips met in a fireball of explosions as his tongue danced tantalizingly around her neck. A tingle went down my spine as I watched his right hand gently caressing her breast before teasing her with a playful slap to her buttocks.

I closed my eyes and imagined, for a moment, what it would be like to have Kennedy McCormick do that to me. He seemed to have a way of supernaturally commanding her to his will, and I longed to have that kind of spell over me. His wiry beard, t-shirt, and blue jeans that he always wears. I just had no idea what he did, but I saw him everywhere.

They have their own kind of reputation known throughout the town, as well as the nearby environs. With just a glance or a come hither gesture with his finger, she precisely obeyed his every unspoken command as I intently watched. I listened very carefully, hoping that the wind would carry their voices over the water and wondered why they seemed to be so different from the all-too-common unfulfilled contemporary couples, so par for the course in a post-modern materialistic society. I also pondered why it was that I was so stuck to my windowpane, trying to see what was going on across the lake.

The erotically passionate shrills that rang out each time I heard them make love utterly captivated my already vivid imagination, carrying it to much greater sensual heights in the heady spirit of the moment. I was practically hanging off the front porch dangerously near the tipping point as I watched the highly erotic spectacle unfold before me in the mid-vernal clime. "It's the best-kept open secret in town with my own private view, and it surely beats watching porn," I thought to myself as I watched with bated breath.

The penultimate excitement of peering in on them soon exacted its own toll on me, and I could not help wanting to touch myself as I threw my inhibitions to the restless winds. Rushing back to my four-poster bed, I intensely imagined what he was doing with her. Wishing that I had a live security cam trained on the love scene, feeding into my HD TV. Sighing for a fleeting moment, I dismissed the idea for purely legal reasons, as I had a professional reputation to protect.

I closed my eyes as I listened to the highly explicit sounds echoing off the lake. The ladies at the post office all swear that he beats her, but I am not so sure. I can hear the clamoring of lids in her kitchen as she no doubt has him taste what she prepared for him and the ensuing commotion as it bounced across the water into my waiting ears. My camp sat caddy-corner to their compound of six buildings that are mainly hidden in a cove by a massive amount of maple and pine trees, blueberries, and raspberry bushes, popping up rather haphazardly.

A bright fire of spiritual passion was always glowing on their beach at night amid the rousing sounds of the native drums, rhythmically beaten across the lake. Often, the local old hens would bustle around and call her names as they chatted it up around the post office and general store.

The thick woods often were my shelter, as I shamelessly spied on them, pretending I was gathering blueberries or tapping one of the maples that connected our lands. Always wanting to step closer to their world, I watched as she hung her sheets on the line, seeing a different set every morning. I sorely ached all over, knowing that she was getting "IT" every night while I proverbially wandered in a "loveless desert."

One night, I worked up enough of my courage to walk over to the camp. I just wanted to find out for myself. What if he is beating her? What if she needs help? The smoke from the chimney swirled through the woods.

The shining light of the full moon illuminated my path as my feet crunched down on the fallen leaves and twigs. The pine needles graced the front walkway as I encountered a sign that read: **WELCOME to the *Center of Love Club*.** It nearly took my breath away!

A beautiful white birch that had nestled itself as a chair of sorts sat rather close to one of the windows, giving me a grand view of their living conditions. The open space where the kitchen looked over the living room with a sturdy table made of a single slice of oak. The bark was still around the edges as platters of nuts and fruits dotted the dining arrangement. I watched them as they looked at each other, lovingly sharing and kissing, as they placed the food into their mouths. I nearly fell out of the tree when a flash of light burst out of the window, and I struggled to see.

I felt a strong electric tingle as I saw her long, sexy legs wrapped around his back as he suddenly mounted her right on the oak table. The hearth fire threw their fleeting shadows against the wall. While he slowly and deliberately thrust and moved deep inside her walls, she writhed, twisted, and moaned in ecstasy.

Struggling to keep my legs wrapped around the birch, I began to ride the tree trunk back up, shimming myself back up to my perch. From my angle, all I could see was hair that seemed to look like a ragged mane as it curled down his back. I kept rubbing my eyes, straining to see more, as her hands ran through her hair and her gorgeous body heaved, thrusting her chest into his face. The wine spilled onto the floor, and his eager mouth buried into her more than ample cleavage as I rode the branch some more.

It was as if I was looking into a night sky, filled with shooting stars of all types and colors or a diamond with its entire spectrum of red, orange, yellow, and blue. The scene spun in front of me, twirling in my mind and exploding out onto the walls. In what seemed like another flash of ethereal light, my eyes blinded as I tried to figure it all out.

Sprouting out of his back was a large span of black feathers as wings came out of his back. Descending onto her in an explosion of sights and sounds, I gasped out loud and screamed as the crack of the branch sent me tumbling into darkness.

I awoke to find myself on a bed, a hand-sewn quilt wrapped around my body. The room had a soft orange hue as the beeswax candle on the nightstand burned. I looked up, astonished to see the voluptuous woman over the top of me, running her hands along the side of my hair.

"Are you okay?" she asked me with the sweetest voice I have ever heard. I stammered to get my thoughts fully collected, as they obviously caught me spying on them. She handed me a cup and said, "Here, drink this."

It turned out to be a homemade infusion of cannabis and Chagas mushroom. I began to sip the tea, sweetened with maple sugar and a cinnamon stick. Many times, I have watched her pluck the mushrooms off the birches, and her herb gardens were always brimming with basil, parsley, and cannabis.

It is rumored that she healed her master with the emulsions that she made for him. I once got close enough to her at the post office when we happened to be there at the same time, and her flowing red hair and hazel eyes seemed to put me in a trance that day. Once again, I seemed to be back under the same spell as her fingers lingered down my cheeks.

Though I knew she was only mothering me, the intensity of her touch was overwhelming. I was rapidly spinning into her vibrant, enchanting, and enthralling world. If she was some sort of strange creature that eats women alive, then I would surely become one of her willing victims.

Frankly, I could not say that I would even fight to get free. As her dainty, soothing hands moved back up to my forehead, my eyes closed again, and I rapidly drifted off into a super-regenerative dreamlike state. Somewhere in the Twilight Zone, I heard her ask me if any part of my body hurt.

My head moved back and forth on the handmade goose-down pillow, and all I could seem to do was whimper back a blissful "No." I felt the heavy quilted blanket being pulled up over my body as I was tucked into the four walls. The burning candle was the only illumination, as the fireplace had long died down. The dim glow of red flecks gradually faded, as one by one, they burned out, taking me with them into a deeper journey of the mind.

The breeze of cool air spilling in from the window chilled me, and I burrowed down deeper into the mattress. I have watched the moon rise over the lake many times, but this time was radically different. It was as if I was on the moon itself, gazing down to Earth below and floating as the night wind took me to recesses of the lake I had yet to visit.

A part of me knew I should just get up and leave. The other part of me that has wanted so bad to be inside these walls just could not seem to muster the energy. It was warm and safe, and I just wanted to stay where I was and savor the most pleasant moment.

I closed my eyes, telling myself that it would be just for the next few minutes and that I would wake up and leave and promise never to come back. The next time my eyes fluttered open, I beheld that the sun had already come up over the lake. I could hear a melodious humming out in the living room as the scent of sausage and maple wafted into the room. I put my hands on the latch and, with my right thumb, released the lever, opened the door, and stepped out where I could see them drinking from a mug, rocking in chairs overlooking the water.

"Loading message ... Undo ... She arises," said Kennedy. There was something about the way he was looking at me when he asked, "Would you like a cup of coffee?"

I could also see by the way he winked at me that he knew why I was so interested in him. It was almost like he was reading my mind. I had a whole clear picture in my head of what it would look like as I blushed inside. I watched as the so-called "Town Witch" flowed over to me. Smiling, I said, "Nice breasts, Oops… I mean nice dress," as I severely fumbled over my words. Her cleavage was the biggest I have ever seen, as they nearly burst out of her nightgown. As she handed me a mug filled with coffee and sugared cream, I stumbled, trying to recover and opted to just take a sip.

"My name is Karissa," she said as she fluttered about the kitchen. "The man who carried you in is my husband, Kennedy," she stated.

I brought the mug of coffee closer to my face, desperately trying hard not to stare, though I was embarrassed by the whole turn of events.

"We found you outside lying on the ground, next to a broken limb off our tree," he said softly, as a slight smile escaped his lips.

"Oh, I must have bumped my head while I was hunting for raspberries", I mumbled out rather unconvincingly.

"We thought you may have bumped your head," Karissa said. "I saw the bracelet that said you have epilepsy, so we figured you must have had a seizure."

I was mortified but grateful that she gave me a recovery that was halfway believable when I said, "I'm sorry, I must have lost track of my hunt." "My name is Charlotte Bennett, and Bennett and I live across the way at my Aunt Anne and Mabel's old place," I said, reaching out to shake her hand with nervous energy. "I've been a chef for almost twenty years, climbing my way up into the ranks of the culinary industry," I continued.

"Did you grow up around these parts?" Kennedy chimed in, curiously.

"No, I grew up in South Carolina on the shores of Lake Wylie. I left when I was sixteen, when my mom passed away. I dreamed of going to culinary school. With few choices at the time, my heart was set on Johnson & Whales in Rhode Island. Why did you ask?" I inquired.

"Oh, I was just wondering; as you speak with a Maine accent, I thought you were native or something," he said.

"Ayah, I guess I do, I hadn't thought that I did. I guess, the lingo somehow picked up on me," I said. "So, where do you guys live in the winter?" I asked, desperately trying to change the subject.

Kennedy looked over to Karissa and said, "We do a lot of traveling for our business, but we hail from Delaware."

My eyes must have grown big for a second or two, for they were looking at me intently as if I knew something. I scanned around the room, hoping that some random feather would reassure me of what I saw when I took a deep breath. "I lived there for about two years, a long time ago," I stated.

Karissa handed me a bowl of granola over yogurt and fresh fruit when she asked in which part of the state I had resided.

Taking one bite, I looked at her and said, "I lived out in the country near Middletown. Did you put Cannabis in this?" I inquired.

"Yes, I did, along with some other little secrets," she said.

Beaming, Kennedy rose from his chair and said, "That little bowl of granola is getting ready to go public."

I was so excited that I blurted out, "I also cook with cannabis, but more on the savory side." "I work at the inn in the next town, and my recipes are starting to create a draw," I continued.

Kennedy's head looked up, and he said, "You mean the *Moose and Deer Inn*"?

"Yes," I replied.

"Well," mused Kennedy, "I think I may have already tried your food." Looking over at Karissa he said, "I do believe I ate there with a friend of mine one day," as he nodded his head rather mysteriously.

Suddenly, I felt like a deer caught in the lights, as I knew that he ate there every week, usually with a different person sitting with him.

I looked down at the floor trying to hide what I was thinking to myself.

"We are looking to acquire that property for the *Center of Love Club* Inns," said Kennedy.

My mind flashed back to the day when Chef Paul was trying to talk to me about purchasing the inn, and I began to wonder if that was the real reason that I saw Kennedy there so much.

He got up, placed his dishes in the sink, and said, "Let's get you home." He turned to Karissa, kissed her on the lips, grabbed the bag she prepared, and handed it to me. Inside, the ribbon-tied bag was a small sampling of chocolate cannabis-infused treats with a note that read, "These are for the Sacral, enjoy."

I looked at the note and thought to myself, "The Sacral … What is she talking about?" as I speculated further upon the ramifications of the impending business acquisition. I could virtually feel my breath cease as the thoughts I had been imagining all year long came back with full steam. I had a whole clear picture of what it would look like as I shook my head and said to myself. "NO, no, he's a married man."

"Follow me," he said as we walked out the back door kitchen that doubled to a showroom floor to his Golden Goddess, as he opened the car door for me and shut it tight. "She sticks sometimes," he said. Kennedy opened it again to make sure that it was firmly latched before he headed around and started her engine up after pumping her pedal a couple of times just to prime her motor.

As the car flew down the back roads, my hands held onto the paper bag, just like the lunches I had packed back when I was a kid.

"What is she talking about?" I asked Kennedy as he gently pulled the 1979 dream machine into my driveway.

"What do you mean?" he asked, slightly puzzled.

"What is a Sacral?" I questioned as I took the chocolate out of the bag and pulled the orange tin foil off.

He put the car in park and turned his body over towards me. My heart was nearly beating out of my chest as the man of my dreams began to show me by running his fingers from my belly button down about two inches. I nearly creamed myself when he said, "Your sacral chakra is located right here."

Coughing on the chocolate that was now drooling out of the side of my lips, my body reacted, and if I did not know any better, I would swear I just had an orgasm.

"The Sacral is an energy center or Chakra inside of your body that governs your sexual reproduction and oversees your libido," he continued to explain.

I closed my eyes as the thought of my carnal desires began

to flash before me.

"You have seven major chakras all running along your spine," he explained, as his fingers drew an imaginary line in the air up my body.

I felt Joules of energy surge through me, and I imagined what he could do to me as I bit into the chocolate ball that was calling me to finish what I started. He gazed and pointed at my old Firebird sitting next to the shed and asked, "What are you going to do with her?"

I looked back at him and said, "I really don't know but my fantasy was to clean her all up and make her run like a champ again."

The sounds that emitted from his lips and the way his voice captivated me had lured me into his trap when he asked if I would like a heart calibration.

I immediately accepted his invitation, not even knowing what it was, when he placed his left hand between my breasts and his right hand on my back in the center and instructed me to take three deep breaths.

Suddenly, a strange new regenerative wave of energy enveloped me, and I sincerely thanked him for showing me an easy path to a new and pleasurable healing experience.

Somehow, I had reached a new spiritual plateau as I shut the car door and watched him drive away.

31

3
Ball of Sacral Fire

As I unwrapped the second candy and let the chocolate melt in my mouth, I began to go on a mystical ride. Within moments, my body was pulsing, and I realized that the first one was strong enough when I felt a rich gong-like beat resound over my abdomen. I made my way down to the hammock overlooking the mountains and lake where I saw Kennedy standing on his dock looking over to me. Each fluffy cloud in the blue sky felt like a hand caressing my skin as waves of pleasurable sensations came over me.

In my mind, it felt like I was being massaged, as if some angelic creatures were floating around with hands shaped like leaves had a hold over me. I could feel the life force of the maple tree that was towering above me, calling me to new heights and daring me to ascend.

Lying back further, I began to hear a voice inside my head, lucidly telling me to relax, whereupon I took three deep breaths, drawing from my belly, as shades of red began to flow into my mind. Then, I began to see an orange hue as the colors flowed from one to another. At first, it reminded me of the orange shade of a Bird of Paradise before the waves of blues and purple washed over me. As my mind watched the flower open, I could feel my own body follow. The energy intensified, and I began to feel a bright ball of yellow hovering over my skin. I watched as the orb of light floated over me like a giant sun in the sky. It was almost as if I had been suddenly transported to Planet Eros and freed of unnecessary inhibitions. In my inner mind, the transcendental countdown to new awareness of an inner universe began inexorably and irreversibly.

As the ball of red energy expanded at the base of my spine, I felt a warm sensation overcome the confines of my physical body. The sphere of orange was spinning in front of me, pulling sexual energy from every region of the world as my body began to explode.

The fingers of a hand started to trace in my mind, and I found myself dancing in a sea of sensual emotions when the lure of the Sun rested inside of my naval. Tiny drops of liquid honey mixed with lemon zest danced on my tongue, and I inhaled its aroma.

My body trembled as I felt a strong tingling energy come in between my legs and travel up the center of my spine, reaching for my heart.

The pressure intensified as I felt the spirit of three energies engulf my throat, beaming bright blue lights. Allowing moans to escape my vocal cords as my hands clawed at the rope of the hammock as if it has a hold of me. The electromagnetic pulses were now throbbing at the base of my brow, churning and intensifying, as its vibrant violet hues settled into my third eye, renewing my mind with a new life force.

Just then, a bright explosion of lights erupted from the top of my head, bursting into thunderous convulsions from every orifice, as the mystical presence was completely inside, releasing its healing essence throughout my entire being. Waves of euphoria rose within as the orb of higher energy came over me.

Suddenly, I jumped from the hammock, and my bed lured me back to my thoughts of finding love. Often, while looking out to the lake, where occasionally, a boat would zoom past me, I hoped that a charming man would just happen to walk up my steps and take care of the growing need welling up inside me. I pulled my leggings off as I began to think of the dark and handsome man who was with Kennedy that day at the inn. As I hopped back into my bed, my hyperactive mind raced back and forth between the two men until I found myself sweating and panting like I had just run a major marathon.

I could hear the laughter again from across the lake as groups of men and women were gathering. There I was, with my binoculars, just spying on them instead of putting on my clothes and going over there. I read through the brochure that was tucked into my nightstand as I got ready for work. I pulled my new automotive pony out of the driveway and rejoiced as the roaring of her engine came to life.

My black convertible had red leather seats with a sound system that rattled my windows. I belted out song after song before Jewel Carter's *New King of Funk* was playing on the radio. As we sang the cords together, I made my way up to the city of Auburn, where a new wedding destination, B&B beckoned me.

The warm summer air hung over the lake as, each week, I watched a new group of people arrive and depart. As the couples gathered around the outside fire pit, I began to wonder what was in store for the group of lovers across the shore. The scent of cinnamon lingered across the lake as the sounds of laughter bellowed out. The enticing glow of the fire coming from each window at night sparked my own desire to see what really happens on these week-long retreats.

I firmly decided that I wanted to get to know them better

and determine exactly what they do. As I burrowed down into my bed, I told myself that the next time I was on that side of the lake, I would knock on their door and find out. Later, I awoke to a most powerful thought that told me to go to their house immediately.

As my Mustang® rounded the bend, I found myself in front of the *Center of Love Club* again. There, by the door, was a basket filled with brochures. The parking lot was full of cars, and I could hear people talking. As I walked up the steps, getting ready to knock, the front door opened, and Kennedy made his way out. He looked at me joyously as he opened the door to let me in.

I felt a bit foolish as I was standing there, feeling like a mouse caught by a cat.

He pulled out his wallet and handed me a black card that read, ***"What's Your Fantasy?"*** etched gold embossing, with the phone number boldly printed in script. As I put the card in my pocket, I watched him drive off, thinking, "If only he knew," as I shrugged it off.

Walking onto the front porch, where a window display case was filled with fruity pebbles cookies and white macadamia chips, I saw some gummies in pot-shaped leaves and peanut butter balls dipped in chocolate. I also saw hard candies that looked like stained glass and some banana and walnut muffins, all infused with cannabis. All along the shelves were gift baskets and soaps, massage oils, bath bombs and salts.

There was a plethora of crystals and bundles of herbs hanging from the ceiling when Karissa came out with a new tray of confections. Her face lit up brightly when she saw me as I fumbled for the money in my pocket. "Hi, Charlotte … Our guests have just arrived … Come on in and see what happens here," she said.

As I peeked through the open door, I saw some people talking. Suddenly, I felt my body start to sway forward as if something was trying to push me through the door. "I want to, I really do, but I am just super shy," I said as I picked out a few more chocolates. "Besides, I'm not in any shape to be dating anyway," I continued.

She looked up at me as I watched her weigh the chocolate and on the scale. "That will be $17.52 with tax," she said as she completed the sale. "You know, Charlotte, it's not what you think this place is," she said as she placed the chocolates into a purple bag with a white ribbon handle.

I pulled out a twenty-dollar bill and told her, "Oh, I know, I'm just not ready to deal with it yet," as I motioned for her to keep the change.

Smiling, I waved goodbye as I walked out the door and got back into my car.

The taste of the walnut and maple ball dipped in dark chocolate melted in my mouth as I headed back home. The hints of orange with a black pepper finish rounded out the dessert. It was so good that I was kicking myself for leaving the club. "I could have at least stayed for a few more minutes," I scolded myself.

The summer season was busy, and with my long hours at the restaurant and selling my cookbooks, I made excuse after excuse as to why I could not commit to the *Center of Love Club*, but the positive cash flow was good. I began to travel all over the country and hired a company that handled more of my social media accounts when I found myself again longing for love.

Soon, the Fall began its descent upon us, and one by one, I watched as each house was closed for the winter until only the last one remained open. "Odd," I thought to myself as I lay in bed wondering why they did not close the last house up. I just could not do it.

I went over the brochure in my hand as I read about the *Center of Love Club*. It is a place where you learn to love yourself while you advance mind, body and spirit utilizing the teachings of healing arts, guest speakers, a wide variety of instructors, vision boards and writing classes, all with an underlying theme of searching for your soul mate.

It starts off with a Grand Gala Meet and Greet. From there, you sign up for week-long retreats in states where recreational cannabis is legal until Mastery of Maschakra is obtained. "Traveling is what I am a master of," I said to myself as I continued to pine out the window, watching the leaves begin to turn colors. I supposed that I would not mind taking classes and meeting new people at world-class resorts, and it sounded like something right up my alley as I continued to dream about joining. I navigated through the website, and I saw that the next step was to sign up for their monthly present club at $19.99 a month.

The package arrived a week later, and inside, I found a container of pleasant surprises. Each month, another present came, and before I knew it, I fell in love with each gift. As I lit the paraffin wax aromatherapy candle by ***FooBellas***®, the music played, and I was guided step by step. I opened the container, where the scent of jasmine and lavender with gold specks took hold of me.

I bit into the cannabis-infused chocolate ganache and let it melt on my tongue. Its rich dark chocolate gave way to a toasted almond, with flakes of coconut, sending my sense of taste to a whole new level. As my tongue licked its creamy center, I imagined myself cooking inside the *Center of Love Club* kitchen.

As the water filled up the tub, I unwrapped the ***Goddess Within* soap** and began to touch myself. I felt the cleansing of my skin as my new flesh was revealed, and the voice guided me to each area of my body. With the shimmer of the gold, my body began to sparkle, and I felt a heightened sense of smell.

The cannabis and amaretto-infused chocolate that made up the second confection soon took me to the next level. The circular motion of my hands glided over my skin, meshed with the strings of the violin. Each note sounded like it had been orchestrated just for me. I got lost in the sounds and succumbed as the bow ran down the length of the strings. I was painfully aware that I was captivated by the vibration it made as the friction grew impatient, sending me to new heights, until the crescendo of stings mixed with the piano tempted me again.

It really feels like it is only letting me catch my breath before descending upon me again, teasing me with its chords as it vibrates throughout my body. I began to glow in a state of utter tranquility when the sensation suddenly shifted indescribably. BAM! The eruptions came back in waves of increased intensity as the water splashed onto my hardwood floors, whereupon I was completely lost in ecstasy!

42

4

The Frustration Mounts

Strumming my fingers along the black card with the gold embossing, I looked out the window across the pond. Listening as the sounds of love were heard around the cove as Kennedy made Karissa purr. Oh, the vibration of shrieks startled even the owls as I crumpled up my soaked bed cover and headed to the washing machine.

Menopause was steadily driving me insane, as it sounds like a "pause on MEN!" This made absolutely no sense as I opened the lid and began stuffing my comforter inside the machine. The more I stuffed my blanket down, the more I screamed. I did not want a pause of the men; I wanted men turned on! As I closed the lid and hit the button, I listened closely as the water barely trickled from the relic sitting in the hall closet. "Great! Now what?" I said, opening the lid.

Already frustrated with where my love life was going, I had

to pick up the phone and play tag when my plumbers could not seem to show up for work when I needed them the most. The construction project I started had all been all but abandoned by the slapstick, slapdash excuse for a carpenter down the street. I reached out for my phone in desperation and sent Kennedy a message.

The burning question of my fantasy was: What if they changed the name of menopause to *"Men o' Plenty"*? Maybe then, I could get my plumbing fixed! That is when I got a text back from Kennedy saying, "I'll be right there."

"Yeah, right," I texted back, as the washing machine sounded like it was a twin-engine airplane ready to take off. The clinking and clanking got out of hand when I jumped on top of the machine and held my hands up against the frame. The spin cycle was eccentrically out of whack as it rumbled around like bumper cars. The vibration virtually accelerated to warp speed and began to get a hold of me.

Before I knew it, I was panting at the top of my lungs, crying out to the Love Gods, "Look at what I've become!" I sat there with my body bouncing as the machine nearly rocked out of the closet, clinging to the walls. I was getting ready to explode when I thought I heard a knock at the door. Mortified that someone would see me getting off on the laundry machine,

I pulled myself together, peeked out the back door, and headed back to the kitchen, pulled a bag of clams out of the fridge, and filled the sink from the only faucet that worked around here.

The cold water pumped in from the lake as I poured some salt into the pot and placed a bag of ice cubes in it. I fumbled down the hall to my bedroom to put on something clean to wear. The heaps of laundry all over my room reminded me that my cookbooks were consuming me.

I heard a ding on my phone, with a message from Kennedy, "I'll be right over there." When I threw my clothes into the corner, my nylon underwear still clung to me as I tried to negotiate it off. Throwing them into the machine, I hit the start button again. As I fumbled around the kitchen, desperately trying to fill the insatiable need that was welling up inside of me, I texted Kennedy again and said that my fantasy is someone who can fix my hot water heater right now!

"I'll be right over," he texted again. I looked back down at his business card where it read, **"Kennedy McCormick, what's Your Fantasy?"**

My Aunt Anne's death landed me the camp free and clear, and I began to contemplate what I could do with the place when I saw a message from Aunt Mabel coming in saying, 'Checking on you, love.' I smiled as I sent her back a message,

"I'm OK, Auntie Mabel. How do you like your new digs?"

"Loving it, sweetie," she replied.

"OK, Auntie, I'm getting ready to make some chowder. I'll bring you some in the morning when I head up to Presque Isle for the cooking contest I entered."

"OK, love," she said with a little heart, "I'll talk to you later."

I concluded by sending back a string of hearts and made my way to the ball and claw tub that looks out to the lake that opens in the upper half of the two-story Cape. There was an old wooden black chair along the side. This is where I began my ritual for at least the last three weeks now.

At first, the water was getting colder, and I thought it was just going into fall. That is when I tried to turn the thermostat up on the hot water heater. Damn, it just was not working. I texted Kennedy again, thinking that he knew someone who could hook me up with my pipes. I laughed back when I texted in all caps: "MY FANTASY IS SOMEONE WHO CAN CLEAN OUT MY PIPES AND FIX MY HOT WATER HEATER!"

"I'LL BE RIGHT THERE WITH MY BIG WRENCH," he typed right back in loud, bold print.

5

Transparency at Its Finest

Rounding the bend, Kennedy saw the glow of her fireplace through the window and thought to himself, "I should not do this," as he caressed the handle of his shifter. He slowed the car down to park down in her drive, pausing at the mailbox and staring at her camp. His fingers began to sweat as he contemplated going down there. The old Firebird® was still sitting around the back side of the shed as I said to myself, "I need to get an estimate on restoring the Blue Bird back to its former glory," That would be the icebreaker now.

"Go ahead, Kennedy ... You got this," a deep voice bellowed in my left ear, with the imp sitting on my shoulder with a pitchfork in his hand. A black top hat that covered up most of his hair, leaving a strand of red curls running down his chest. He was wearing rainbow suspenders that hardly covered his nipples, with his beer belly hanging over his belt line sporting a pair of tweed knickers. His black compression socks went all the way to his knees. His large clown shoes dug into my sternum clavicle.

"Damn right, I got this, Lucius," I said. As I gripped the steering wheel, the smug little demon bounced on my shoulder, digging his rod into me. "You know you want to bump her starter and take her for a spin," he said, as his childish laughter bellowed throughout the Trans Am®.

I sat contemplating my next move when my guardian angel appeared on my right shoulder dressed in a white mother of pearl. Her long blond curls ran down her back with white wings fluttering when she scolded me and inquired, "Are you sure you want to go through with this?"

"Tatiana, what the hell are you doing here?" I asked as I flopped back into my seat.

"There is a lot riding on this deal, Kennedy," the beautiful little angel said as her eyebrows glared at me. Just then, the imp grabbed the angel's hair, telling her, "Shut up, Blondie! I've got my own deal I'm working on."

In a flash, the Angel in white was rummaging through her very own white leather tool bag as sparks began to fly.

"Hey, rascal, is this your ratchet?" she asked as she threw a ten-millimeter socket in his lap. "Take that and be gone!" she commanded.

The little wretch grabbed his crotch and shouted obscenities as he tumbled down to the floorboard of my car.

My guardian angel looked down at me with her arms crossed and said, "What's it going be? Kennedy, are you next?" Looking at her as my hand accidentally on purpose hit the switch to lower the passenger window, I began to shift gears.

Just then, the little devil slammed his pitchfork onto my gas pedal and yelled, "I don't think so, Buddy Boy, you're doing this," as the Trans Am® roared down the drive. My guardian angel screamed, "I'll get you this time!" and dove in between my legs. As the wheels chirped, my Golden Goddess was heading straight for Charlotte's back door., I could not believe what I was seeing as my guardian angel's heels wrapped around my neck. In a flash, the angel and the imp began to roll around on the front passenger seat, duking it out in spades, when I quickly slammed on the brakes.

The car's wheels locked up and slid for what felt like miles, stopping just before I reached the back door. I jumped out of the car and slammed the door shut just in time to see Charlotte standing under the light of the porch in her bra and underwear with a large wooden spoon in her hand. "Yes, a hot meal tonight," I thought. I turned to see my guardian angel riding the little imp like he was a stallion, and she was the jockey heading for the win at the Kentucky Derby! Utterly horrified at first, I then laughed and said, "I knew they were in bed with each other".

I turned back to Charlotte, noticing the high beams were on and said, "Everything is fine," when she turned around and ran back inside. Screaming something about needing clean underwear. As I stood there in what felt like purgatory, the horn on my car started to blow. I knew that there was going to be a major mess when I looked back to see the angel's wings fluttering over the steering wheel. Lucius' hat blew out the T-tops. Then, I ran right behind Charlotte, screaming, "You got any paper towels."

As I followed her into the house and stood in the hallway, watching her, she ran back to her bedroom and rushed around to find anything to wear. Throwing a nightgown on that she grabbed from off the floor, she scrambled to find clean underwear. Sniffing each pair frantically until she found something that must have been clean, whereupon she put her toes in the holes and pulled her granny panties up. She frantically ran out of the room and slammed right into me!

Bouncing off me, she stumbled onto the floor. "Holy crap, I nearly shit myself when I saw the Trans Am® coming straight for me with the devil in the front seat!" she exclaimed.

I helped her get up and could not help but laugh.

"What's the problem?" I asked, laying my tools on the kitchen table when the unmistakable sound of my horn blowing out of control came piercing inside the house.

"What's wrong with your car horn, and what was that out there?" Charlotte asked, stammering.

"Oh, nothing, nothing at all," Kennedy replied as the horn began to blow wildly out of control. "Sometimes, my horn just sticks and does that. It will all be over in a few minutes," he said. The energy of the room changed as Kennedy tried to get me centered back on him. "What seems, to be the problem here, Charlotte?" he asked.

"OK," I replied, "my hot water heater is ice cold, my washing machine is banging, the carpenters have not finished what they started, and to top it all off, I now have three cars in my driveway that don't work."

"All right, calm down, Charlotte," he said, with his arms caressing my shoulders. His burly salt and pepper beard nuzzled my neck, and his fingers continued to scratch my arms up and down as he calmly breathed reassurance into my ear. "We'll get this fixed … I'm a master at fixing things and unclogging pipes," he said.

A shiver ran down my spine as I imagined his snake unclogging my line. "The septic tank is out back. Do you do that, too?" I said, laughing as I whirled my wooden spoon in the air. All I could imagine now was me bent over the kitchen sink, my legs spread wide, just begging for his pipe wrench under my faucet while I tried to unclog the garbage disposal.

"Let me look at them," he said as he turned around and headed out the door. Startled and confused with what was happening, one minute I thought he was fixing the kitchen sink and screwing me when, in the next moment, he was running out the door asking for the car keys. What was I doing as I went chasing after him? The horn had stopped blowing as Kennedy made his way back outside.

Standing next to my car, sitting there collecting leaves, he turned to me and told me to get the keys. I ran back into the house, fumbling for the set. I ran back out to where he was standing and handed him the keys. I listened as he sat down in the older Mustang® and started her up.

He took my pony for a little spin and came back. "Sounds like the transmission is slipping," he said as he shut the car door.

That is when he set his sights on my Firebird® and asked if it was the starter.

I looked back at him and just laughed to myself. "Is it the starter? How the heck would I know? Do I look like a mechanic?" I replied.

"I'm just asking you a question, Charlotte. Don't get your panties in a twist," he said.

"Well, in all reality, my engine is in high gear, my transmission is slipping, I'm leaking oil all over the place, and I can't get anything around here to work, including the contractors that I hired to build me a new bathroom!" I replied.

"Wow!" is all I heard back. "I'll take a look at your Firebird® and look at the cars in the light when I can see better," he said. He took my hand and said, "Now, let's go look at your pipes." He made his way back into the house with me, running and panting like a lost puppy dog. As he stood with his tool belt cocked right in front of me, I could hardly take it anymore. "What the hell are you doing, Kennedy?" I screamed, blowing a gasket.

"Why haven't you joined my *Center of Love Club*," he said back to me, with his fingers pointing to my chest. "You know this is what you need!" he exclaimed.

"I've just been scared to spend that kind of money on myself," I hissed back.

"If you can't spend money on bettering yourself, then how do you expect to get any better?" he quipped back.

"Gee," I stammered, "I didn't think about that," I replied, knocking my hand on my head.

"Do you think what I do warrants no compensation?" he asked.

"No, I just don't know what you do," I said as my feet shuffled along the floor.

"Don't you think if you showed up to a class that you might be able to figure it out in time?" he asked.

"When I sent you a text and said my fantasy is someone who can fix my hot water heater, I didn't realize you were a plumber," I replied.

"Well, Nancy," he mimicked in a Ronald Reagan type of voice, "Ya know, I didn't go to school for this, but back in the day, I was known for cleaning out the ladies' pipes," he said with a click of his lips. "I did give you my business card when I took you home, didn't I?" he continued as his fingers trailed my countertop.

I just stood there frozen as I tried to mentally process everything. I looked back at him and said, "I don't remember what your card said that day. I must not have paid it any attention," *I* said, knowing damn well right that was a lie, as vivid thoughts of Maury Povitch flashed before my eyes. Flustered again, I said, "I thought your business card said **Kennedy McCormick—What's your Fantasy?**" I was virtually falling over my words as I fumbled in my night shirt. "I didn't realize you were a plumber and master mechanic, too," I said as he stood in my door.

He laughed, "That's really not what I am master of," he replied with a twinkle of an eye as he looked at me through his cheaters. He whirled his ratchet in his hand like it was a nine-inch wand of vibrating steel, and I knew in an instant what he was talking about.

I had become mesmerized by his wrench doing somersaults when I calmed down and asked in a softer voice, "What are you a master of then?"

A tantalizing smile erupted on his face. With that, he pulled the hose off the back of the washing machine, with his thumb clamping down on the gush of water as it started squirting out at me.

"I can tell you right now, it isn't plumbing; I forgot to turn the bleeping water supply off!" he said, laughing in the hydro-comedic moment.

"You don't say," I replied, knowing damn well that he did it intentionally. I laughed, watching him swirl that old hose in his hand like he was twirling a baton.

"Don't worry, it's under control," he said reassuringly.

I stood there, my head spinning, water dripping down my neck, and my erect nipples poking through my nightshirt. "What the hell is this man doing in my kitchen?" I thought to myself. "He needs to be in my bedroom!" I mused.

He looked over at me with my nightgown drenched with water and smiled back at me. "Looks like you need a new night shirt on; go get changed while I fix this," he instructed. His eyes twinkled as he looked up at me; his glasses fell down his nose, and he slid them back up again. "I wear the cheapos," he laughed back at me.

I went to my room and rummaged through the drawer, where I found a new sexy nightgown and a pair of black lace underwear and slipped them on. I slinked back down the hall just as he finished tightening up the hose, wearing my best lingerie. I watched him out of the corner of my eyes intently as I minced up the celery, knowing that I was testing him. Hooking the water back up, he hit the button, and, in a flash, the cold water came pumping in from the lake intake.

Kennedy looked at the hot water heater and said, "It's the thermocouple," he said, as he got back up from his knees. "Let me see," he said as he read the name of the manufacturer and model number from the panel. "I keep extras in the trunk of my trunk," he added. He got up, headed to his car, came back again in a minute with a new package, and said, "Just happened to have one," he said as he got back down on the floor.

"Of course you did," I replied, as I rolled my eyes and hit the button on the washing machine. I was so relieved to hear the flow of water filling up the tub when I asked, "What was wrong with it?"

He smiled back at me and said, "The hose was clogged with debris," he explained.

I headed back to the refrigerator and pulled out two ears of silver queen. Shucking the corn over the kitchen sink and pulling the husk off, the dark brown silks reminded me of my own crop when I ran the kernels under the water using my hands to wash them off. I was acutely aware of Kennedy's stare as my fingers glided up and down the golden rows and how I wished he would take hold of me.

I bent down to tease him as I shuffled through the drawer, looking for the lid to my pot. I took the glass dome off the cake plate and let my winning recipe for cupcakes boldly tempt his nose.

"This is going to affect my blood sugar," he said as he pulled the wrapper off.

I pulled the plate away, not wanting to make his blood sugar spike, when he stopped me in mid-flight.

"I don't give a damn. I know I'm not supposed to be here either," he said as he pulled two cupcakes off the plate, peeled the wrapper off, and stuffed one in his mouth.

I offered him a glass of water and squeezed a lemon in, letting the juice run down my fingers, knowing that would help to keep his numbers from spiking up. He drank the glass down and handed it back to me when I asked him, "Would you like to have a cup of clam chowder?"

He looked at me and smiled, "Is this my reward for fixing your water supply?" he asked.

I smiled, and within a matter of minutes, I offered him a bowl of my clam chowder and filled him with another glass of lemon-infused water. I was thinking that I finally had the man I had been craving in my grasp when he said, "Can I ask you a question?"

"Sure," I said, clearing my throat. As my eyes grew shy and buried my head back into my legs, I waited for what felt like an eternity when Kennedy patted my shoulders and said, "On second thought, you're good now," as he grabbed his tool bag and headed out the door.

"I'm good now? Is that what he thought?" I reflected. As I watched him walk out the door, he had to have known what I was looking for. The sheer frustration now began to sound like a gong as my pelvic floor began thumping, sounding successively louder as each footstep headed out the back door. By the time I had made it to lock the door behind him, my whole body was heaving and craving, practically begging for him.

The night ended rather abruptly, not the way I had planned. At least I had hot water while I waited for my construction to finish. "It figures," I thought, chalking it up to its experience. I went back to the kitchen to put my soup away, shut off the lights and headed back up to the bathtub, where a jar of cannabis-infused sugar scrub was waiting for me.

That is when he sent me back a text, "Sorry Charlotte, I had to go before I went overboard," it read.

"Overboard would have been nice," I texted back assertively. I climbed the steps deflated, wondering what was wrong with me. Intensively, I looked in the mirror, paying attention to the lines that were now creeping up on me. As I beheld the crow's feet around my eyes, I wondered aloud if I was too old. I peeled off my underwear, let the night dress fall to the floor, and turned the hot water on. Curiously., as if on cue, I peeked out my window just in time to see the headlights light up the property at the *Center of Love Club*. "Oh, Kennedy, Kennedy, Kennedy," I winced in sheer frustration.

This would have to do, as I lit the candle in the jar and turned on the CD player. As the hot water filled up the tub, I slid back and took a few deep breaths. I opened the lid of one of the products I had been secretly working on. An upside-down pineapple and cherry sugar scrub made with a blend of THC to keep the body pumping. It felt like a good long hit, as I started with small circles, running it along my legs, circling up around my hips, trailing my breasts as it lingered up my neck and finally letting the blend run around my lips. I knew if I could just get Kennedy McCormick to try one of my products, maybe, just maybe, he would be so impressed that he would offer me the job of my dreams and hire me to make a line of products for the *Center of Love Club* that would make the men get down on their knees!

I could see it now, my cannabis-infused sexual editable products being the talk of the world as I imagined three mounds of whipped cream standing in the center of a cannabis-infused chocolate-covered banana when I let the massage oil infused with cocoa and cannabis enter my vertical smile, allowing the sweet sensations to cover up my defeat. All of it together just smelled like a sundae as I lovingly began rubbing the sweet oil around my mound, letting my fingers slip around the bottle while wishing it were a man as I furiously rubbed myself.

The black card sitting on the chair seemingly called out to me as I sat there looking at the phone. For what seemed like an eternity, I tried to fashion the words. "What do you charge to join your club?" I texted and hit the send button.

As the water level rose, I slumped further back into the tub. The off-lighting from the small lamp was enough for me to see my skin shimmer. Shuddering in the tub, I felt myself release as my walls clamped down on the bottle that was filling me. The harder I rubbed on my strawberry cake, the more I started screaming, "I know what my fantasy is!".

I could not take the ache as I managed to get out of the tub. Heck, I could hardly handle the steps, as each one I went down sent me into another dimension as I screamed inside for someone to take this need away. By the time I made it to my bed, waves of tremors had come over me as the erotic edible from *The Center of Love Club* began to take full effect.

Reaching for my battery-operated best friend, the hum of the machine vibrated as I hit number nine. I was thrilled to death that I lived deep in the woods, where no one could hear my screams, writhing at the top of my lungs as I begged for a spirit to fill me! Then, a thought occurred to me, and I wondered that if I could hear them, then they could hear me. I flopped back down in my bed, beating my sheets with my fists. My voice seemed to shudder every window in the house, and I could hear the charges of deer as they rolled along the hills when my tongue bellowed out. Reaching out to my cell phone, I sent Kennedy one last text. "My next fantasy is: FIND ME A MAN!" I cried over the keyboard.

6

Captain Switcheroo

As the sun was rising, I found myself making the four-hour ride to Presque Isle in preparation for the first cannabis confections contest titled "Slopped". I stopped by Aunt Mabels, who promptly pulled out a bright and clean new jacket with my name and a cannabis Fan leaf embroidered on the breast. When he eyed me up and said, "Better bring me home the winning cake," he gave me a wink. I barely made it in the kitchen before Chef Shane cut me an eye. In his heavy British accent, he bellowed, "You're late, now drop and peel twenty sweet potatoes, as a playful wink graced his face. It is the way the Crooked Spoon hit the table that sent a shiver down my spine. My phone beeped, and I saw a message from Kennedy waiting for me. My mouth nearly dropped when I saw what he asked for: a one-year commitment, 4 classes, $2499 paid out in monthly installments. The more I pondered his price, the more I realized I was not getting what I wanted on my own, so maybe this was not so bad as I sent the next text back, "Okay, I can do that."

"Monday night or a Saturday?" he asked.

"I'll never get off on a Saturday," I said to myself as I typed in "Monday."

His next text came in, "I will have an initial meeting with you where we will go over all your desires and put together a plan to help you achieve all your goals."

I texted back, "OK," not understanding the world I was entering but knew I needed something, so I succumbed and set up my payments. Lost in my own thoughts as I set everything up, I looked up just in time to see a few more chefs come in and pick a station. That's when it hit me: my first televised contest! I was very excited as my head got back in the game, scurrying around and setting my workstation up. As Chef Shane went over the contest rules on "Slopped," I glanced around the room, checking out each chef I was up against. As each contestant stated their names and what they were cooking, the tension began to swell, knowing I was going to have to beat each one of them if I wanted the coveted golden cupcake on the shelf. The mixers were on high speed as the timers kept buzzing; the scent of cinnamon and vanilla permeated the air.

I looked down at my jacket with my name stitched in black, then looked down the line to each other chef. There was Chef Kat putting what looked like red velvet in the oven, and Chef Trevor from Buds Tavern was taking hard candy he fashioned out of maple and molding it into flowers. The more I sized up each chef, the more nervous I became when I began to smell the faint scent of burning sugar. I look up to see Salem taking her batch of cupcakes out of the oven. The over-baked gluten-free lumps of chocolate coal that even cannabis could not have saved had she even put it in. I glanced over to the judges as I watched Salems' cupcakes cling to the pan, begging to be released from whatever news article that was sure to print when Salem hit the pan on the counter, sending the burnt offerings flying. The reviews of restaurant patrons past hanging off her chef coat, a ghoulish spectacle that, at first glance one cannot help but gasp. Even the wrappers had a tinge of burnt around the edges as she desperately tried to hide what was sure to be a humiliating defeat with a goat cheese frosting. There was no turning this around, and she was the first in the contest to lay her bagged goods down. A corpse of a cupcake panting as she clings to the sparkling wine that she infused inside her confection. Desperate to be anywhere but here as the bottle hits her lips, trying to drown away what was sure to be another embarrassing display of culinary ineptitude. A stark reminder of all the bottles once reserved for special occasions now fermenting in the basement, eating away at her soul. She had been preparing for years for this moment when her burnt tower came crashing down literally at the feet of Cupcakes by Kat with her Chocolate Grenache and Infused tart cherry cordial cakes. I focused my thoughts once again as I pulled the cinnamon and cannabis-infused gummies out of the mold and placed her on the mountain of whipped cream cheese frosting that was nestled on top of the sweet potato cupcake that was sure to be my best confection to date, pumped full of peach preserves and cream she was a southern men dream as the judges bit into her flesh. Salem was furious as she watched the faces of each judge lit up as they bit into each baked sweet dream. It was the infused peaches that took my sweet potato cupcakes over the edge and I knew I was that much closer to winning the contest. Though the room was full of commotion as Chef Kat placed her infused cherry cordial cake that she got second place, you could hear a pin drop when Chef Shane declared Salem had been "slopped." A part of me felt bad for Salem as this has got to me the most embarassing defeat she has ever had as her cupcakes were placed inside the trough, knowing they were now pig food. I held my trophy in my hand, happy to beat Trevor and Cupcakes by Kat. However, it was the green eyes on Salem glaring down at me that told me this was not over. I decided to rent a cabin along the banks of the Mattawamkeag and take a day to rest and see what Aroostook County has to offer before I head back home.

Within a week, a product arrived in the mail. A bar of soap called **The Goddess Within** and a bottle of massage and bath oil in the same scent. A few weeks had passed while I answered every question he had asked when the day marked on my calendar arrived. The small Cape Cod has been overrun this week with plumbers and carpenters finally working on the last of the bathroom renovations. I was running around trying to clean up all the mess before Kennedy arrived. Sliding into the powder room, I fumbled with my makeup and clothes one more time, hair spraying my dirty blonde hair, trying to look my best.

Then, I heard a car pull down the driveway and looked out to see a black Range Rover® with tinted windows drive down the gravel road. I was expecting his gold Trans Am® and wondered when he would get his new car. Flustered, I ran back to the bathroom just to check my lipstick one more time. I ran to the pantry and quickly popped a few chocolate chip cannabis cookies that I baked on a plate and one in my mouth when I made my way back to the door.

I heard the door shut and excitedly listened to each step as my heart thumped up against the wooden door as he made his way down the wooden ramp leading to the back doorway. Going over the list in my mind, I made sure I had carried out each instruction as stated. The kitchen table was clear. The only illumination was the fireplace. His lobster bisque was on the stove. I peered out from the side window as a uniformed man with a brimmed hat came up to the porch and knocked on my door.

"Holy shit, the police," I shrieked. Running around with the plate of cookies in my hand, jumping up and down, "Holy shit," I kept mumbling. He was much taller, broader, and was dark! I thought that this was Kennedy coming when I told myself to get a grip when I hollered out the door, "Who is it?"

Standing outside the door was a policeman while I was eating a cannabis cookie. My nervousness was starting to get to me, and I began to wonder if I had made a mistake. The money had already been wired in to pay. I supposed that I just could not answer the door, when it dawned on me, I am in Maine, and I can legally have this here! That is when another thought hit me, "Oh man, is this prostitution or what?"

I took another deep breath as his fingers wrapped on the screen again. His body was impressive and taller than mine. That is when it hit me. He was the guy from The *Moose and Deer*

Inn! I opened the door and let him in. His dark chocolate eyes matched his skin as he walked in, taking command of the room. He moved to his left and right, scouting out all the rooms with a flick of a light switch. As he took his hat off and placed it on the hall table, I could see he was bald as his head shone in the light of my kitchen. He was incredibly handsome with lips that looked delicious as I led him to the kitchen, fumbling over my feet.

"Good evening, Charlotte," he said as he slid a set of keys across the table. "Take these, go to the trunk and pick out what you want. Can I use your bathroom?" he asked.

Not knowing what to do, I walked him around the bend. The powder room window was slightly open as the scent of the candle filled the room. "Here you go," I said as I closed the door behind him, falling against the frame. It was beyond confusion as to what was happening, but I distinctly remember him from that evening. This was not who I was expecting, especially considering everything that had happened in the last week with all the text messages and answering all those fantasy questions that Kennedy sent me. The more I thought about it, the more intrigued I became.

His body was so much more different than Kennedy's, and he had a presence about him that aroused me, and I wondered if I was even ready for someone like him. I took another deep breath as I began walking out to the crisp air; then, I hit the remote that unlocked the supercharged black machine.

A set of aviator glasses rested on the dashboard as I walked around the back. The briefcases in the trunk first caught my eye. Each case contained a different item. I saw whips, chains, handcuffs, a baton, leather straps, wigs, and some feathery things. Oddly enough, I also saw a bag of groceries and an empty bag, whereupon I began picking up what caught my eye, placing each item therein. My fingers were trembling as I made my way back into the camp.

I did not get two feet in when I felt him come up behind me as the items in my hands fell to the floor. His left arm wrapped around me as he firmly held my neck up against his chest. He whispered in my ear to take the tie off his neck and use it to wrap my hands together. "Oh boy, it's happening, I gasped as his left hand came around my waist.

"We need to establish a safe word," he said.

The mirror reflected the scene as I watched him suckle on me. I clumsily untied the knot from his neck, looping the dark blue material around my wrists. His blue suit with gold stripes still clinging to his body as he guided the baton between my thighs, sending shivers up my spine.

My mind began racing in search of the safe word I would use when all I could think of was to say, "Oh God." That would never do; that would stop things now, but 'Oh God,' a safe word, a safe word," I kept mumbling in my head. My legs began to tremble as I felt the first slaps of his hand, as they came down hard on my ass. The sting, at first, was a bit more than I expected and I soon felt my first release. My fluids squirted out, copiously splashing his trousers with full intensity. The strength of his hands further aroused me as each slap sent me to another realm, and the tears ran down my face in a mixture of pleasure and pain that left me begging for another strike.

In a swift move, he cradled me into his arms as he led me to the room and set me down on the comforter in the center of the bed. I watched as he took the end of the tie and wrapped it around the bedposts, securing my hands up above my head. The ivory silk sheets and pillow were embroidered with lace, and the black feathered boa bound my feet together as his fingers trailed up my thighs.

"Close your eyes," he commanded.

I could feel his breath in my ears as he told me to relax and gave me the safe word to use and asked me to repeat it.

"Clinton," I moaned out, waiting on his cue, "is that what you want me to use as your safe word?"

He whispered in my ear, "Is that what you want it to be?" he reiterated.

The more I thought about it, the more I wanted his name to be safe for me, "I will use your name," I said softly.

Knowing that I needed to get over my past and face my own demons, I let the tears fall down my face and said, "Yes, I understand the instructions." Not knowing what was going to happen next was the most exciting part for me. I felt gratified as a feather began to circle around my face and trace down my skin. In my mind, I began to see images of the man that had been haunting my dreams. I saw this man in uniform as he entered my head space.

The hat and blue coat triggered the mood as my fantasy began to take off. I opened my eyes again and let him touch my quivering abdomen. I had always wanted to have sex with a cop. I wanted to feel the touch of the handcuffs. First, he showed me his gun and safety. There were no bullets inside. My breath panted eagerly as I watched him unbutton his shirt and take his clothes off. The sound of the snap on the black leather case, as the metal clamps came down on my chest of drawers. The clicks of his gun as he took the holster off his back and the thump of the metal as it hit the closet rack.

He used his t-shirt to cover up my eyes as I drew in his

scent through the material, all the while laughing to myself, thinking I was a hound dog. He began by kissing my cheeks and tapping my upper thighs. The musky scent of his body grew stronger as he began rubbing up against me. Each slap of his strong hands sent a wave of emotion as I shivered while he spanked me. My mind exploded with every thought of what I did do. How could I have paid someone to beat me? Oh, but if you only knew!

"Just do it," I yelled, as the tears fell down my face, my words choking to come out. I wanted it to be over with as fast as possible now! The desire for pain was consuming me, and I needed to release it. The more I tried to force myself to do it, the more I resisted. I began thrashing around the bed, screaming for it all to stop.

I felt deflated as his body relaxed up against me, and he said, "I don't think you're ready for that stick yet."

"I know I am not," I said.

"What's the magic words?" he said.

I continued to defy him, waiting for him to beat me again. He began to untie my hands from the bed.

Again, he asked, "What are the magic words?"

I looked up deeply into his eyes, daring him to beat me again as my body started to writhe.

He bellowed loudly, "Get dressed," as he untied my hands.

Oh no! He was better than me. He was the master, and I was the puppet, as I quickly thought of a recovery.

"Do you have my Lobster Bisque ready?" he asked.

I ran down the stairs, wrapping my robe around my shoulders, to the kitchen where the Lobster Bisque was simmering. Apparently, Clinton, not Kennedy, had requested a New England favorite and one of my specialties. I quickly ladled the creamy base with chunks of lobster inside the little crock. I headed back to my bed, asking him to come out and join me on the porch overlooking the lake.

I liked the softer side of him, and as he smiled, I could see all of him. I could see all the love that was in him, and I wanted so badly to just feel his heart. I walked up to him, with my hands reaching for his chest. I just wanted to see if he would let me in.

When he put his arms around me, he pulled me into his body. I could feel him breathe into me. I knew I was safe with him. I knew he understood me. I looked back up to his eyes, the shiny head with beads of perspiration, closed my eyes and waited for it. I felt his fingers wrap around my face and felt this intensity like a thousand horses were galloping with him leading the charge. I could feel the horse stop in front of me, with his men behind him, waiting to charge when he said, "Why do you want a beating?"

"I don't know why," I answered. As the cannabis began to enter in, I could feel myself wanting to climb on top of his horse. I stood up on my tippy toes, trying hard to get closer to his lips, as his face came closer to me, and I felt his right hand on the back of my hair, as he clenched my locks. I closed my eyes, and I felt his lips against my cheeks. My breath was panting, and I was tingling inside.

Then it hit me, like tiny little bursts of light, as his lips danced so close to mine that he was asking me with his kiss to let him come inside. I tried so hard to contain myself, as I did not know this man from Adam, but in that moment, in that instant I wanted him in. I closed my eyes as I heard the music play. I wrapped my arms around his neck and felt my fingers run up and down his chest. I closed my eyes once again as the kiss I had been waiting for entered my lips. I was in with a thousand kisses from all eternity like fireworks were exploding in front of me. I asked him if he was really a police officer as he whirled me around, bending me over the kitchen table and spreading my legs with his knee.

"I'm with the Delaware State Police," he said as he panted in my ear, hammering me from behind. "Six more months and I retire," he added as he padded my body down. In between each driving kiss, he revealed that he was heading to Rhode Island to do private investigations. In an instant, I felt like I was in an interrogation room when he flipped me back around and lifted me on the table, whispering in my ear.

"What state were you born in?" he asked, as he smothered my neck with kisses.

Feeling his baton, I started yelling out, "Miss, miss, miss ... oh boy," and hissed, "Mississippi, Mississippi State," as if I was in the marching band. By the way, my legs were running up and down his back. "How'd you meet Kennedy," I clamored back.

"I've known him for years," he replied as he whirled me back around and placed me in the chair.

Questioning his integrity, I asked him if he would drive four hours for a night of sex with a woman.

He looked back and me and laughed and said, "No, I drove four hours to have the woman that has written two cookbooks fix me a home-cooked meal, now get to it," he pulled me up and slapped my ass.

I was way beyond puzzled as I rubbed my butt.

"Kennedy called me the other day and he gave me a heads up of your fantasy," he explained. "He knew that I wanted to meet you. Let us just say either way it went, I was game for it, he continued. Putting my hands over my face, I uttered, "Oh, I am such a fool. I thought Kennedy was a Don, and when I texted him, I thought he was coming over here."

"A Don? Kennedy? No way, not him," responded Clinton.

As the thoughts of the last few days kept running through my head, I chalked it up to experience. Looking down at the floor, I said, "I'm signing up for the Meet and Greet, and I'm going to be out your way in a few weeks for a few book signings in Delaware. Maybe we could try this again ... I mean if you want to hang out or something."

Clinton smiled back with a wink. "We could arrange that," he said, "you never know where I'll be at.

I ladled some bisque into his bowl. "How'd you like it?" I asked.

"Very impressive," he said, "I don't think there's a place on the island that could beat it."

Smiling back at him, I said, "Yeah, I thought the same thing. It's one of my most favorite dishes; it's my calling card, so to speak." I went back to the refrigerator and opened the door. The Romaine lettuce was nice and crisp as I pulled out my wooden bowl and drizzled some olive oil on it. I watched him as he went for the bag still sitting in the front hall, when he pulled out a ham and some potatoes. I took a pot from under the sink and began to heat it up on the stove. I placed the ham inside my pan and added five pounds of sliced potatoes. I melted the butter and added the flour in with the heated milk until it made a nice thick creamy base, spooned it over the sliced potatoes and placed it in the oven at 325 degrees F. Knowing that it would take a few hours for it to bake, I began to cultivate a new plan.

I washed my hands as he helped me clean up the kitchen and looked over at him. "I know this is probably going to sound stupid, considering everything. I have this sugar scrub in my bathroom that I've been experimenting with. Would you mind putting it on me, or perhaps I could put it on you?" I suggested.

Clinton smiled and said, "It's what I have been waiting for."

7

Missile Accomplished

The water pumping in from the lake was now connected to an on-demand hot water system as he led me into my master bathroom suite. The marble floors were warm to the touch as the heat radiated from inside the rafters. I stepped inside the two-person jetted tub overlooking the water from the nine-foot cathedral ceiling as the glow of the moon reflecting off the water ricocheted all kinds of lights.

The large ferns in massive ceramic pots seemingly transformed the bath into a tropical oasis as exotic flowers blossomed in every nook and cranny. The crystal chandelier suspended from the ceiling threw prisms of colors all around the room, and matching wall lights dimmed with a slight touch to the hand instantly set the mood to romantic, along with the sound system with speakers hidden inside massive crystal rock formation of white crystals and Amethyst.

The massive two-person shower with pulse jets oscillating from the ceilings, walls and corners and the built-in shelves of glass rock and flowers inside the natural stone imparted the sensation of standing under a waterfall. The double vanity sink was built to look like a Victorian-era antique dresser with over eight feet of granite counter-top from the Maine mountains with shades of green tourmaline running in the veins. The separate lavatory attached to private dressing rooms ultimately made the room a veritable lover's paradise.

The smell of real maraschino cherries and pineapple tempted my taste buds as I opened the jar, "This is my own special blend," I said, handing him the container.

He gave me a look as he dipped his fingers in the jar, pulled some out and let it linger on his tongue for a minute before giving me a "thumbs up" and said, "So you want to work for the *Center of Love Club*?"

My mouth nearly dropped when I heard him say those words. I had not told anyone about that fantasy of mine when I said in an aloof tone, "Well, yeah, if a position were to come up, I would seriously think about it."

He took a sniff again and began to taste the emulsion

inside and asked, "Is this an editable sexual body product?"

I was so delighted that he knew what I was doing, lost in the moment when he instructed me to stand up.

Starting with my feet with his hands glided up and down my legs.

"Yes, yes, it's my own secret that I've been hiding for some time now," I said.

"Interesting," he said.

"Yes," I moaned as his large hands began rubbing my other foot, and the water continued to rush out of the brass faucets. I loved the way that his hands continued to rub the sweet scrub up my inner thighs, teasing me with his fingertips, alternately taking me over the edge and bringing me back down again.

His chest muscles began to stand out as I scooped some of the sugary mixes all over his pectorals. His naked body glowed enticingly in the light as I rubbed the sweet concoction from his feet to his thighs. The background music worked well for him, and his body swayed to each strum of the strings. I kept time by circling the scrub with my hands into his back, letting the water caress his body.

Whatever he does has served him well. His body was

beyond amazing as I began to kiss him up and down. The lighting from inside the ceiling was enough for me to see his skin shimmer as he pulled me up to him. The palms of his hands danced as he polished the sugar around my chin. I found myself drowning in him as he ran his long arms along the side of my neck.

I took another scoop of the sweet scrub and started running my hands up and down his back, lingering as I felt the firm outline of each muscle of his glutes and could not hold back any longer. Shuddering, I felt myself release whatever was holding me back before. The waves were so strong that I was hardly able to hold myself up as the first tremors came over me, with each one increasing in intensity.

Using his magic hands, he lathered up my hair, letting the suds flow down my back. His kisses were so powerfully alluring that I could not help but follow the trail as he motioned, "Come here" with his right index before snapping his fingers. I took the towel off the rack and got down on my hands and knees.

With his legs spread apart, I used the towel to slowly wipe his legs clean, making my way ever so slowly up his shank. His baton grew longer the more my hands worked the cotton fibers into his flesh when I thought about how good this blend would taste on his ham.

His glowing, shimmering skin made him look like a God as he walked me into my dressing room. "Why don't you put something sexy on, and I'll meet you downstairs," he said as he closed the door behind me.

I scoured my built-in cabinets until I pulled out a long black silk gown with feathers around the neckline hidden underneath a bodice. I slipped my toes inside the black shoes and began to cascade down the steps and make my way to the living room.

Standing in front of the fireplace, he took my hand, and as he placed me down on the bear skin rug, his lips tasted of cannabis honey wine as he nourished me with his tongue. The bottle of The **Goddess Within** massage oil was now in his hands when he opened it up. "So, you want to cook for the *Center of Love?*" he asked.

I felt my flower open as my legs obeyed the invisible command. I said over and over, "Yes, I want to cook for the *Center of Love.*"

He squeezed the Jasmine and Lavender massage blend into his palms and slowly worked his way up my limbs as he entranced my body in a way I had not expected. His tongue darted in and out as he teased me wildly.

My body no longer trembled from fear, and I opened to

him. His big body felt weightless as he danced on my skin, with his rock-hard dark meat all over me. Putting the bottle of oil in my hands, he got down on his back and told me to massage him.

I watched as the shimmering blend of oils dripped down my hands. In the glow of the fire, I saw every scar, every mole on his skin, as I ran my fingertips up to his chest.

His pectoral muscles flinched as my palms rubbed the fusion into his flesh. His legs shimmered in the firelight as his quadriceps flexed. "That's right," he moaned.

I gently encouraged him to roll over as I watched his flesh roast in the glow of the fireplace. Starting with his head, I massaged his back from the neck down. Then, I playfully squeezed his cheeks and dug my fingernails into the flesh of his mountainous rump. Pretending his leg was a ham shank, I ran my hands up and down his thighs, wondering how he was going to feel inside.

"You have a good touch, but you need some more training when it comes to massage," he said, switching his position.

He must have read my mind as he guided his smoked meat into my pot and, within seconds, pounded his manhood deeper inside me. His full circumference felt like a cucumber that had been hidden in a field a full week after it should have been picked.

As each thrust went deeper, my muscles clamped down hard, and my walls felt like suction cups latching on to him. I could feel my muscles spasm with each hard push, sending my senses over the top. My bear rug had never felt anything like this, as waves of tremors came over me.

Each thrust sent him deeper, and it felt like he was hitting my lungs. He was like a hungry bear coming out of hibernation and running for a meal. "Get on top of me," he moaned. His teeth bit down on my cantaloupes and sent spasms all through my body.

My gurl was so sore from the pounding I had endured when he flipped me around. The whole length of his manhood came quickly into me, taking my breath away as I tried to take all of it in. I gasped for air as I felt his hand slap my ass again, pumping me harder as he begged me to respond.

"Is this how you like it ... you like it rough?" he asked.

The pain was incredible as I delighted in his task. Struggling to obey his commands, I responded, "Yes, yes, I like it like that."

"You're such a bad chef," he said as he hammered me some

more.

My hot juices were splashing all over my floor as I became delirious with his attention. Desperate for some refreshment, I stopped to fill the glasses that were sitting on the side table with raspberry and lime aid that I made before he got here.

His rough voice grew softer as he pulled out of me and sat down on the couch, his shaft protruding skyward.

Struggling to move as the orgasms seemed to be on back order, I crawled on my hands and knees, trying to deliver his refreshment. I saw his whole mast in the glow of the fireplace as he guided it into my flask. I could sense my own elixir moving up and down on his pistol. Hints of pineapple and sugar mixed with the cream I had been releasing as I tried to take all of him in. The more I let my mouth go all the way down the glass, the more excited I became.

His head was like a boa constrictor that had just eaten a rat, and I felt my mouth start to twinge, and I knew that I wanted to taste that.

Flurries of expectations came over me again as he matched each thrust that I gave him. Never had I experienced an orgasm by just going down on a man! When his veins began to swell like a gorging river, I knew he was getting ready to explode. I backed off, not wanting it to end, not knowing what had come over me, utterly delighted in the way he was handling me when he pulled me up on top of him.

Slowly, I felt myself slither back. With each breath, I felt him go deeper. As I looked into his eyes, a different feeling came over me. Waves of emotions flowed like the Gulf Stream as I reached my hands around his neck. The rhythm increased, and I felt myself released. I knew that my couch was done for, but I simply did not care. I never felt anything like him before and did not want it to end.

As I rode his staff, I could see the moon shine down on the lake as the breeze swirled in the room. I slowed myself down and paid attention to each gyration as I watched his body glisten with sweat. I needed a new safe word as I murmured his name in his ears, the veins that felt like they were streaming fast. I knew he was getting ready to blast me with his fully loaded weapon when I took a step back and said, "Hold up."

I looked him deeply in his eyes and said, "Not yet, not yet. I have waited too long for this." I was just beginning to get used to the giant piece of meat that was taking over me when I pulled him back down to the floor, down where my bear was begging for more.

Our bodies danced in the firelight as I felt him explore my

lotus. "I don't want a safe word right now, Clinton, just let me feel everything," I whispered.

He looked back up at me and asked, "You think you can handle me?"

"I don't know that I can, but I'm willing to try," I replied.

He stood back up and made his way to the couch and sat down in the center with his arms spread wide over the back end. "As you wish," he said, placing his hands around my hips. "Get on top and ride me," he commanded.

I do not know why I smiled at this, but I looked at him like he was a horse on the mounted patrol at an amusement park with no lines waiting.

He was like a jackhammer with a full trigger release, as I lost all sense of time and space. I rode his shaft like I would never see one again. With that, I felt an energy inside my body suddenly expanding, as I felt tremors, like progressively louder drumbeats. I could feel the French horns as they trumpeted inside the room. I was lost in my screams as I shouted out his name, "Oh God, Clinton," as I grunted harder on him. I felt our bodies shoot through the roof as the deepest explosion I had ever felt blasted right through me.

The gates of heaven opened when we burst into the

chambers. Rows of books and feathers, harps and angels passed by. All glancing at me, saying, "You are getting it. Take it one day at a time." It seemed like hours before we were able to come back down to Earth as I lay on the couch, catching my breath.

The night stretched beyond the early morning as we cooked in the kitchen and screwed on the counters.

I collapsed from exertion in what would undoubtedly be the best night of my life! Breakfast would not happen until almost half past Noon. I could not help myself from making him some home fries with a western omelet and baked him an oatmeal custard with a praline topping studded with some raisins, apples, and coconuts. I packed all the rest of the bisque for him, the three o'clock in the morning ham and scalloped potatoes offering, watching as he put his uniform back on.

His black Rover pulled out of my drive when suddenly, I realized it was Tuesday afternoon and I totally forgot about the job in Auburn. "Who cares?" I said to myself, "I got laid today."

I felt utterly amazing like something had freed me during the night, and I got back into the ring, ready for a fight. He was not what I had expected, but well worth it, as I watched him drive away. I ran to my laptop, looked up the *Center of Love Club* and registered for the meet and greet in Jamestown, Rhode

Island, coming up in just two weeks.

I rapidly looked through the recommendations, saw that a massage table was needed, picked out one on the site, and ordered a dress from the local seamstress and hired a manager.

8

It is Time for Butter Cream

My cookbooks were selling over a hundred a day now on every outlet imaginable, which did not even include all the book signings that were lining up all over the United States. People were suddenly coming out of the woodwork with copies in their hand, asking for a signature. It was a strange feeling to have people recognize me, but I began to get used to it, and with each passing day, my confidence grew stronger. I knew I was ready to face the camera and really started praying for a phone call for my own cooking show.

I headed to the auto mall and began to run my hands down the rows of cars begging for me to take them home. The racy side of me was still not tamed, though the XT5 was calling my name. There she was on the showroom floor, beaming from all sides. That was one hot woman, as I peeled her white dress back, barreling down hard with the beach underneath her as I took her for a spin.

Wednesday arrived, and I started my drive down I-95 in a brand-new 2020 Mustang® GT with a White Pearl finish. The leather upholstery and power seats made me want to flick it. I slid my ring finger up and down her seat and rubbed her flesh tenderly. The black wrap extended all the way back, revealing her pretty skin once again.

"Oh," I heard you calling, as a message displayed on the navigation screen, "I got you in a book signing scheduled for a cooking convention in Atlantic City in just a week!" I hit the button on the steering wheel for the hands-free cellular system. "Thank you, Taylor!" I replied, "You are amazing." I pulled into my driveway, where a cardboard box was pushed up against the front door.

My massage table with the *Center of Love Club* emblem embossed with a set of gold rings and two sets of flannel twin sheets arrived in less than a week. A plush purple blanket made of fleece rounded out my ensemble. I did not remember ordering this when I looked at the piece of paper tucked inside the tissue wrap.

There was a picture of the crew waving that did all the sewing for the *Center of Love Club* with a note inside that read, "Thank you for your purchase of our table and sheets. Please accept this gift of a plush blanket, proudly made by the *Angels of Las Vegas,* and know that when you support the *Center of Love,* you support all of us."

I read that over and over as I choked back tears, knowing that this was the kind of company I wanted to keep. I kept looking over at the gown I ordered, the fabric of red chiffon that felt like silk as it went up my hips.

I packed my car and headed down the coast, where more book signings were lining up. A stop in New York City on the curvy couch, where live on national television, I made my cooking debut with cannabis! I hit Atlantic City for a three-day convention, where every name in the business was there.

All the cooking stars who I modeled my life around were walking around the conference floor, and the excitement of being at this event, selling out my cookbooks on the first day, was mind-blowing. I tried to be cool when I saw what looked like Anne Burrell and Bobby Flay walk past my booth.

I took the Cape May-Lewes Ferry, where the last book signing for the week was scheduled in Rehoboth Beach, Delaware, during another festival on the beach. I booked a private home in Lewes, then spent a few days walking up and down Rehoboth Beach, trying to come to grips with what was happening and what I really wanted out of life.

I made a fast phone call to my publisher and ordered three hundred more books, marked it **RUSH** for general delivery to the Lewes post office. The famous beach fries were calling me as the ever-wary seagulls wagered bets on which one would win them or me. I sat down on the bench and looked out to the sea, wishing that I had some ketchup to dip my fries into.

Some powerful emotions surfaced as I went through the checklist for the Meet and Greet in Rhode Island and watched the ocean crash up to me. I must admit that this approach to finding love was a bit out of the box. However, the more I thought about it, the more I began to wonder.

What would it be like to learn to read the psycho-physical language of the body? Was it possible to evolve both physically and spiritually? Would I be able to find my soulmate on one of these retreats? The more I thought about it, the more I realized that if I took the class, I would learn. Who knows? Maybe even Clinton would be there.

I got back into my car with every intention of relaxing in my mad race to catch the ferry, when suddenly, I saw a most beautiful woman standing in a green and golden delight in her culinary dress, who I just could not wait to meet. She was so hard to resist, with her beautiful wavy hair tempting me with her stare. The scent of cannabis was lingering in her hair when

I asked her if she could get me a gram.

"Sure, I'll take you there," she replied as she opened the passenger door and got in.

Damn! That girl had a killer voice with the way her light shone as I brought it home for the win, making her scream as I hit the pedal to the floor. Taking her around the bend, tires screeching, I gave my pony some more gas while she took me to her secret cooking stash. The little bungalow was hidden on a dirt road where Jersey cows lined every crossroad.

"Damn, girl ... How did you do these so good?" I asked as I picked out each little cake. Hidden inside from maraschino cherry to pumpkin pie with her cannabis love brewing inside.

"It's in my genes," she said back at me as she waved goodbye from the front porch.

How I wanted one more bite, damn If I did not hold on, as I pulled a one-eighty and clamped my mouth down, running back into her little bakery. I just needed a bigger stash as I bought a few more things. I told her about the club I had joined and that she should give it a try. I gave her my number and said that she should look me up.

Suddenly, she started complaining about her current boyfriend. Yeah, I bet she was flustered, and I could tell she was trying to leave him. I gave her the address of where I would be and begged her to come up. Apparently, I had landed right in a rose bush. She was thorny, but I did not care. I would fall face down in that purple Kush rosebush anywhere. I was not even out the door when she ran down the steps and hopped back in my car.

The rain pelted loudly as it pinged off my vinyl top, barreling down hard on the finish line, the lightning bolts in the sky as he ran down the steps chasing her from behind. I drove to Long Neck Road, where we slipped inside a development. Mobile homes lined the streets as we made our way to the peninsula overlooking the water, and she directed me to park on the beach. We pulled out her stash of cannabis confections and began to talk about life in general. The more the high began to set in, the more I questioned my future as I pulled the wrapper off another cupcake and wondered how I got here.

Lowering the seat back, I started to dream of myself being one of the head chefs at the *Center of Love Club*. I knew, for me, that cupcakes were not my thing, as the savory side of me came out, but I could hold my own and cook whatever I wanted. Olivianna was a hell of a ride, that yellow cake baked with green love inside. Oh man, what a dream her buttercream was, as I licked the frosting in the back seat. "See, it would take me years to perfect what you do with these," I said as I polished off another cupcake and let the buzz come in.

Olivianna turned to me and asked, "Why don't you open your own place?"

I started to think that she might be right and wondered out loud for a few minutes as the thoughts of a food truck turned around my mind. I had no idea how long we sat out there, but long enough to know high tide would come in soon as I backed the car out and drove to another spot to watch the sunset. We giggled and talked about all our dreams. The windows had frosted up with our breath when I heard a tap on my glass. Looking up, there he was in blue, his lights flashing. Damn! Now, what did I do?

Mermaid with Green Rose Bud Wings

Barley missing

that large tree

by a landslide

he rescued me

as our tongues collide

I count as the tree

Grows inside

blue and red flashing lights

glowing to my delight,

are going down on me tonight

oh, the chocolate one

with a Ganache cream

in a blue and gold Dream

then moves away so easily

It is as if we are writing in synchronicity

Oh, the dance

the swirls in my mind

the white linen embodiment

as his hands spin me round

lighting the path for me to see

I have been stung again by this bee

wanting his stinger inside of me

as I holler out arrest me

put your cuffs around me

this was not the way

I was hoping for

The Delaware State Police Lure

As he shut the car door

He is the Angel

I have been waiting for

I cannot believe

us three

Rescue Me

Rescue Me

Rescue Me.

The Lure of The Sea

A Fisherman's Delight

A sea Captains Flight

The Narraganset in all its rights

A place to come and seek refuge

A place to learn a thing or two

Our Nation's History

Forged right here

From Steam liners of the sea

To coal grinding along the Allegheny

The Rich and Famous came for Hospitality

Many years later

The history still churns

The mansions clamoring

For you to learn

All these crazy entrepreneurs

Newport Rhode Island

A place of Serendipity

Many things to do

While you sit under its Wisteria tree

The ocean slamming with all its might

Calling you out to its delights

The Unique Restaurants that line the streets

Fish n chips and lobster treats

Clam Chowder contest a winter bet

The best calamari you will ever eat

All these things beckon me here

To teach me what this country is about

Innovation and creativity do here sprout

Walk the steps of the buildings

Designed by all the great men

Every party was led by an even better woman

Networking, they knew what to do

Gossiping about a thing or two

Newport, Rhode Island, what can't you do?

9
When Your Past Comes Back to Haunt You

Pulling into the parking lot of the inn on the shore of the Narragansett, I made my way in and waited in line for the desk man to check me in. There was a picture of a sea captain hanging on the wall, who used to own the house way back when it was just a home. The dining hall along the front looked over the bay. I sat down, ordered a cranberry and vodka, and went over the menu. I downed my drink, asked for someone to bring my dinner to Room 313, and created a tab. I had scheduled a three-o clock appointment at *The Spa* over in Newport the next day for my nails, make-up, and a blowout.

The four-poster bed in another separate room reminded me of a small home. With a mini refrigerator and microwave, it was simply perfect. Even if Olivianna did show up, I would have more than enough room to accommodate her. I crawled under the white linen sheets and set my alarm for eight thirty in the morning when there was a knock at the door. I had completely forgotten about the sushi I ordered when I sprang up to grab the handle. I pulled a five from out of my pocket and handed it to the woman as I flopped back down in the bed.

"The mad rush was over, and it's much better this way," I thought to myself, puffing out my breath. As I dipped my sushi in the soy sauce, I began to fill the bathtub and resigned myself to just relax. I hit the music station on my phone and focused on my breathing, concentrating on just getting in the zone. It was not long before I headed off to bed. I woke up the next morning, got dressed, and headed over to Narragansett to see who was open for breakfast.

As I crossed the bridge into Newport, the lighthouse to my right caught my eye. Smiling as I remembered the times back in Newport when I was just wet behind the ears, those hot summer nights when fishing tournaments and racing boats cluttered the bay, as I pulled down Long Wharf. The boats were still dotting the marina, which was bustling with herds of people walking up and down the streets.

Looking at my phone, it was only half past ten when I settled down for breakfast. After driving all around the island

and sitting up against the shore writing in my diary, I headed back to town to see if any of my old friends from *the Pub* were still polishing the wood.

Out of the back kitchen came Tammy, carrying a plate of food for the couple snuggling in the corner when she recognized me. As soon as she came back, we hugged for a few minutes and caught up on life real fast.

I ordered a drink as I pulled one of my cookbooks out of my bag.

She eyed the cover up and down, laughing, "Damn, girl, you're in the big league now."

Smiling back, I said, "It's been a long road to get here; it's not easy doing this," as I dropped a ten-dollar bill on the bar. Then, out the door, I went.

It did not even take a minute until I was standing at the reception desk with my dress over my arms as I checked in. The pretty brunette receptionist fixed me up a cup of tea and then escorted me to the dressing room, where a robe and slippers were waiting for me. I sat in the chair, sipping on my Earl Gray®, and began to look around the room, wondering if any of the people in here would be at the meet and greet.

I took notice of this one woman who was lounging in the

chair, sipping on her tea. I struck up a conversation with her and soon found out she was a baker. She handed me her business card that read, **Velvet Cakes by Gwen by Monique Outerbridge.**

"Are you up here for vacation?" I inquired as I tucked her card into my purse.

"A little bit of both," she replied, "I am going to an event today with the *Center of Love Club.*"

I nearly blew my tea all over me when I excitedly responded, "Me too!"

Within seconds, a woman breezed in, announcing she was my nail tech. I quickly shook Monique's hand and said, "I will look for you tonight." I walked the hall until I saw a display of nail polishes lined up.

Picking out Big City Red polish, she filed my nails, spruced them all up, and got every length to match. Lord knows how she did that as I held them up to the light. My toes were long neglected, at least that is what she said, as she slathered a moisturizer and paraffin around my feet and covered them in plastic wrap as a heated booty to let my feet rest.

I began to think that I was the cowardly lion in the *Wizard of Oz* when she pulled out a tool that looked like a knife sharpener. I darn near came out of the chair when she said, "Relax, it's just a file." Instinctively, I closed my eyes once again and concentrated on the warmth of her hands. "I could really get used to this," I thought to myself reassuringly.

While my nails were drying, I was introduced to a woman named Cheryl, who placed me in her hair chair. I watched as she blended some foundation and then dotted it along my face. Within minutes, my color started to change as I felt the brush running down my mane. With the tickle of the makeup brushes lining my lips, the lash extensions that I somehow was talked into were glued into place.

Before it was all over, I had a bleach kit in my mouth. What started off at two hundred fifty dollars had made its way up to four hundred before the woman helped me get on the red dress and zip it up. Staring at myself in the mirror, I did not feel like such an awkward duck anymore.

I looked at the time and realized I was running on schedule for once in my life. Then, I made my way back over the bridge back to Jamestown and followed the onboard navigation system until my car pulled up the stone-lined driveway, where a tall cedar tree was perched in the center. The entire entrance was lined with cars from up and down the East Coast, and one tag even read SYRNDPTE when a man opened my car door and took my keys. I began to walk the purple carpet, and that is when I noticed the step-and-repeat banner with the *Center of Love* logo, **FooBellas®** and a host of other sponsors and wondered what I had gotten myself into. The purple carpet flowed right to the front door, where another doorman greeted me and opened the door, letting me in. I heard the vigorous voices of laughter as the wait staff ran around prepping everything. My first instinct was to grab a plate and start hustling when I realized that this was not my ball, and I did not need to do a thing!

The fireplace was glowing and liberally adorned with flowers. The cathedral ceilings and exposed wood gave this house such an ambiance, as the twinkling lights that laced through its beams reminded me of the stars. I walked over to the large window overlooking the grounds out to Mackerel Cove at a lavender-laced trail dotted with hydrangeas and hostas. The salty air, mixed with the scents of the food, excited my palette as I felt called out to the water.

I tasted each appetizer that went past my nose. Trays of succulent delights from land and sea were brimming in each nook and cranny. Karissa, the host, greeted me, and I was taken aback. In a full-length evening gown with her hair fashioned up, I was almost blinded for a moment as she was just glowing in her white dress with whispers of feathers and diamonds all around her neck. Standing by her side was her Master, Kennedy, who sweetly caressed her back.

This time, seeing him in a tuxedo all slicked back was a radically different side of him that I had not seen or imagined before. His sheer confidence was staggering, and the radiant energy emitting from his body was almost intoxicating. Though it was glaringly obvious that he was enamored by his prize, I was quickly reminded as to why I was here. You could tell in an instant that this was her ball.

As I stared out at the men in tuxedos and military uniforms, I was amazed at how handsome they all looked. All eyes seemed to turn on me, and I quickly realized I was the first woman yet to arrive. The stares from the men made me blush, and I quickly looked around for someone I might know.

As the seven o'clock hour approached, the sun was beating off the ocean. More guests steadily began to arrive as the composition of the room balanced out between men and women. As the wine poured and conversations flowed through the room, I excitedly chatted with each one.

Off in the distance I heard the strings, and beckoned me out to the veranda, where white lights entranced me. There in the center was the woman I had met just a few hours earlier with her display of desserts and mini cupcakes. I came up to her again and said, "Monique Outerbridge, correct?"

Her smile was captivating as she beamed with pride when she said, "In the flesh!" I looked at her display, and the strawberry and red velvet hit me right away. *The Moyln Minis* made it so easy to enjoy each delicious treat, and before I knew it, I had several other flavors sitting on a plate. I grabbed another business card and programmed her website into my phone, velvetcakesbygwen.com and knew I would be contacting her soon.

As the night lingered on, I found myself in a circle, dancing with every man and woman. The little castle on the hill reminded me of a legendary land of romance, where dreams of love splendidly came true. As I inhaled all the aromas that floated in the air, I was reassured that I was taking the right step. One could not help but get the sense that love was built into this program. Karissa and Kennedy made the announcements for the weekend schedule of events.

Karissa's voice took over the room, and her words echoed through the night air as she spoke. "This is not a place for you to meet the love of your life in one night and ride off happily ever after. Tonight, it is about learning how to love yourself in a new way. This program takes as long as you need it to. Commitment is always first to you. We want you to look at these retreats to the universe we live in. To learn how to heal, using the ancient techniques of laying on hands healing combined with chakra energy. Eventually, as you master each level, we will continue to journey and heal, teaching the arts of massage in our Maine location, with the hopes that your inner peace, strength, and joy has emerged," she said.

Her voice came out louder this time. "The second reason you are here is to find your soul family as you learn to read the energy of the others in the room. Trust in the process of your own system. Once you have completed the classes, if you find your life partner and choose to make it official, we can take care of that, too," she continued.

I looked around at the people in the room and suddenly realized that we were all here for the same things: Leveling up, networking, and finding the man or woman that we could propel with.

From there, a new woman walked up onto the stage and hollered out, "Hello, entrepreneurs, extended guests, members of the military, and anyone else. My name is Charlotte McBride, and I am so excited to be here tonight. I am a Reiki Master and specialize in sacral healing."

I went over to the table where the fliers for each guest speaker were all lined up, scanned the list of names until I found her card, went over the materials in her brochure, and saw that she was also a tarot reader and oracle. That made my heart sing at that moment, and I knew she was what I needed. I saw that she had an opening for a session, and I decided to book one for the weekend. I wrote my name down in the available time slot, wrote it in my calendar, and then headed back to the party.

The claps roared through the room, and Karissa turned out to be so much more than the "witch" that I had once thought before. I could now see her as a Goddess of Love with her trails of feathers as she flew around the room while the night continued, exploding with sights and sound. The music tones rang higher and higher. As the Gods of the Sea roamed around, the passion in me began to rise. Lost in the Sea of Love as Neptune came flying by, I was utterly spellbound in the house overlooking the ocean as an apparition enchanted me.

As the God of the Sea was flowing down on me, I opened my eyes to see a man. This was no ordinary man. No, this was a seaman. It felt like I had flown down the Atlantic Coast and was back inside the living room of my best friend Tina's place. I felt the miles he traveled and felt his desire to kiss me again.

My eyes closed once again, not sure about what I was seeing. Traveling with him as our hips collided, the fireworks shot upwards inside my body, igniting as his hands held me tight. I could feel the length of time he waited for this special kiss, the seas he had crossed, the battles he fought, and the wars that raged on the ground and in his head.

All that pent-up passion accumulated in my head. It was like fire, exploding from the floor all throughout my body as if he flew right through me. I never thought that I would kiss a man so intensely and feel a surge of electricity, but something just happened to me. I opened my eyes again, expecting to see the man from way back, when I scanned the room, not knowing where he went. I thought that by now, he surely must be a captain as I inspected the sleeves of their white dress jackets, looking for stripes.

Of all the things I knew right now, for sure, if that man Kennedy touched me again, I might be head over heels in love. I looked up at Kennedy. What stopped it? Was it me? I cannot make the same mistake again. He is a married man, and I turned away. I continued to walk around the room, introducing myself, and then, out of the corner of my eye, I saw the captain again.

As I struggled to get clear, a surreal haze fell over my eyes while I made my way closer to the man in white. I could tell that he remembered me, and as my mind began to race, I started seeing shrimp in my head once again when on further inspection, it was just the waitress offering me a plate. I closed my eyes once again, forcing myself to just concentrate on the task at hand. "Was this man named Bob the man I met that night in Tina's house?" I thought to myself, as my memory flashed back to nearly twenty-seven years ago, desperately trying to remember what he looked like.

"This time," I listened attentively to the voice inside my head, crying from deep within, "Please do not deny me again, oh, my God," as the words escaped my lips. His jaw ever so softly danced around my chin. In what seemed like lightning speed, perceptive energy descended on me, telling me with his tongue the details of what he could deliver me. My legs were crumbling when I blacked out. I came to moments later, trembling on the dance floor. I had never felt anything so powerful in my life before when Kennedy helped me up and instructed me to catch my breath by going to the ocean.

I looked back at him, not understanding what he meant. I smiled and said, "Thank you for that," as I continued to walk all over the property, just trying to figure out what was happening to me.

The waves hit the rock that I am standing on, setting a trap for you to find me, "Come to me, goddess of the sea, I am waiting for you; the sea is calling out to you, too." I held my head tight, just wanting the voices to stop when, from out of nowhere, I felt it again.

Kissing me with all his might, the ship captain appeared, hovering down upon me in the moonlight, his stripes in plain sight, showering me with a kiss that a thousand years could no longer deny. The next kiss is going to be dynamite. I was nestled between the couch and the fireplace, as the wind blew me off to some far-away place as his hands gently caressed my face.

"I remember that look you had in your eyes that night. I knew that once I did, I was done for. That once I kissed you, it would be forever more. I would never be able to experience another person again. I had so many that I wanted before I really committed," In my mind, I heard his spirit say.

"I needed teachers, too. I was in no way ready for you. You were so much more woman back then. Me fumbling with the frying pans. I was not equipped for your heart. I would have broken yours all apart. I am here now, whole as I reach out to you. I've been following you," his spiritual voice continued.

I felt that I was being lured in, crawling to my lover's cravings, but I could not see him. As the mist formed in front of my eyes, I reached out and touched his face. I fell into his trap; it was like I could smell his scent once again and was being called back by the perfume of his hands as it wrapped around the bait. His tentacles entered me, and I was engulfed by his raging curiosity. It is like I was making love as I danced in the house by the sea. The ghost in my head lingered as he talked to me.

Once again, I found myself in another dimly lit hotel room. There was no choice anymore, as I grabbed his necktie and dragged him with such force that we landed on the bed. His arms ripped my dress off with all his might. I fumbled with the buttons, trying hard to win this fight. I could not help myself anymore as I ripped off his shirt.

He put his hand on my throat as he gently brought me higher. I could tell that there was going to be a big fire, as I was exploding before he was even inside. His right arm rested on my navel as he connected to my jeweled crown.

"You're driving me nuts," I thought, succumbing to my mind. I was once again the crab as my body bent back, feeling his spirit enter me. As my eyes fluttered open, I was spellbound, spinning under a canopy as the orchestra played.

Shooting stars lit up the night sky as the eternal sounds of the sea crashed all around me. I felt supported by thousands of seamen as they made their way towards me, dancing in a cove of love as the fragrance of hydrangeas and roses perfumed the air, and I knew it was all in my imagination.

As I made my way back up the stone steps, the scent of lavender began to slowly bring me back, and the sounds of the orchestra reminded me that I was at the *Center of Love* Grand Party. The Specter had vanished once again. I began to wonder if the fantastic kisses had ever happened. It was as if my whole life was a dream and, alas, I quickly walked astride the cold slate path back into reality.

The night played on for hours as I watched the love unfold, the sounds of pleasure hiding around the corners. I looked around the room, hoping to connect with someone, but alas, it was not going to happen tonight.

Our hosts ended the night with one final toast, and we all began to file out. My eyes glazed piercingly through each white dress to see if the captain was hiding beneath. I fumbled for my keys and headed back to my hotel.

Lying on the bed, my mind began to replay everything again as I freely let my hands explore myself. Dreaming of Clinton walking through my door, I longed to feel him again. I simply loved the way he bounced from sheer brute strength to gentleness in a flick of a switch. As I drifted off into a heavy sleep, I wondered once more if the night was real or just my imagination on overdrive.

Who Am I?

I swear it is like

a cook calling out to me

You are here with me

time beyond time is what I hear

That time is what you make it

Come with me, dear

Captain of the Sea

make love to me,

You are confusing me

it took many ladders for me to climb

submerged submission

Peeling potatoes was my first commission

Oh, how I loved that job

As I reach out in front of me

each thing over and over

it is like my mind

playing tricks on me

running with a lace of ribbon around my feet

A gown of red bounds me

My flower opening to you

your spectacles as they beckon me

make love to thee

My body can hardly take

this tease you are giving me

Which one was that in my head, you or me?

My body writhing, as my back climbs the helm

The captain spinning my body around

With his finger pointing right to my heart

His eruptions each tearing at my belt

Oh.... like popping corn

Drizzling me with his buttery flask

Sprinkling that sea-salty blast.

10
Confusion Says

I awoke the next morning with the sun shining through the windows. Looking over at the clock, I was shocked to see that it was 8:11. I had less than two hours to be ready for my first attunements, so I grabbed a bite to eat and made my way down Highland Drive. The morning sun beat down upon the steep slate roof. The stone walls inside the court gave the house a regal feeling, while the colorful trim gave way to the more tranquil lure of the sea with its ever-changing blueish-green schemes.

Karissa and Kennedy greeted me as I carried it to my massage table. The main dining area transformed into a classroom, as the massage tables were set up. Some sheets billowing in the breeze had made their way outside and dotted the landscape. The place was amazing and provided an atmosphere of great peace and love. As I joyously walked around and soaked in its energy, I could feel my roots wanting to sink in here.

Anxiously, I waited for all of us to arrive. In my mind, I was looking for the captain again. I hardly even recognized the man who came in. As our eyes locked, a sudden wave came over me as Clinton embraced me. "I don't remember you being here last night," I said to him as I pulled back, looking into his eyes.

"Oh, did you miss me?" he asked, with a questioning look to his brow. "I had some pressing business that needed my immediate attention, and I didn't come in until late last night," he explained, pulling away.

"Come in," I replied, "I thought you lived in the area."

"I do, or I will rather shortly," he said. "I just travel all over for business, and I didn't fly," he continued.

"You didn't," I asked.

"Nope, I took the scarab," he said, pointing down to where the boat was floating.

I tried to observe the vessel from where I was standing, but the pitch of the hill blocked my view, and all I could see was the stern when, around the corner, a beautiful woman approached us. She wrapped her arms around his waist and smiled at me.

"Let me introduce you to Charlotte Bennett," said Clinton, "this is Salem Bloemfontein."

As I reached out to shake her hand, her green eyes glared at me, and that is when I realized I had met her before. She gave me a perfunctory glance over without saying a word. I could tell she did not like me, and I really did not know why unless she was afraid of me. Why would she be afraid of me? What did I do? That's when I realized she was the woman in the cupcake war on "Slopped" and that I had beaten her that day. I looked back at her, knowing full well that the show was on.

"Where's your friend?" Clinton asked.

"My friend?" I stammered back, not knowing what he was thinking.

"Yeah, you know, the blonde I met the other night," he replied.

"Oh, Olivianna," I blushed. "Yeah, I do not know where she is at." Something came over me, and I knew I should just walk away from him. Let it go, a one-night stand, nothing more than that. But I must admit, it was harder than I thought.

I looked over as Kennedy made the announcement that

class would be starting and to partner up. I was relieved to break away from Clinton and Salem and decided I should look for someone else. I walked away from them, but my eyes could not look away from his, with a powerful stare until I looked back at Salem; the look on her face was priceless. I could almost feel her claws scratching my face, and I knew she had her talons sunk into Clinton. Imagine the relief I felt when the door opened and in walked Olivianna. We hugged for a second, and she gave me a wink.

Kennedy stood on a platform and scanned the audience in the room of about fifty people when he started the introduction and later led us into a mediation that lasted for fifteen minutes. As waves of calmness came over my soul, I knew everything would work out in the end.

According to Kennedy, the history of Maschakra is something he and Karissa coined, a blending of massage, messages, reiki, stone therapy, plant medicine, and an open and willing acceptance of the sensual side of the body. The teachers went around the room saying prayers over our heads, "opening us to the universe," according to Karissa. Next, we picked our stone necklaces by feeling which one was "calling" us.

I looked carefully around the room at the mix of people present. I saw a Native American man whose hair came down to his hips. A sizable group of people appeared to be from India, as well as what appeared to be a team of banking executives by the way they carried themselves. I could see hotel representatives as our eyes met and a whole boatload of Navy men and women. I counted five executive chefs standing around **Monique Outerbridge from Velvet Cakes by Gwen,** and I nearly peed myself!

I fumbled through my purse, knowing I had her business card, and there it was. I realized this was way bigger than what I had originally thought. "Oh my God, can you imagine all the iconic chefs of television right here?" I thought as I took a few deep breaths and told myself to calm down. I turned my gaze back to Kennedy as he demonstrated the first one with a beautiful woman who sparkled with shimmering lights.

I was in a state of tranquility as I watched his hands hover over her body. In an instant, I was entranced and transported inside the whole thing, vicariously feeling the energy exchange. They went through hand placement on the knees and ankles, explaining what each chakra meant, and I was amazed at what I was perceiving. I deeply felt myself release emotions that I was not even aware were mine as I saw various corresponding shades of colors envelope and fill my body.

It was virtually a dreamlike dance, back and forth between

partners, and I began to experience the silent language of being still and knowing.

As I looked over the questions, some seemed so personal. Kennedy explained everything further, and I began to feel more at ease. I was a bit offended at first, until I realized that I needed to thoroughly find myself, so I decided to answer the questions truthfully. If I could not be honest with myself then why bother? I began to answer each question as accurately and forthrightly as I could. Then, we took turns explaining what we felt to the group.

All day, I wanted to work on the Captain in White who kissed me last night to see what I felt, but he seemed to be nowhere in sight. No one's touch even remotely compared to his all day, and I realized I was losing sight, but I clearly felt his energy last night. Once again, Clinton was nowhere to be found, and I resigned to focusing on myself, not worrying about what was going to happen, and just experiencing and being happy in the moment.

Karissa and I paired up together, and I felt an energy exchange that blew me away. Sensations I never thought I would feel again came flooding back in. As my brain tried to wrap everything around my head, I went out back. I took a few more deep breaths before I was ready to head up the stone walk. As I looked up the stairs, there stood a different man.

The way he was waving that got my attention. He introduced himself and said that he worked for Kirkland Construction. We seemingly talked for nearly an hour in our souls, although in actual Earth time, it was only a few minutes. He told me he was a carpenter, and I smiled and asked if I could have his business card. He said that he was fresh out of cards, and we decided to Facebook® each other instead. The day was spent exchanging with different people.

Each experience seemed to open another door to communication that I was not aware existed on this plane. We broke for lunch, and I sat down by the water. The leftovers from last night tasted even better than what I remembered them being when I caught myself looking up at the clouds and remembered I had that appointment with Charlotte McBride.

I quickly walked back up to the house, where Kennedy guided me up the stairs and to a room where Charlotte was sitting at a table with a candle lit. The scent of sage was burning in the air as hints of lavender and geranium wrapped around me. She gave me an initial card reading where she said my heart chakra was bypassing my solar plexus, and deep inside, I knew what it was. I laid down on the table and relaxed as her hands passed over my body while she explained what she was feeling to me. The session was over in an hour, and I walked out back where the rest of the members were gathering, deciding what they were going to do for dinner.

Some were going over the bridge where hundreds of restaurants lined the street, proclaiming that theirs was the "best fish n' chips you'll ever eat." As I reached for my keys, I almost gave up when I spied out of the corner of my eye, none other than the captain leaning up against the side of the house. I do not know what came over me as I reached into my purse, pulling out my hotel key. The closer I walked to him, the more he was gliding over to me until I was right in front of him.

"You're Bob, right?" I said, as my hands extended out to him, "My hotel has a bar. Would you care to join me?"

He reached out and took the key from my hand. I turned away as my body began to shake at the sheer stupidity of what I just did, and I quickly got back into my Mustang® and headed to the inn. Nearly forgetting about Olivianna, I beeped the horn. She came running out of the house with a joint hanging out of her mouth. The more I kept thinking about what could happen, the more excited I became.

"I got a date," she said. "Don't wait up."

My fingers trembled as the motor ignited, and I nearly

cringed at the thought of getting laid. Stalling the car twice as my feet fumbled with the clutch and the gas pedal, I ripped my shoes off, threw them to the side and feathered the gas pedal until I was out of the driveway. I felt like a bumbling fool as I finally got the accelerator to work, and the car took off with a jerk. The house with the large bell made me laugh as the radio started playing "*You Can Ring My Bell*" by Anita Ward.

I walked into the inn and let the man at the front desk know that I might have a guest tonight. I sauntered over to the restaurant and perched up at the bar. "Eddie, I need help," I gasped as I plopped my head on the polished wood.

He promptly slid a cold drink over to me.

My fingers tapped the rail as I put a Sushi order in. I watched and listened as the front door swung open with each guest strolling in.

I made small talk with some of the locals, and one man told me about his brother, who can always be found down at the lighthouse with a bottle of wine. I was intrigued by a man who sat by the water with some vino, but tonight was not the night for socializing, so I paid my bill and headed back up to my room.

The warm, pulsing shower water flowed down all over me,

and I heard the beat of the drums as the violin played. At first, I was not sure what was happening or if my imagination was playing tricks on me.

His hands were large and rugged – yet soft – at the same time. I closed my eyes, and I felt the plastic oil bottle in his hand as he took me from behind. His palms rounded my shoulders, gliding all the way down my back. I felt his magnitude, and I could not wait to feel his generosity inside of me again. My frame arched after waves of musical notes crashed down on me, and my torso continued to contract as I felt the full metal in his vest.

I turned and slowly began to raise my arms up into the air as his chocolate eyes stared back at me. I closed my eyes and felt the smooth emulsion on his hands glide down my skin. As my hands crossed each other, I felt his manly strength.

His veiny muscles were hard as steel as he pressed his palms into my wrists up against the tiles, where he slammed my fist.

In a flash, we were lying on the bed with his mouth descending on my neck, sucking me like he was a vampire draining a victim. Even if he were a vampire, I would still readily agree to be his prey. His dark chocolate skin glistened with perspiration as I clamored to let him deep inside me.

Just to be able to feel this right now, this supercharged Captain of the Sea, the other man that is captivating me. It was like his fingers were laced with golden dust, and his energy was all over me as he securely tied me again to the bedpost. The boiling water nuclear reactor of the passions dwelling within me trembled to be released. With my arms firmly bound and my legs untied, I could not wait to get on his ride!

His fingers began to feather my skin so lightly, taking me back to the morning when he first put his ham in my greens. I watched as he took the stone pendulum off his neck and placed it over my pelvis.

The faster the orange calcite spun, the more intense of a release I felt until I finally gave in. Bucking wilder than any horse I have ever met, I even thought that I could take my own pony for a bet.

My motor was not only running, but it was sitting on the start line with my feet on the gas and the clutch at the same time, and my right hand was firmly held around the eight ball of the gear shift, which reminded me of a pool table. I was just waiting for the Christmas tree to go green as the roaring of both engines got the stadium jumping. The machine to my right, traveling nautically last night, has embraced me with his 70's era Chevy® 454 Big Block, alright.

His dark brown skin ignited a passion within that I could no longer hide as it shimmered in the light, traveling to further dimensions as each blast of energy took me higher. My instrument was not going down without a fight as my tongue took flight. Plunging deep inside, I give him my best. It felt like I was hitting the wall, with fluids spraying up on me. The white light shined down on me, reaching maximum intensity.

The indescribable source of energy was calling, screaming to God to release his heaven in me. My voice hollered out to the Chocolate God shimmering on top. My goddess was in resplendent pink as her torrential rivers flowed and the stones spun wildly out of control. The harsh slap of his hand spanked my ass and commanded me right out of the bed, spurting my elixir on the floor. As I raced to the bathroom, I heard a knock at the door.

Bill of Rights

My lover from my past life

It was not until I kissed you

I realized who you were

Not until you kissed me

Did I know about this curse?

please release me

The essence of healing

Is coming to thee

Stop fighting your luminosity

I release you Marijuana

My sweet Mary Jane

That heals my pain

release the plant

Let love flow once again

I release you from your bitter stain

Make love and live while you are on this plain

I love I love you, my sweet Mary Jane

I release, I release, I release you of this pain

Free your soul, yes you will

When you release the Marijuana Bill

seeds shall dot the lands

Let the American Spirit

Determines who wins

Let the entrepreneurs usher in

That is the only way America Wins

When Imagination can grow within

The Spirit of the Warrior a deep walking

Clamoring to get to the other side

Fighting my way each step every day

Determined in the end, I will get my way

11
One Mixed Drink Coming Up

Looking over at the alarm clock, it was almost ten as I fumbled in the dark, making my way to the hall light. Damn! As I looked around the room, it was all just a dream again. I opened the door to a shiny pair of black dress shoes. Oh, God! Could it be Clinton? Oh, please let it be him, as my breath started to rise. The more I continued to follow up his torso, the more I realized this was not the man I was dreaming about.

He took his hat off, tipping it to me with a nod and uttered, "Charlotte." His full head of hair confirmed in my mind that it was not Clinton this time. Standing there for a moment, frozen in time, his chocolate brown eyes reassured me I was in good hands. He looked at me and drew his next breath. "Do you always give strange men your 'key'?" he asked.

I looked at him as a nervous smile escaped my lips. "No," I said. "I don't."

"My name is Jerrod," he said with an Indian accent. "I am trained in the healing sensual arts and have penned many books on spiritual enlightenment," he elaborated. "I've come to you tonight to teach you," he continued.

I looked up at him rather puzzled, with my eyes slanting down, as I concentrated on reading him.

He started moving closer as he flipped the hotel key through his flanges. "What I'm going to share with you is an advanced class," he said softly. He put his hands in prayer, nodding Namaste, as I opened the door up and invited him in.

"How did you know what I need?" I asked as he came in and sat on the couch.

"Your eyes tell secrets that you think you have hidden," he replied as he began to chant and encouraged me to join him.

I did not know what to think as the OMs began to vibrate off my lips, and I felt myself connecting to a deep space in my heart.

He led me to my bed and instructed me to lie down. Every vulnerability I had was shaking off me as his hands hovered over my skin. He started with my feet with slight hand pressure and encouraged me to inhale deeply, then blow out to a count of ten, controlling my release. Tremors erupted as my body shook from my feet to the top of my head.

Memories of when I was molested as a child began to surface as I found the courage to say "No." The little girl, too young to know the difference at the time, came back out. She was too young to understand that not to show other people your behind.

As his hands hovered over my pelvic region, my body relaxed, and I was sequentially released from highly negative memories from past incidents. Each insecurity I had was being serially addressed as his hands rested gently on my navel, and my tears fell copiously upon the bed.

He whispered in my ear the name of each chakra as the vivid spectrum of corresponding colors floated into my head.

My body was heaving as his hands moved up to my heart space. My whole chest lunged forward as his fingers pressed, ever so lightly, into my nightdress. As his hands glided up and down over my body, successive waves of emotions poured out of my eyes. Conventional time, space and mass seemed meaningless as I entered an altered state of consciousness, wherein my soul transcended to a new level.

As the hours passed through the night, a fluttering of sensations came over me. I found myself suspended in a weightless atmosphere, where our bodies floated in the air. That is what his love felt like. That is the only way I could describe what happened that night. Our bodies never merged, yet we flew like angels in the midnight sky.

Jerrod did things to me that I have yet to understand in the exact way that his lips touched my chakras, breathing new life into my soul. He thoroughly moved me that night, for I felt healed and loved without fright. In the end, he was the most beautiful soul I had ever encountered. His use of alternative medicine is what intrigued me the most. We talked for hours about how personal energy needs to be freed and how the lakes and oceans are the birthplace of healing.

I asked his opinion on cannabis and told him how the herb has been helping me. No longer on any type of pharmaceutical medicine, I refused to believe I had epilepsy, as the tremors simply felt too glorious to me, like sexual explosions from my toes to the ends of my hair. It felt like I was in the movies as the spaceship of my essence and being hit warp speed. Why would I want to take that away?

"That damn bipolar curse," he said. "Why can't they see? How did you think I could have written all these books if we were not connected to His divinity? That is the reason you do not need as much sleep when you are writing; you are in God's Grace. Who do they think writes the music and songs, the lyrics we sing?" he reflected.

"He was the most brilliant man I had ever met," I thought to myself. As I breathed inside his chest, I instantly remembered when I was in heaven, writing my birth script. Now, I was clearly seeing that I had planned all of this. I came here to do a task.

The Messengers are angels underneath, I realized, as he continued to breathe. I felt more wisdom when he blew into my crown chakra like barn doors opening from the ground. Like magic, it was as if doves descended into my head. Their wings fluttered rapidly as I heard them sing the Songs of the Sages. Guiding my words as best as I could, I was seeing my very future unfold when I touched him. Was he really Metatron underneath?

His lips were like honeybees in a garden of brilliant colors and scents. I woke up early in the morning, refreshed, knowing nothing was breached — just a new enlightened paradigmatic exchange of spiritual energy underneath, spreading love across the land.

I drove back into the house on Highland Drive to the next

class in spiritual development and wondered what more I would learn today. Once again, I strained, looking to see if Clinton was there. The harder I looked for him, the more disappointed I felt, and I decided to put him out of my mind for now.

I was paired up with Jaxson, and we had rivers to ford, mountains to climb and deep seas to explore in the infinite multiverse of the soul. A wooden case of different-shaped pendulums was brought out, and we were all shown how to read the body, with a different teacher. As the crystal swayed back and forth or rotated in a circle, it indicated what the individual chakras or energy centers were doing.

It was utterly amazing, knowing the questions that one can ask and receive an answer for. Equally impressive is that the more I was focused on the body, the more I could read it. I would see things and whisper, "Does this sound familiar?" as the images appeared.

When each release was happening, I felt the emotions as they went through me, and my body shivered or shook. It might appear as if it is painful at first, but it is rather ornate. It was as if God was rewarding me with a dose of his divine embellishment. As my mind expanded, it became more open to the rest of the people in the room. I began to pay greater attention to their more subtle movements and could sense the differences in and unique qualities of each person's energy configuration.

In parallel light, my spiritual consciousness expanded to learn to be close when you are so far away and to see people not just for the color of their skin but what was on the inside. The light behind the skin was so cleverly hidden, thinking that the soul could not be seen.

The town was still as perfect as I remembered it to be. The shops were lined all up and down the streets. It was a genuinely nice week as I strolled through the streets, getting to know everyone and me. I paused and thought about that as I walked all around the wharf, looking at all the lobster boats. I remember the days when I would watch the boats that all came for the Americas Cup race, the lobster traps piled on top of each other, when it suddenly sank in that what we all needed was each other.

The connections that I was making with all kinds of people were staggering. I met media executives, actors and singers, hotel managers and real estate tycoons. I met divorced women who were finding themselves to figure out if they preferred men or women or realizing that they liked both.

I registered for the full-week retreat in August at the Maine location, as well as several other two or three-day retreats around the country. As I went through each level, I went over the scheduled locations and decided where I wanted to visit, coordinating with my scheduled book signings as much as possible. As I looked at the map of all the different classes I had to sign up for, I was nearly delirious. The Vegas class was just two months away, and I signed up for that week's retreat before it was booked up.

I knew as the classes continued from levels two and three that eventually, I would take the massage class with the idea that I would find someone I felt safe with to begin massaging on my own. For the first time in ages, it was time to come out of hiding. I spent the next weeks working on book tours across the country, making my way around the malls of America, selling my brand in every bookstore that I could get myself into. My days were long and filled with traveling. I welcomed the thoughts of another vacation, so I began to look up and plan what I would do when I was in Vegas.

I Am Free

A red like nothing I have ever absorbed

the orange-like sparks of fire in the sky

the yellow that reminds me of clover honey

trails of green luminosity

shades of blue that still haunt me

the violet was like blueberries and cream

whisking its energy into my dreams

then white as bright as you could see

So, blinding you, brace your eyes in its beams

All of that spinning in a vortex, uniting all eternity

12
What Happens in Vegas

The room was filled with a broad mix of celebrities, regular persons looking to advance professionally and some who just wanted to focus on personal development. Others were there just for healing throughout the day. I remembered one gentleman, thinking that he looked like a cowboy when he walked in wearing his black hat, with his full beard hiding most of his face. His eyes spoke to me, and I could tell he led a fantastic life back in the day.

I was drawn to him in an instant, even though he was a good ten years older than me. It felt like, in some small way, that I could mend his heart. As soon as Karissa said to partner up, I made my way to him to introduce myself. I liked the way his jaw cracked a warm smile as his right hand patted my shoulder.

Laughing, he said, "I knew I would have you before the night was over."

"You keep thinking that," I said as I shook his hand. I would not dare to tell him that I was sure I had him pinned to my walls as a teenager growing up. I positioned my hands in Namaste and invited him to the table.

As my hands ran through his hair, I could not help but start to massage his scalp. His muscles were still well-defined, and his sun-ripened skin felt smooth under my hands as I began to massage his neck. I closed my eyes, rubbing his shoulders, as my hands trembled over his delicate skin.

There was something so magnetic about his energy. It was only a Reiki Two class, but my natural inclination to massage his body was taking over. In my fertile mind, I was already unbuttoning his shirt. All I could think about was running my hands down his chest, as it just felt like his muscles were tense and needed a healing release.

I composed myself and asked him if he minded if he took his shirt off so that I could kiss his chakras. He lifted his shirt off, revealing a trail of hair surrounding his navel, and in an instant, I was taken back to when I saw him many years ago on the big screen. It felt like electricity was coming out of my hands as my nails began to massage his scalp.

I began by asking him to take three deep breaths in unison with me. As our bodies continued to connect, I could not help but go back in time with him. My mind was racing as I was trying to figure out which man from the television set or movie screen was under my fingertips. His jeans made me think of Burt Reynolds, and then his smile took me to Sean Connery, and as I watched his t-shirt come off, Richard Gere exploded in my mind. My legs began to tremble, as I was so nervous at the thought of it being any one of the iconic fantasy lovers of my adolescent nights. Inside my head, I was dying to figure out who exactly he was.

I had just about forced myself to get it together when he mouthed, "*Don't Start a Ruckus Love.*" Then, I realized that over all the years I spent in the kitchen, all the people I have witnessed, he could have been any of them. He could have been the dishwasher from way back when, for all I knew.

I continued to let my trembling hands be guided, placing them on his heart chakra. Kennedy instructed us to begin by encouraging us to connect our breaths. As I began breathing in, all I could feel was the presence of God going through me. I could feel the beating of our hearts as they fell into synchronicity. I began to see tiny shades of red luminosity and hear the Orient as string instruments were played.

In that moment, he was every man I had ever loved. He was Simon and Art, Gilbert and Bo, he was Elvis in Hawaii and Superman® flying above. I felt my own soul begin to beat to the rhythm of the string section of a symphony orchestra as I heard Rachmaninoff's *Theme of Paganini* play. I opened my eyes and saw that his body was heaving off the sheet as if some mysterious energies were guiding him.

I needed to get grounded right away. I stood back up and made my way to his feet. Holding on to his black dress socks, I began to pray. I sensed in my heart that he was a King and wondered what to do with this information. Just then, I knew what to do.

The Magician spoke in all his glorious incantations, and down on my knees I went. As my lips kissed his heels, I was reminded that with each kiss, I was kissing the King. As the mist seemed to enter the room, I became lost in a fog as I kissed each dactyl. As my mind went back, I felt myself as Mary. I felt the presence of angels as they surrounded me in a glass palace as Jens Cad spoke to me.

I covered his body with a small towel and began with small, tender kisses, melting every wound on his skin. As my lips touched his right ankle, I could feel the energy go through me. As my lips slowly made my way to his knees, I could see how he landed hard on them just to please the stadium and front-row seats. I held on, concentrating right where I was and took three deep breaths. Then, I blew the air up toward his chest with the intention of hitting his root chakra, the first energy center at the base of the spine.

As the music played, I felt a bright light sparkle with each breath I blew, and my sole mission was to breathe life into each of his chakras. With all the love I have in the world, my lips kissed each scar as the mother of all Eternity channeled through me.

I heard Karissa say to Kennedy, "Her wingspan is growing. Look at the gold shine beneath her wings," as my ears tuned in. After the third breath to the sacral chakra, I could feel the spin of energy underneath my hands, and I was in. An explosion of red, orange, and yellow glowed in my eyes. In my mind, I was seeing bananas, oranges, passion fruit, pineapples, avocados, and cucumbers. I thought that he must be another cooking kind of guy.

As I continued to kiss his body, I arrived at his solar plexus. As I breathed into his power, I could feel his essence go into me. Tiny kisses fell from my fingertips as I began to make my way to the center of his chest, the heart chakra, whereupon I next placed my hands.

I began to speak out loud to his heart, "I want you to envision new veins growing. Anticipate tiny feet like tails, making their way into the lining of your valves. Imagine volts of electricity streaming out of my fingers, getting the blood flowing to your chambers. Imagine as my air comes in breathing love, light, peace, strength, vigor, and vitality with every breath I blow".

As my mind continued to transmit healing energy, my lips made their way to his throat, and the sensation of his five o'clock shadow grazed my hands as my lungs breathed new energy into his voice. Making my way with my lips puckered, I gently kissed the brow chakra and imagined that I could feel inside his mind's eye. I saw musical notes dancing by, sending a clear channel to the station he requested as I breathed my love inside.

His hands were on his hips as I made my way to the front of his head. His thick hair ran through my veins as I began to hear rain. As I traced his eyes with a light touch, his body began levitating off the table once again. I felt the exact same energy source as my own body began to spasm from deep within.

Continuing to breathe, I was centered again in what seemed like some sort of acrobatic stunt. My body shook vigorously from within. As I lay on the floor, I looked up to see two men working on me at the same time. I was encouraged to stay down as I felt a pair of hands softly go over my eyes. This time, I looked up again; I knew the energy as I had felt it before. It was the conductor from the party in Rhode Island.

As the spasms continued, my body reached for the lights, and I awakened to see Karissa at my feet. The out-of-body experience had taken me to another dimension. As my soul vibrated in the light above my head, I experience the combined power of three people as they worked on me. In my mind, I could see the fire come out of their hands, as one at a time, their wings emerged, dancing around me, bathed in red and blue lights.

As the light expanded in me, my senses were taken to new revelations as the orange ball of light began swirling above my head. This warm ball of liquid energy reminded me of orange zest, with its sweet juice squirting on me, leading me to my destiny. The now dripping fruit squeezed over my lips released its scent and opened as Kennedy walked past.

The orange energy created a wave of releases that resonated and vibrated in my sacral region. Next, as my body arched up to the sun, yellow lemon zest, in turn with its brilliant light, flooded my soul as liquid sunshine, igniting my power. Feeling myself channeled to some higher dimension with the beat of my heart as the drum sounded, the emerald, green lights now illuminated my flightpath. I knew that my plans were arriving as the aroma of lime embraced and imbued me.

Waves of love cascaded over me like a blanket of pink roses, as drops of sweet sweat mixed with sandalwood dripped down on me. The blue light descended upon me as my lips tasted of elderberries. I could feel them as they dropped down hard on me, flowing like air through my lungs and breathing new life into me as my body spasmed responsively under the sheets.

Royal Purple then appeared in all its splendor, and graces were showered down upon me. Hiding in the most amazing of places, the oval jewel encased in platinum hovered over my Third Eye, transmitting secrets from ancient eyes as my eyes were imbued with new life energy. The lavender ice cream and honey dream fragrance were all around me as I tasted it in the wine that was circulating.

Finally, the white light of protection flowed inside me, exploding as I called out to the Goddess Within. My body fully released its pressures and tensions, as my yoni could no longer deny the volcanic lava flow burning inside. Waves of emotions surged out of me as a multi-colored kaleidoscope of colors burst from every orifice, like millions of shooting stars in every color of the wheel, as we continued to mouth breathe. Indescribable colors that I have never seen before emanated from my vertebrae.

I felt brilliantly enlightened as I floated up towards the light when I looked around the room and my eyes fixated on the man whose music I had been singing. It took a few moments for me to gather myself, then I got up and walked over to the man who I knew as Jewel Carter, the King of Funk and extended my hand. "I have been listening to your music for years," I said as our hands met, and he nodded his head.

"That's cool, baby," he said as he took my hand, "I appreciate you." We decided to partner up when the class broke for lunch. As the cannabis high began to lull its way in, he started talking about the dealership where he picked up his new ride. He looked around and said, "We've got time; come on, let's go for a ride."

I jumped up without a care in my head, knowing full well that all one must do is say "car" to me, and I am down on my knees, begging the car gods to give me what I need! I slipped into his Maserati®, and it was a dream, with the engine purring as I rubbed its leather seats. Oh, man! It was so amazing as he pulled around the bend, feathering the clutch and the petal. He gently rolled her over the plate, and down the rows, he strolled, flaunting his new fly ride. I was thinking Mercedes® when he caught my eye. I clamped my hand down on his thigh when I yelled, "Oh my God, Stop the car!"

My legs began to shake as I saw him on the stage; I opened the car door. I was drawn to him like he was an alien's spacecraft, and I was caught in its energy field. I was totally mesmerized and lost in his grace. The more I ran my hands down the sleek curves, the more I started to moan to myself. I soon lost all sense of my surroundings as I drooled on the cool metal. I begged the car salesman to let me in, and within moments, I heard a click when another salesman came out with the keys, looked me in the eye and asked if I wanted to take it for a spin.

"Oh my God ... YES," I nearly squealed with delight. I slipped down into the driver's seat when I felt the stick. I closed my eyes as I caressed the shaft. "Please, car Gods, let me have this!" I prayed as I pressed the button, and he fired up. The excitement of it all nearly blew my top off as I looked over at the man Jewel to my right. "You ready to go for the ride of your life?" I asked.

"Fo'sho," he said, "let us do this right." He fastened his seat belt and lit up a joint.

The Bugatti® Divo ™ engine roared as I hit the gas pedal and left the lot on Sahara Drive. All I could think of was to get him off on the highway; one wrong turn was all it took, and there I was on Harmony Drive with this sweet car as my ride. The roar of my engine surged as we hit the strip. "Oh my God, I can get used to this," I thought.

As I rubbed my hands around the steering wheel, so absorbed in the mechanical pleasure of the moment that I had almost forgotten about the class I was in. Adding this to my list, I said back to him, "Mama's working on a plan," as I rolled him in. I ran my hands along the gear shift one more time, imagining that the car was in my driveway this time. "I'm going to need a bigger garage," I said with hearty laughter.

"Hold on, let me catch my breath," I said, turning to Jewel, the music icon that took my breath away. I looked at the salesman and asked if I could have just a few more minutes alone with him.

"Sure," he said as he got out of the car shutting the door.

I watched as he talked with the man to his right. It only took a second before I could hear the Bugatti® speak to me through the rumble of the idle as I watched the gas meter slide. I sat there running my hands down its hard, sleek body when I closed my eyes and saw it all vividly in my head, the blue and red lights so far in the distance reminding me that I just cannot have it yet.

"Oh, but I want you, baby," I kept saying to myself as I let my hands rub the seats, screaming out, "I want you, Bugatti® Divo™ ... I want you," as I rode the seat. I ran my hands eagerly along the instrument panel as I whispered in the gear shift. "What do I gotta do to get you?" I asked silently as my fingers traced the leather casing that covered up the steering wheel.

"Make me fuel efficient," I heard back in the sexiest voice I have ever heard in my life. It sounded like Barry White and Sean Connery with a hint of a Spanish accent as his tongue rolled when it yelled out, "Antonio!"

"Jesus Christ!" I exclaimed, "am I nuts, or does this car freaking talk?"

The car salesmen nodded their heads in unison, and one of them said, "Yes, he does, and his name is Geronimo."

I was so glad I wore a pantie liner today, with the roar of all 1500 horses running between my legs. The sound of hemp came screaming in my ears, "Fuel efficiency baby ... I'm coming, my dear." I could hardly stand it anymore, as it automatically started up just to give me a roar.

Kissing the gray man of steel one last time, I held my legs tight as I got off his ride. I was in love with him for sure. "I will have you someday," I said to myself, running my hands down the back end. I stood behind, holding to the tail end, when I felt a wave of energy go past. The emission was going to be fantastic; all it was going to take was a little hemp lubricant in his gas tank!

"Fuel efficiency," I heard Geronimo say, "I might have to sacrifice a few horses for that."

I rubbed the rear end once again and said, "That's OK. I can't ride fifteen hundred horses at the same time, anyway". "Until we meet again, boyfriend," I whispered, blowing "him" a kiss.

We got back into the Maserati®, and the iconic music legend, Jewel, skillfully sped away, glowing in the pleasure of the moment, as we pulled back into the parking garage and made our way to class.

The men and women cried out in the room. Some wailed about babies dying long ago in their wombs. Some grieved over the loss of loved ones. Some whimpered as they released a rape memory. Others had crosses too great to bear. The men in the room were holding on for the nation's sake. One of the women across the room was having very traumatic releases, just like mine had been. One could tell from her sobs that she was releasing some dark memory of being violated.

Our eyes locked on each other as we were both somehow connected to the same experience. From across the room, we breathed together and resonated as the healers continued to hover over one another. We could tell by just looking at each other what the other one had gone through.

"Hi, my name is G'anacia," she said, introducing herself. She reached out her arms wide, and we embraced warmly. She smiled and asked if I wanted to pair up, and I eagerly took her up on her offer. She went to the table first as my mind wandered off in the distance.

This time, I traveled even further back into the past. Through a tunnel, I was walking with people who I seemed to know but could not place. Off in the distance, a wrought iron table with chairs was waiting with two tumblers filled with lemonade. I saw the sprigs of lavender and mint infused into the ice as the facets reflected the crystal glass. A voice in my head nudged me to sit down, and I waited for my visitor to arrive.

The cushions cradled my body as I wondered who was inside. In my mind, I felt a wave of security come over me as I fell deeper into the ongoing conversation in my head. As the chimes sounded, I was brought out of the tunnel with resounding speed while I held still to her feet. That was when I realized she was someone famous with her own private security details.

The food was incredible, and the cannabis editable, which I was lucky enough to sink my teeth into. I watched as the man spoke candidly at the podium about how he used to be addicted to all kinds of prescription pharmaceuticals, how cannabis saved his life and how he was now devoted to making it legal. He came out to Nevada to get a head start on his company while he waited for Delaware to pass legislation legalizing the adult recreational use of marijuana.

When whispers in my ear, that seemed like a typewriter in my subconsciousness. Suddenly, I heard a camera shutter flick and looked up to see Eddie Bell, the famous photographer from the Las Vegas Strip. Knowing I needed a new headshot for my next book cover, I excitedly asked if he could fit me in.

"I got you," he replied, as he turned to his assistant, "Schedule her for this week."

I was so excited to get the famous Eddie Bell taking my headshot. That is when it began to dawn on me that the *Center of Love* was way more than a love club. They were a networking agency as well. I sent the money to his account to confirm my time slot and decided on Mt. Charleston for our next meet-up. The *Center of Love Club* members had a few more tricks up their sleeves when the legendary Prince Fleet Easton jumped up on the stage and started singing the songs of yesterday.

Cannabis for the Win

My body convulsing

overwhelming me

I cannot help but spasm.

I cannot help but want to be free

As the pineapple fields enters in

A hefty shot of jasmine tea wins

As my mind is open once again

Two men healers

Working on me

Oh, this, by far

Is what is exciting me

Two men and me

In a fantasy freeze

The Garden is tempting me

To invite them both in

To relax as the hands hover and win

As waves of emotions

That long to be free

Release themselves from me

As the tears flush away

All the pain of yesterday

I am asking, you to do you want it too.

Do you want to be free once again?

Close your eyes and count to ten

Let the color spectrum explode within.

13

Virginia Is for Lovers

Old Man winter was still holding tight even though it was the first of April. The snow began falling over my camp, reminding me that mother nature still calls the shots, as I made my way up to the master bedroom suite. The large set of windows overlooking the lake made the decision for the King bed to be placed in front of it easy. With a remote control to bring the whole bed up, I could sit in bed and keep writing for hours.

The halo of the moon was trying to peak through the snow-filled clouds, but it was no match, and the snow was winning. The branches of the trees were heavily laden with white powder as I listened to their loud creaking and placed a few more logs in the fireplace.

In Bath, Virginia, was one upcoming class, where the Reiki

symbols and their meanings would be taught while we floated in the mineral springs and let the water naturally do the healing. I was trying to give up on hearing from Clinton, but that night, the thoughts of him just kept creeping back into my head. When the tug inside my underwear began calling me again, I reached over to my phone and sent Kennedy a text. "My next fantasy is to meet someone who wants to see the world with me," it read.

Within a few minutes, he replied, "Go join *The Center of Love Club* message board".

I rolled my eyes but was relieved to see there were no grueling psychology tests to take — just an open communications board with the user's names and the areas that they live in. I downloaded the last picture I had taken when I was out in Vegas. It cost me a few bucks to have that shot, but Eddie Bell was worth every penny to me. The more I began looking at the connections, the more I began to see the pattern. Each person was either famous or high profile, and I sat there, wondering how the hell did I get in when the thought finally occurred that I was one of them!

I had never really thought of being famous (at least, that was not my motivating factor) as I started the rough draft of my next book — a collection of recipes with the stories behind how they were made. I was contemplating naming it *"My Sweet Rosemary"* when I heard a ping and looked down at my phone. The icon of Clinton had appeared, and I nearly blew my tea all over my brand-new sheets! My hands wrapped around the phone, contemplating my next move when the green light vanished, and I fell flat back again. Shrugging my shoulders, I decided to just give up on him.

"I guess I should have never had sex with him," I thought to myself. But then again, how do you know what you want if you are not willing to try a few things? I put out a blank message to the group just to see who would respond. You would have thought I would have been over this already as I typed the words "Is anyone up who wants to talk?" and hit send.

Within a few minutes, I got a response from one of the guys I had met in Jamestown named Jaxson. Previously, we exchanged phone numbers and texted for a bit, and I told him that I just signed up for the Bath County retreat in a few weeks.

"Me too," was the response back. "Do you want to carpool?" was the next message.

I had seriously thought about flying due to the long trip when I got a text message from Olivianna that read, "I saw you just signed up for Virginia, "Can you pick me up?" Two minutes earlier, I was sitting here all alone, and now I had two people wanting to go. I typed back "Sure" to both. That got me wondering where I was going to put them.

I heard a sound that, at first, I thought was butter sizzling in a frying pan. The more I listened, the more I realized it was no longer snowing. I got up from my bed and looked out the window and, to my horror, it was freezing rain. I cringed when I ran back to my bed, as my early morning meeting with the producers would probably have been rescheduled.

I rolled over, closed my eyes, and repeated in my head, "Trust the process … trust the process," over and over.

The next morning, I woke up in an ice castle. I headed down the steps to the kitchen, made a pot of coffee, went to my old bedroom that was now my office, and turned on the desktop computer. The bitter cold temperatures outside were a stark contrast to what I was feeling inside, and it felt good to walk around the house without a massive layer of clothes on and still be warm. It was almost a quarter past ten when the phone rang with my agent on the line.

"Your book's sales are doing fabulous, and I have an interview for you lined up with a major network in New York City. Do you think you can be there? It's scheduled for the second week of April," he said excitedly.

I flew through my calendar, looking at the dates, when I saw that it was in the same week as the retreat. "I can do it," I replied, as I envisioned myself in the studio. I took a deep breath and began to dance around the house singing: "I want a Cadillac®, plenty of room for my groceries in the back, I want it, I want it. I want a Cadillac®, sugar maple steering wrapped sound system that does not hold back, and I want it! I want it! I want a Cadillac®, go cruising down the track, I want it, I want a Cadillac®!"

I belted out the last notes, watching as the ice-encased my house. The ball was really rolling now, and my next cookbook was getting ready for release. A news flash went over my phone that they were predicting another round of ice storm, when from the corner of my eyes. A new Cadillac® XT5 popped up on my screen. "Predicting," I said to myself, "Where are their heads at? It's been freezing rain all night."

The quiet stillness of the house lured me back to my bed, where the message board was calling me. There on the screen, was a message from Kennedy. I clicked the message open.

"R U, OK?" it read.

Reluctantly, I typed back, "Yeah, I'm okay, why?"

"Just didn't know if you needed anything," he typed back.

"Yes, a man would be nice. Got any handy?" I replied.

"I got plenty," he shot back.

I stared at the message for nearly five minutes when the thoughts of Clinton popped back into my head.

I went over my bank account; the buffer I was seeing was looking good, and I started to contemplate my next move when the Cadillac® flashed me again. I could not wait to slide my thighs down on those seats as I clicked on the website.

The images of the wide tires clinging tight to the road and the maple sugar with black accents were getting me excited – not to mention the cooling and heating options! No way was I selling my Mustang®. I waited for a few hours to see what the storm was going to do. By eleven o'clock, the temperatures dropped, and I knew I was simply going nowhere. I did the unthinkable: I looked up my Cadillac®, and it led me to a company that would deliver it to me.

My heart melted when I slid down on the leather chaps. Damn, he reminds me of Clinton! Maybe this Cadillac® is not a woman this time! Maybe, just maybe, it is a man. Oh yes, I can see him now. Long and wide, comfortable, strong and confident in his Black Passion Tint Coat! Oh yes, "My Caddy," as Daddy would say. That Black Caddy was the car of my dreams. The wood grain was stained with gold and brown sparkles lacquered to a high finish. The leather-wrapped steering wheel begged me to wrap my fingers around it and massage its hard finish. It only took one push of the button to know that I had arrived. That feeling you get when you know it is time to upgrade – when it is time to get serious about your life and where you see yourself. That is what I said to myself anyway when I decided I was well worth it.

An official Currier dropped off a letter from the Governor, wanting to feature me in a video welcoming people to experience *"**Maine, on the Higher Side!**"* These were all the tell-tale signs that something amazing was coming around the bend and the things that strengthened my faith while I was negotiating my own cooking show featuring the delights of *Cannabis Culinary Infusions*® – in short, the stuff of which dreams are made and realized.

I left Maine and headed down the coast, feeling as confident as ever, as I rapidly made my way to Jaxson's condo in Connecticut. Getting into the car, he smelled of coffee and cologne as I programmed the next address in Rockefeller Plaza, New York City. My legs were shaking when I first met my agent in the lobby.

Looking at me up and down, he said, "You look perfect.

This is just a small meeting, nothing major, just an introduction, and we'll be out fast." I sat down and waited patiently until the receptionist called my name.

Walking into his office, across the aisle was a man not much older than me. He quickly stood up and reached his hand out over the desk. "I'm Jack Kent, Research Executive for the *Cannabis Network,*" he said. "Would you like a cup of coffee?" he asked.

"Yes, thank you … cream and sugar," I replied as I handed him my resume.

He rapidly looked it over. "So, you want a show on the *Cannabis Network,* do you?" he asked with a twinkle in his eyes.

I simply smiled back and said, "I most certainly do, sir."

"*Cooking with Cannabis,* I see," he said. "Do you think you are ready for the big league?" he asked seriously.

I cleared my voice and said, "Yes sir, every bit ready as I can be."

"Good response," he said, smiling back at me. "We've got a few more people we are looking at, so would you relocate for the show?"

"Yes, sir," I replied reflexively, "I'm not married to my

house, even though I just spent over a hundred grand on renovations," I thought to myself.

"Good," he replied. "We are thinking Las Vegas ... Tell you what we are going to do ... We want to put you on one of our shows, just as a guest celebrity chef and see what your ratings look like ... Are you up for that?" he said.

I nearly flew across the desk, overjoyed with that request as I nodded my head, "Oh yeah, I'm more than willing to do that," I replied.

"You'll need some polishing up. I'm going to make a few phone calls, and you'll hear from us soon," he continued.

I stood up and shook his hand. "Pleasure doing business with you," I said.

"The pleasure is mine," he replied before I walked out the door. My agent was sitting there with his hands in his lap.

"Well, what happened?" he asked.

Keeping my cool, I walked to the elevator and waited for the doors to close. As soon as I heard the ding, I was jumping up and down, "I'm going to do a guest show!" I exclaimed.

"Way to go, Kiddo ... I did not think that would happen so fast," he replied as the elevator opened, "you are on the move."

Outside, in the car, Jaxson was still waiting when I jumped in and said, "Guess what!"

"You just got booked on a show," he said.

"How did you know that?" I questioned.

"Did you get a show?" he asked, with an incredulous look on his face.

"No, not yet ... just a guest appearance ... but, again, how did you know?" I asked.

"I am psychic," was all he said.

I started my Cadillac® as I punched in the next address, and off we headed to Delaware to pick up Olivianna.

Our communication was a bit dry at first, but as the miles passed, the more we chatted. Time itself seemed to lose its duration, and in what seemed like minutes, we were on Long Neck Road. My whole body felt refreshed. "It must be the comfortable leather seats," I thought to myself. I pulled up to the tiny trailer, dodging golf carts full of dog passengers.

There she was again, Olivianna, the pastry chef I met that night in Lewes. I met her boyfriend, Daryl, who owns a hemp farm outside of town. Loading their bags into the car, I asked Jaxson if he minded driving the rest of the way to Virginia.

"Do you trust me?" he asked, taking the keys to my car.

"If I didn't trust you, you would not have been in my car this long," I replied cynically, looking at him half-cross-eyed.

After Olivianna was packed and everyone was ready, Jaxson pulled out West on Route 24 to RT 54, then South on Route 13 and West on RT 50 to the Chesapeake Bay Bridge Tunnel.

"It sure beats the Beltway," I said as I opened a bag of hard candies that I bought last week and passed it around. I started sucking on what tasted like strawberry.

Jaxson started to suck on a piece, twirling it between his teeth, making me wish I were a candy mint right now.

The drive to Bath County, Virginia, dotted with some newly formed wineries here and there as we made our way down the byways. Fields of lavender were seen, wafting their healing fragrance as the mountain ranges spanned for miles. We collectively gasped as we pulled up to *The Victorian*, with its large wrap around porch.

I lugged my suitcase to my room. The garden tub in the corner was calling me. In my mind, I saw Jaxson wrap his knuckles across my door. A few minutes later, I heard a sharp knock at my door, and there he was, standing in front of me.

"Charlotte, I know we have not talked that much, but I would like to exchange more reiki with you sometime this weekend, if you would like to," he said.

Standing up next to him, his body seemed almost a foot taller than mine. I looked at him and said, "I did not bring my table with me. Did you mean just us or in the classroom?" I asked.

Looking at the wall, he said that it really did not matter. "We can start tonight if you like, as the class does not start until ten tomorrow morning anyway," he added.

Looking up into his eyes, I said, "How about let's start with a walk?" I quickly changed my clothes and put on a different pair of shoes.

Olivianna had brought down her mini muffins, but there was really nothing mini about them once they finally kicked in.

The B&B was close enough to the Jefferson Pools, so we decided to walk it. His long legs gave him a rapid stride that kept me on my toes. I just hollered for him to go on ahead, and I would catch up. Naturally, it did not help that I was still not anywhere near what my ideal weight should be. I kept telling myself that I should start to learn to run now, as I began to pick up my pace. I was certainly no match for him, so it was silly to even think of competing. It seemed that he could sprint a block with just his stride.

As I made my way up to the pools, I noticed that **NO Trespassing** signs were posted everywhere. I could hear water splash as I whispered, "Jaxson." A voice from within called out for me to come in."

I pushed on the old wooden door as the heavy hinges creaked. The large pool of water, known as the Jefferson Pools, opened in front of me. "How did you get it unlocked?" I whispered.

He pointed to his head and said, "Mind Power, baby."

The moonlight was cascading down through the gaping holes throughout the roof of the old Jefferson water hole. His wet body glistened in the moonlight as he beckoned me to come in. I took each article of clothing off, slowly trembling, as I second-guessed myself. I was sure that he was thinking that I was being seductive as I pulled my pants down when, in truth, I was just trying not to fall.

Leaving my bra and underwear on, I walked down the steps and into the ninety-eight-degree water. The slippery feeling enticed me, as the bubbles tickled my legs, and I decided to go under and swim. As I ran my hands up his arms, the muscles in his arms were like bulging balls of steel. The scent of his testosterone mixing with his deodorant had been driving me virtually insane all day in the car. He was so strong as he lifted me up against his body. My underwear drove a very thin wedge between us. His nose as it caresses my skin through my red lace bra. Just the thought of his manhood being inside of me sent shivers down my spine as my fingers trembled from the inside out.

It was almost like I had some hidden chastity belt when my underwear somehow glued itself to me. The more I denied it, the more I wanted it. It was like a drug high that I felt calling me onward. He was like no other drug I have ever felt in my life. I saw flashes of lights as they flickered off the water and escaped through the roof openings. It was as if we were floating high in the air, and my soul was dancing around the room as magnetic charges tingled in the air.

His fingers feathered my skin, taking my senses into a tailspin as his heavy accent began to lure me in.

I felt his hips rubbing against me as his hands slid down my arms, and his body trembled. I sensed that his physique was completely tuned into the sensations. Our minds seemed to be in sync as our bodies floated in the air. The dazzling illumination emanating from his skin reminded me of looking up into the sun too long – of the kind where one can be blinded by its power if one dares to investigate it too closely. Yet, it was an energy so intense and enticing as to be virtually irresistible. Even if the mind wanted to, the body would, by far, lose the dare.

Soon, I willingly succumbed to him, his hairy chest, the tattoos that made me want to think that he was a badass when deep inside, he was as scared as can be. I held my hands to his heart space when I breathed in and out with him and felt the beating of his chest as his heart nearly jumped out of his rib cage.

His body was lean and felt like a tiger as his strong arms engulfed me, and his long tail vibrated up next. I have never felt anything like this in my life, as the energy surged through me. I could taste the liquor floating in his system when I felt another surge of energy.

He looked at me and said, "It has been years since I had a drink, and now, the only drug I do is cannabis – and I am hard-pressed to call that a drug".

I understood what he meant and did not need to say anything anymore, when I noticed lights flashing. I felt my body begin to shimmer; the more I looked at the transform, the more I started to panic, thinking that I was spontaneously combusting, when my body floated off, as I felt his hand. Suddenly, I felt the pulsing of the energy, trembling like a generator, building off the elements that were floating in the water.

"I've been wanting to feel the touch of his hands," I thought as he caressed my back. It was all I thought about as I ran my hands through his pecs. I looked up at him and whispered words that I never in my life thought I would say to anyone, "I have known for a long time now that you are an angel of love, and I've been waiting for this moment with you."

Immediately afterward, his wings roared open, and his whole being engulfed me with his strength and vitality. I was so intensely blinded as the spectra of lights suspended me, reminding me of the grand finale at a firework show. It felt like a symphonic crescendo as the strings from *Saint Madonna* melted my heart. Oh, can you imagine that, as his blonde hair fell upon me?

His nose touched my cheeks as his lips kissed me. Watching as his wings expanded out of his back, I felt his resplendent life force hover over me, glowing into the night sky, shooting rockets as the energy propelled us up through the woods. We virtually traveled at the speed of sound, as our eyes became one, seeing exactly what the other was seeing simultaneously, even though we were viewing from different angles. Oh My God! It was so exciting!

It was like a 360-degree 3-D camera in my head, spinning in every direction at the same time, with RADAR never experienced before, as my senses attuned to the frequency of the Universe itself. I continued the indescribable transcendent voyage of discovery, riding the waves of energy beams as lightning bolts of colors pierced me, propelling me onward and upward to a much higher ethereal dimension, where there is no sense of mass, time, and distance – just infinite space and knowledge, as in a new paradigm shift or *Feldraum*. I did not even know if I was still alive, but something told me that I needed this now, more than ever, as I felt yet another spiritual energy spurt.

My eyes fluttered open, and I woke up surrounded by pink roses as the wallpaper print became clearer. The sunlight peaked into the room, though the heavy green curtains that were drawn closed most of the way. I lay there frozen, wondering if Jaxson was still here or was it all a dream. As I reached behind my back, I felt the sheets, hoping that I would feel his flesh.

Running my fingers up and down the sheets, my thoughts drifted back to my doctor. He was trying to tell me that I had some sort of delusional fantasy happening – that I was seeing things that were not there. I had been having trouble distinguishing between what was real and what was not, as I had thought that I met a man in Jamestown who was the Captain of a ship. When I inquired about him, no one seemed to know who I was talking about, and there was nothing about him on the Internet.

I previously met him back in Rhode Island at the Gala on that most amazing night. I could see him, his beard gray with age, looking like a mix of Captain John Smith and a guy I once knew back in the day. Honestly, I thought that I saw his name tag on his coat when we danced. It all seems like just a distant memory now: his white hat, shining from the polish on the rim and the stripes on his arm, indicating his rank. I could have sworn that I said "Bob" when I handed him the key to my room back then – when, instead, it was Jerrod.

The "Captain," or Bob, or whatever his name was, seemed to randomly appear and disappear as he pleased. He almost reminded me of Clinton in a way, coming in and out of my life when it suits him. Just when I gave up on him ever showing up again, he would reach into my mind and take me to places to which only a captain of the sea could take me. His chest muscles flexed as it flashed again in my mind, and the markings on his arms as I watched him roll in the white sheets.

I closed my eyes again and felt Clinton breathing down my neck, the sensation as his hand spanked my cheeks, and I was again lost in the race. I could see him in his blue shirt and aviation glasses, running across the desert in a race against time. I knew then that he was a King, a Pharaoh from long ago in ancient Egypt, as the thought vividly crossed my mind.

I realized now that the captain was merely a ghost or apparition with his crew of seamen scurrying around him, all loyal to the fold. It took months for me to figure it out. Were these the ghosts of the era back when our ports were bustling with vessels, crews, and sea captains in the Age of Sail? I knew some of the inns I had worked in before were haunted, but never did I ever feel a presence like the one I felt for the captain. My only other question was, "Why did the captain take Clinton's shape?"

It was as if I saw two people in one body. Then, I realized, after talking with a few other people, that what I have been experiencing is a crazy ghostly gift. The more books I read on the topic, the more I knew that I was not alone. Other people have witnessed and reported experiences that were like mine.

For now, I was thankful that I heard Jaxson releasing his bladder in the bathroom. I rolled over as I watched him walk back to the bed. He wrapped his arms around me, and I felt safe in his chest. The moment his hands were in the center of me, we breathed in unison, and as our hearts beat as one, I knew that it was not a hallucination or a dream.

As he began chanting OMs in my ear, telling me he would make me forget about what I was thinking, I became completely lost again in his energy. All senses of time and space just disappeared as my body merged inside of his, as if our skin disappeared. All I could see was a brilliant burst of light. I do not know how long it was that I was in his embrace, but it was evidently long enough that we were late for class.

Karissa and Kennedy were already at the bathhouses when we walked over and met with everyone else. As I looked around the room, I saw some of the faces from past classes, and we hugged. There were a few women that looked familiar to me, but I could not quite place them. We all paired up for the next hour. Olivianna wore her tight little bikini. "How did that baker get away with it, eating all those baked goods and still looking so skinny," I wondered, silently.

The pools had a much different look during the day. I was chatting with some of the women, and they talked about the local news. Apparently, some strange lights were reported over Virginia, and there were talks of UFO sightings.

Jaxson gazed at me with an anxious look to keep my mouth

shut for now, and I quickly slipped under the water. The warm, healing water was crystal-clear as I watched the bubbles float out of invisible holes.

One by one, we began to break up in teams of six. One person was receiving while each person was holding on to one another until we formed a circle. One woman had recently lost her husband, and the grief of what she was processing was extremely hard for her. Her sister had taken the class with her to help her out. I felt so bad for her that I was compelled to reach out.

There was something magical about the Jefferson Pools, the way the bubbles would come up from the floor and tickle our bodies. I was so incredibly happy to have found a man who appeared to have the same type of energy that I was learning about within myself. He was obviously way more advanced than me, and that was a comfort, knowing I was not alone in all of this. I had floated to the ceiling before but never thought that people flew. This was much different than what happened up in Jamestown at the Gala on that fateful night with the captain. In fact, I have not even seen the specter for weeks, now.

We all gathered for dinner down at *the Homestead*, where the talk in the dining hall was of the strange lights that were reported to be shooting around the skies of Virginia last night.

I could barely sit at the table, as it was the buzz of the whole room. Each time I tried to drink my water, I would hear someone from another table say, "Hey, did you see the weird lights in the sky last night?"

I looked up from my menu to see my waitress, and I asked her for a strong drink. A few moments later, I had a whiskey and pineapple under my lips and tried drinking it as fast as I could, hoping that it would somehow drown out all those people chattering about the lights. With my thirst for chatter attenuation not yet quenched, I waved to the waitress for another drink.

I nearly blew my liquid escape across my plate when Kennedy asked, "Did anyone see bright lights coming out of the pools last night?" As I desperately fumbled to put my glass on the table, my drink went down the wrong pipe. "Cheap whiskey," I spurted, beating my chest as I pointed to the glass. "What the hell was I just saying?" I thought as I looked back at my glass, knowing damn well that it was Hennessy® I was drinking. I shook my head, nearly coughing up a lung, still wondering what I was thinking and utterly taken aback at what I was hearing in the aftermath of last night's events. Discretion demanded silence, as there was too much at stake.

Keeping my eyes focused on the menu as the whole room

repeatedly erupted over what each person saw, I pulled the menu up further over my face, pretending I could not read it, even though my glasses were right on my face. In my mind, it felt like a thousand voices clamoring at me. I headed to the bathroom, walking quickly as Karissa followed me in.

She handed me a towel, and I wiped my face as she looked at me and winked.

Grabbing the towel, I looked at her for an instant and just put my face into the sink. The warm water coursed through my fingers as the information suddenly flooded in.

"Are you getting a download?" she asked perceptively.

"All the stars are lining up in my head if that's what you mean," I replied softly. I flashed back to the night I was up in their tree. I knew that I saw wings that night and bright shining lights.

"You were with Jaxson last night, weren't you?" she asked, as my breathing suddenly got heavier. "In the pool, right?" she said, pressing on with the investigation.

I nearly fainted as she led me to a lounge chair in the next room. I lay there for a few minutes, waiting for the room to clear, as the lady washing her hands nearby stared at me and threw her towel in the trash.

Karissa took my hands and firmly led me into the sauna. "Come in here," she whispered. Quickly opening the door, she pushed me in, and shut it to not let anyone else in. She turned up the dial, and as the steam came loudly hissing out, she jumped up and down, rubbing her hands in anticipation. Her sparkling eyes bulged with excitement as she asked, "Did you get your wings last night?"

Looking in her eyes as deeply as I could go, I mustered the strength to say, "I think so ... I am quite sure I did ... I mean ... I do not know ...   Maybe." "You are one also, aren't you?" I asked as I continued to stammer, "you and Kennedy both are, right?"

"Of course, I am," she said, as a broad smile came across her face, "I thought you knew."

"I did not know," I replied, "I thought you were a witch; I mean, I thought something was up the night I fell out of your tree".

"Fell out of the tree?" she asked.

Putting my hands in the air, I whispered, "I thought your husband was beating you, and the town ladies all say he does."

"They do?" she said, laughing. "Well, I would not put too much stock in what the old ladies say as they have been wrong a few times before," she continued.

"Look, it is not a problem," explained Karissa, "you're coming into your superpowers, and you're learning how to use them. When we get home, we will set up a time where I can sit down with you, and we will discuss more. In the meantime, you are in good hands with Jaxson. He is highly skilled. He has had his wings for some time and is a strong leader."

Judging by the light show, I thought that it was incredible. I just remembered looking at her, not knowing even what to think. We walked back out of the lady's room and could tell the conversation in the dining hall had changed.

I ordered a Cornish game hen that was served in a honey and orange reduction, with mashed fingerling potatoes, roasted garlic, and grilled asparagus. My highly trained palate picked up undertones of thyme and sage as the poultry just melted in my mouth. I was in heaven once again as the balsamic honey that braised the asparagus entered.

Jaxson and I decided to walk back to the inn along Sam Snead Highway. Looking up at him, I asked, "Should we keep to ourselves for the rest of the weekend – you know, lay low so as not to start any more controversy?"

He reached into his jeans pocket. All I could see was my

own reflection as I stared up into the lenses, hoping I was looking into his eyes. Kicking a rock with his shoe, he told me that he loves controversy. "As far as I am concerned, I made the papers and the Six o' Clock News, and so did you, I might add," he said with a twinkle in his eyes and a jab to my rib cage.

"I guess I did, didn't I?" I said, returning the jab.

"What do you say we go for a hike, up along the side up over that hill?" he asked as he pointed toward the sky.

"Lead the way," I replied.

As we continued, we took a path, cutting through the woods. The sun was just beginning to set as we reached the mountain peak that he had in mind. Even though it was only mid-April, the weather was so nice; the lilacs were blooming, and the temperature was wonderful compared to Maine, where winter still beset the landscape.

Out over the hills in the distance, we could see the leaves and the start of the wine season protruding out from their vines. Lying back on the ground as we looked up at the stars, we seemed to talk for hours about our lives. The orange and gold streaks gave way to midnight blue, and the stars appeared more brilliantly in the sky as the Pink Moon hovered over us. As I looked up, I could hear his voice in my head, asking, "What are you waiting for?"

I rolled over and sat on top of his waist. I watched as he reached down and took off his shirt. The bright moonlight illuminated his whole body as I reached down and began to kiss his lips. I could taste the coffee that was still lingering on his breath as his hands reached up for mine. Our fingers laced together, and I slowly came back down to his hips.

Each little kiss showered down on his body ignited a fire deeper in me. As my hands ran over his chest, I watched as his eyes closed, and he began to moan. I unbuttoned his jeans and slid them off his legs. In the moonlight, his body locked so much more impressive than what I saw last night.

The aura surrounding his sheath looked like a multicolored light show with hues of pink and green. I could not tell if we were in a meteor shower or if his body was sparking off charges of electricity. Whatever it was, I did not want it to end. Each explosion only made me crave him more and more as waves of release came over me. My body began to tremble at the highest rate I had ever felt, like the supercritical Chernobyl nuclear reactor, ready to explode.

A sharp pain entered both sides of my back along my shoulder blades as I felt a golden ray of light shine back. I looked up at him as my wings emerged. I felt like a cat chasing its tail as I twirled around the mountain, trying to gauge my wingspan. I could not believe it, and I had wings! Rejoicing over my newly resplendent wings of bright white feathers with sparkles of rainbow colors rounding out the tips, I ran around the mountaintop like I was a little kid.

"This was way better than any chiffon dress," I thought to myself as I completely transformed. I opened my eyes to feel his hands in mine.

"Do you want to fly?" he asked.

"How?" I asked with utter astonishment as the R. Kelly song, *I Believe I Can Fly* played throughout my head.

"Let me show you," he said as he took my hand. "It's not the strength of muscles that make you fly; it's your belief in yourself that enables you to do it," he explained. "Do everything out of love," he concluded.

I tried so hard to figure out where the energy of my love needed to come from to propel myself to fly. The harder I tried, the more impatient I became with myself.

Jaxson watched me for a few minutes with his hands on his hips, laughing. "Come over here," he said softly. "Take my hand and let me show you," he guided.

I took his hand and looked into his eyes.

"Are you sure that you trust me?" he asked. "This is the most important question I'll ever ask you," he said.

I thought for a moment and asked myself the question over and over in my mind. I concluded that I did and said, "Yes, I do." As soon as the words were uttered, I felt a swoosh, and we were off in the sky. My wings stayed close to my body, and his mighty arms held me tight as his wings spanned across the sky, soaring higher and higher. In my mind, I heard him say, "Now, try flying." I closed my eyes and let go.

I started falling like a cannonball, as my head made a beeline for the ground in front of me, and my arms and legs flailed wildly in the air. In an instant, I outstretched my arms and shouted, "I want to fly!" My wings fluttered to life as I took off towards the heavens like a Space Shuttle. My excitement sparkled as my wings shed their baby down and a full complement of flight feathers grew out in their place, right before my very eyes!

Of all my dreams of being a fish swimming in the water, nothing compared to this. I saw Jaxson right behind me as he rode the wind of my newly formed wingspan, swirling in the moonlight.

He pointed over to a field off in the distance, where he motioned for us to land. The closer I got back to Earth, the more I realized that I had no idea of how to land.

"Land, Land, Land!" he shouted.

"I don't know how!" I screamed, with my shoulders and wings in an open position, plummeting precariously.

Just then, I plunged into the middle of a pool. As my feet hit the bottom, I shot back up to the surface to the sound of Jaxson laughing his head off like a cartoon clown. I made my way out of the pool, flopping my legs up and down as I surveyed my drooping, soaking wet wings. Suddenly, a flash of light appeared, and as I strained to see where it was coming from, I heard doors opening.

I took off running when I heard the gunshot engage once again, with my gown of white feathers billowing around. I looked back to see a grizzled, white-bearded old mountain man with a big belly, running in his polka-dotted underwear, taking aim with his long rifle. His wife accompanied him with her hair up in rollers, wrapping her belt around her house coat, yelling, "Dagnabbit … I heard 'em ... I heard 'em ... it's them damn Smith boys!"

As he continued firing, I felt the bullet fly over my head as if the Sheriff himself was coming after me.

"Use your love and fly!" shouted Jaxson.

Instantaneously, my wings spanned back. My feet hit the top of the fence, flying *UP, UP and Away* from the blasts, as I heard the corresponding '60s song playing in my mind, hoping that my beautiful balloon would not be punctured.

Taking me back under his wings, Jaxson steered us off towards the Moon. I looked back to see the old man and his wife scratching their heads in utter confusion with the look of scared rabbits on their faces.

"Abner, Y'all better lay off that damn moonshine," bleated the old man's wife. "Ahm a-tellin' ya!" she hollered.

"That there goes double for you, too," he shot back.

"If'n y'all is as good with your gun as you are with your big mouth, y'all just might hit somethin' for a change," she retorted, getting in the last word.

Jaxson looked at me and said, "You're a nut."

"Yeah, a wet nut but not a wing nut," I replied, surveying my water-logged wings. "I think we'll be making the news again ... do you think they recorded us," I said, rolling my eyes.

"Oh yes, most definitely … Did you see the look on the old man's face when he saw your feet running along the top of the fence?" he asked. "It was priceless," he chuckled, "I wish I had a camera."

"Where the hell were we anyway, West Virginia?" I asked most curiously.

"Almost Heaven," he replied with a hint of sarcasm. He paused, letting out a sigh of relief as he wiped the telltale sweat of his brow. "Do you have any idea of the major damage this could have caused?" he asked rhetorically.

"No," I replied.

"Kennedy would be very angry at me if I lost one of his prodigies," he elaborated.

"Whatever are you talking about," I asked, hissing back at him.

"In our flight school, you've got a lot to learn when it comes to earning your wings," he quipped as he pointed me off in a different direction.

"Cut me a break," I retorted. "I didn't have any idea I could do this without prior instruction."

"Tell that to the FAA," he needled.

We flew to another range that faced North and watched as the sky began to change its colors from dark blue to hues of orange and yellow. As the sun climbed over the mountains, I felt his hand go over my shoulder.

He gave me a few pats and said, "Let's go. We only have a few minutes before we are detected," in a much softer voice.

My wings opened with ease as I took flight over the mountain range, swooping back down to the woods behind the Ivy Cottage, waving to Sam Snead as he tipped his hat to me.

The tiny dressing rooms of the Jefferson Pools were moderately appointed. As I changed into my swimsuit, I happened to catch a glimpse of my back. Struggling to see where my wings came out of. I began taking notice of the other people in the room as I scanned up and down the backs of each person, looking for signs of wings or feathers.

The final hours of the energy exchanges were taking place. Karissa demonstrated to Jaxson as she scanned his body with her hands. Occasionally, I would see a ball of light out of the corner of my eye. Sometimes, I would see sparks just dancing in the air. I began wondering if it was light trickery. Occasionally, I would see red or blue, but yellow seemed to be the prominent color today. I was happy about that. I was not looking forward to the long ride home, and I needed to have my power back.

By two o'clock in the afternoon, the class was dismissed, and we all said our goodbyes as the teachers left. We packed up our bags and embarked on the long return home. Jaxson made the first leg up to Delaware, and I hugged Olivianna goodbye.

"I'll see you in a few months," I said.

She ran inside and came out with a bag of frozen treats. "These are my new experiments," she said, "try them and get back to me."

"You got it, sister," I said, waving farewell.

It was nearly eleven pm before we reached Connecticut. I was running back and forth in my mind, wondering if I wanted to stay with him one more night or rent a hotel and wait until morning for the final leg of my trip back home.

"Nah, you're spending the night," he said as we arrived at his parking space, "I promise we'll just sleep."

I looked back at him, puzzled as to why he said that. "I don't recall asking you about staying the night," I said, questioning his intent.

"You're going to have to learn to get your thoughts under control," he replied. "I could hear everything you were thinking," he said, turning to me.

"Wait," I said, rather puzzled, "you can hear my thoughts?"

"Yes," he said. "I can not only hear your thoughts, but I can feel your body as well. It is just one of my gifts. I know that this weekend has been hard on you. I know a lot of new things have happened, and, in truth, I think you just need another night. Three is always the way," he explained.

"Hmm ... three, you say," I responded as I reached for the door handle and stepped out of the car. "Three it is," I said, grabbing my bag.

Presidential Request

You release inside and open the flood doors
juice spilling out
Laundered between the floors
Elixir of Love
For all eternity
Climaxing all over the land
Sending vibrations of love
Is our command
It does not matter
Where we do
All that matters
Is our seeds
Spread through
Send a message
Actions and plans
For making love
Across the lands
Learning to love
Was no easy quest
Loving you has been the best

I'll do this again
I'll do it forever and again
Until eternity expands
Teaching love is
Our abundance plan
All of my love
I give to me first
All of my love
I share your thirst
All of our love
Will abound about
All of our love
We will shout
All of our love
Is our brand
All of our love
We command
I will love you throughout the sands of time
The hourglass is always in rhyme.

14
Fantasy Facial

It was almost nine AM when I heard the blender running from down the hall. The sun was shining in through the window blinds, and I could see out to the Atlantic Ocean. The call of the seagulls got my attention where. Off in the distance, I could see boats positioned in the water, waiting for their crews to arrive. The smell of coffee was so strong that it lured me out to the balcony, thinking a barista was somewhere close. I was caught up in the sun shining over the water, running my hands along the edge of the railing, when I heard Jaxson walk out. I turned around to see him carrying a tray.

"Breakfast is served, my dear," he said as he placed the tray on the little table, where a strawberry and banana smoothie with scrambled eggs was waiting for me. Pointing over to the corner of the building, he asked, "Do you want a cup of coffee?"

"Ha, I knew I smelled coffee," I said as I went over and fixed a cup.

"You're thinking too hard again," he said, sitting down. "Relax," he instructed, interrupting the silence.

"How do I tell this to my therapist?" I responded.

"You don't," he laughed. "They don't understand any of this, and, for now, you're trying to figure out too much too soon. Just chill; you have time. Plus, I have a surprise for you," he said.

"A surprise? I don't know if I can handle any more surprises, and I'm still trying to wrap the whole flying thing around my head," I said.

Jaxson got up from the table and took the plate out of my hand. "I want you to go down the hallway to the last door on your right, go on in, take off all your clothes, put the paper sheet over you, and lay down on the table. Lastly, there is a box with a set of dark glasses inside; put the glasses on and relax," he instructed.

I marched down the hall like a toy soldier in the *Nutcracker Suite* as the giggles came over me, "Hey, did you cook those eggs with cannabis today?" I asked.

"No, I put a pain relief tincture in the smoothie," he hollered down the hall.

My funny bone kicked in big time as I opened the door to the room and wondered why he gave me a pain relief blend. The walls were painted in a soft blue hue, relaxation music was playing, a candle was lit, and I immediately felt a bit more relaxed. What appeared to be a lounge chair was sitting in the middle of the room, which turned out to be an aesthetician's chair draped with blankets that were warm to the touch. A large piece of plastic wrap lying on top, another paper sheet to cover up with. Sitting there was a box with a set of dark glasses inside. Along the counter were jars filled with cotton balls, cotton swabs, wooden spatulas, massage oil from **Foo Bella's™**, and all kinds of other natural-based products.

I began taking my clothes off and hung them on the hook on the back of the door. I laid down on the plastic sheet and pulled the paper blanket over me, looking up at the ceiling, not knowing what I was waiting for when I placed the glasses on my face. The room went dark while I listened to the voices just outside the door talk in a muffled tone and wondered who else was there. I lay there quietly until there was a knock at the door, and a voice that had such a familiar ring to it asked if it was OK to come in.

"Yes," I responded and laid back down. In the darkness, I listened as jars opened. The warmth of the table began to lull me to sleep when that voice instructed me to open my mouth. I hesitated, not knowing what I was opening my mouth to when the voice said, "Open wider and let me come in."

The voice was in a tone that I knew, but it was not Jaxson. I reluctantly began to obey the command as the trays came into my mouth, and I was told to clamp down. The saliva was accumulating in my mouth and pooling into the back of my throat, and I realized this must be a bleaching kit for my teeth.

The trays were taken out of my mouth, and I was told to spit out my saliva into a cup he provided. I heard what sounded like a spatula mixing and was told, "Hold on, here comes the fun part. You ready for the pearl?"

The sensation was warm and soothing as it was being applied to my face and neck when suddenly, he asked, "Are you ready?" Thousands of hairs were ripped from my skin in a move that I was not sure if I wanted repeated when he said, "Too late, already started." The pain was over in an instant when I felt the heat come back down on the other side of my neck.

Over and over, it continued, from my underarms to my legs, until I reached down between my thighs to see if I had any lips left. The more I was feeling myself up, the more I was relieved when I felt the warm, oiled hands run up my legs and all over my body. My skin was smooth to the touch, and the more I rubbed my flesh, the more I loved how it felt when he asked, "Are you ready for that Fantasy Facial?"

I smiled inwardly, knowing there was no way he would ever know what my fantasy was and smirked, thinking that he would never guess it anyway.

"Put the robe on and come down the hall, where we have another surprise for you," he said.

I took the dark glasses off and was grateful that I had them to shield me from the bright overhead lights, wondering what my next surprise was as I walked down the hall and peered through the opened door, where I saw a hair-dressing chair and mirror with a stretch of lights, a shampoo bowl, and a hair dryer.

He gestured for me to get up into the chair and spun me around facing the mirror. "I bet you didn't realize I was a cosmetologist, did you?" Jaxson said with a smile.

"I had given it a thought as to what your occupation was, but sometimes a woman just likes a surprise," I replied, with a slight twinkle of my eyes.

"I bet you do, and that's why you're getting groomed right now," he said while he ran his fingers through my hair. "When's the last time you had your hair colored," he asked bluntly as he pulled my hair and looked at the ends.

"I don't remember … not in years, I think," I responded. "Why?" I asked.

"Just wondering … you got some gray coming in," he said.

I watched as he studied the color lineup and began mixing colors in a bowl. The combs edge zigged and zagged across my scalp as he dabbed the paste and foiled my hair. After an hour, I thought that I almost looked like a space project – a part of the tin hat Soviet. "Ready for transmission," I quipped, using both hands to grab at the foils at the sides of my head, bobbing my head back and forth and doubling over with laughter.

"Very funny," he smirked as he placed a plastic bag over my scalp head. "I'll be back in a few minutes," he said, heading out the door and closing it behind him.

I snickered again, thinking that it was funny.

"I heard that," he shouted from down the hall.

I looked up at the clock and saw that it was shortly past twelve when he came back in carrying what appeared to be a power tool case.

"Damn, am I that bad that you need a jigsaw to do my hair?" I asked.

"Do you really want to guess what's in here?" he asked as he flipped open the locks.

"I don't know ... makeup?" I replied, shrugging my shoulders, "I'm fresh out of guesses, and all morning I've had a very strange feeling that I am in some sort of conspiracy that I just can't put my finger on," I responded.

"Well, you're not that far off track, so I'll level with you," he said, "today was arranged for you by Kennedy."

"Kennedy arranged for my hair to be done?" I asked.

"It seems there was a little misunderstanding between you two, and he wanted to make it up to you," he said.

"Oh, Gee," I said, turning ten shades of red. "I don't even want to talk about it, so let's let it go," I said, as my hands reached for my head.

"Oh, no ... not so fast," said Jaxson. "We're not letting any of this go," he said as he spun the chair around to face him. "There is nothing to be embarrassed about. You obviously picked up on something about him. Otherwise, you would not be here right now. Plus, was not one of your fantasies to be, shall we say, desired?" he continued.

"I must admit you got me on that," I replied, wondering how he knew that when he opened the case. Inside was a series of colors, each in its own tray. Eye shadows, blushes, foundations, lipsticks, and I smiled, knowing I had guessed it right.

I bit down on my lip and knew this excited me when I asked, "How long have you known Kennedy?"

"Kennedy is my coach and/or mentor, whatever way you want to call it, and I've been working with him for a couple of years now," he elaborated, fiddling with the foil on my head. "A few more minutes, and you will be ready," he said.

I wondered what I got myself into but did not care as, for the first time in a long time, I felt like I was being spoiled and was enjoying every minute of it – conspiracy or not.

Jaxon started to pull the foils out of my hair. Blonde streaks were falling all around my face as the foils disappeared. It had really been years since I had done anything with my hair beyond a bowl cut here or there when I blurted out the question, "Does Kennedy do hair?"

"No, Kennedy does not do hair," he said as he led me to a

sink, leaned me over the wash basin and rinsed the paste out of my hair.

"Is this some clever rouse to get me to come back to you and keep up on my hair then?" I asked, mumbling under the flowing water.

"Maybe," he chirped back. "It takes money to make money," he said as he continued to pull my antennae out.

Jaxson placed the towel around my head and snapped his fingers. "Come here," he said.

I jumped back into the chair like a puppet on a string. "Yes, Captain," I bellowed out, as I adjusted my ears.

Pretending that I had a little spaceship commander next to me, barking out orders, I could tell that my little jokes were not going over very well, as I snorted in laughter.

"Go into the room that looks like a giant closet and pick out one of the outfits on the bars," he dictated, "do you understand the instructions?"

Remaining silent, I merely nodded in the affirmative.

"Pick out what shoes you think will fit you and what you think will be good for you to strut in," he said.

"Strut?" I muttered back.

"My understanding is you wanted to be a model, so how do you think you can do that if you are not comfortable wearing something seductive then walking down and showing it off to a group of strangers?" he asked rhetorically.

I stumbled over my thoughts as I pictured myself seductively walking the carpet. "I guess I had not thought of that," I said.

"No worries," he said, "before I am through with you, I will have you walking the carpet and owning it."

I walked back down the hall into a space that literally looked like a wardrobe room for a movie set. Hundreds of dresses in different sizes from designers such as Oscar Della Renta®, Michael Kohrs®, Versace®, and Prada® lined the shelves. I picked out a white bra with diamonds and a label from a designer named **Festival Queen from Miya®**. Silk panels with diamonds were embedded into the bodice with holly leaves embossed with gold. The trails of gold and white silk panels attached to an undergarment were held in place with strings. Underneath were wisps of white feathers emerging from the center as the shawl spanned out.

I picked out a set of high heels studded with diamonds

when I happened to notice the music playing. *I Do Not Want Anybody Else When I Think About You, I Touch Myself* by the Divinyls permeated the atmosphere. With the dress and shoes over my arm, I saw Jaxson staring back at me as I walked back down the hallway over the red carpet, with legends of the screen lining the walls. That is when it hit me: he was a cosmetologist to the stars!

"Oh, Stephanie Miya, I love her designs," he swooned in praise as he hung the dress up on a hook. He placed me back in the chair and whirled it back around, facing me forward. His scissors ran down my hair as his head bobbed back and forth. I closed my eyes when he applied a blow dryer with a round brush, which made my blond streaks turn to curls around my face. I watched Jaxson as he continued to work when I spoke up again and asked the question that was most on my mind: "What does Kennedy do?"

"Kennedy makes fantasies happen," said Jaxson as he continued to frame out my face.

Those words seemed to hang in the air like a thick fog when I worked up the courage to say out loud, "If Kennedy makes fantasies come true, then why did he send me Captain Switcheroo?"

"Maybe he could not personally give you what you wanted,

so he sent the man that could," he replied.

I thought about that for a minute, and it made sense, so I shrugged my shoulders, took a deep breath, and began to drift off to a place in my mind where I relived my dreams.

"What's your fantasy, Charlotte?" Kennedy's voice whispered into my head. The voice startled me back awake as dabs of foundation went on and transformed into a nude beige, and hues of pink rounded out my face. The more I looked in the mirror, the more I was shocked to see my reflection. I felt pretty, despite myself, and my new self-confidence surely must have shown. Naturally, I felt more empowered when I rose from the chair, assessing my new look.

"Good job, Jaxson … I'm impressed," I said gratefully.

"It was not me, he said. "This was you all along, and you just needed a different look," he continued.

"Jaxson, we have a problem," I said.

"Kennedy," he answered.

"Yes, how did you know?" I asked.

"Really, Charlotte … I'm psychic," he answered.

"All I know is that, for some weird reason, I am so attracted to him, and I can't help but fantasize about him," I admitted.

"This is what I know," he said. "One day, I had the opportunity to work with him, but I did not know what I was walking into at the time. I thought this would be a pleasure as usual, like what I was used to with all the other clubs. But they were different, and I had never seen anything like that before. I was fascinated by what he was able to do with his wife. How he was able to bring her to levels I had never seen before, and I thought I had seen everything," he intimated.

Jaxson continued: "The more I talked with Karissa, the more entranced I had become. She has something inside her that I swear is a gift from God. Her capacity to make love to the whole world was something to see. The passion inside of her is something only a rare few will ever experience. I was the one of those rare few. What they were able to do to me healed me from something I was suffering with. I do not even know how they did it, but I wanted to learn. I wanted the skills he possessed. I wanted to do what he did. I breached every ethical and moral code there was in business, and I dove into their world."

"I knew it," I said, squinting my eyes and planting my hands on my hips. "He has this way that he looks at me and smiles, and I just swoon, so I'm in the program because I thought I was paying for him like I thought he was like an escort or something," I continued.

"Ha, well, I guess you could call it that if you wanted to, but he never looked at it like that. He was a natural born healer. It is in every aspect of him. His hands have magic inside, and I would have never believed it had I not seen it with my own eyes. One day, when I was talking to Clinton, he explained something to me that made a lot of sense. He told me that it is broken people who become the healers. When a person begins to heal themselves from their past traumas, they do it by helping others. What he did was give women what it was that they wanted. He took care of needs that were not being met, and he developed a reputation for doing it. You should ask him yourself to tell you how he got to where he is now. The stories will blow your mind as well as your g-spot," he said with a twinkle in his eye.

"My eyes nearly flew out of their sockets with the thoughts of Kennedy McCormick and my g-spot all in the same sentence when I asked, "Does he still do that?"

"Ah, he dabbles here and there, but for the most part, he just teaches what he knows to the others that want to learn," he said. "Did you not get a taste of him?" he asked.

"I tried, but, instead, he left in a hurry," I blurted out.

"Did you get your fantasy?" he asked.

"No, I couldn't do it ... well, I guess I sort of did ... I mean ... like," I stammered, fumbling all over my words as they left my mouth. "Okay, I guess I did, one way or another," I uttered, somewhat deflated. "I have a lot of fantasies, and I chickened out with the first part, but I inadvertently paid for the whole year, so I guess I am getting what I am supposed to be getting, right, Jaxson?" I continued.

"Maybe you requested a fantasy that you could not handle at the time you requested it, and he knew it," speculated Jaxson.

"Well, I could not do what I had originally requested. It sounded so good on paper when I first thought about it, and it just took me a long time to get myself to do it, I said.

"Charlotte, my love, if everybody could do this, they would," he said.

"But what if everybody can do this? What if they just started to believe in themselves? What if they just started to learn a new way?" I asked as I felt my energy rising again.

"All I know is that it takes about three years for the whole process to really bloom, many more years after that for you to develop, as you always are growing, learning, healing, and releasing," said Jaxon. "You really should be proud of yourself," he concluded.

I paused, savoring the moment.

"So, what's the deal with Clinton?" he asked.

"Clinton," I gasped, not knowing he even knew about him. "I, well, I'm … geez, you already know; you said you can read my mind, so why do I have to tell you?" I stumbled back.

"You must tell me so that you are honest with me so that I understand what I am dealing with here," he said.

"Jaxson, have you ever had secrets inside of your heart that, even for you, are hard to get out?" I asked. "Yes, I do. I have things I want to do, yet I do not see a way to get them," I continued. "Well, what if there was a way to get to our dreams?" I finally asked.

"You know, Charlotte, I do believe that you are beginning to understand just what it is that Kennedy and Karissa teach," he said.

"Well, I do not know about that; I'm just sort of suck at the love parts," I said.

"I don't know that you suck at love … I mean, you do suck," he said.

"Really?" I interrupted.

"The more you begin to love yourself and realize you deserve amazing love, the more you will attract amazing love, according to the Law of Attraction," he answered. "Let me ask you something ... what did you think of the past weekend?" he asked.

"My mind was frozen in time, and then ... poof," I rambled. "To be honest, I am scared. I don't even understand who I am anymore. I do not know what to think, and I should be ecstatic with what I learned, but, in all reality, I am probably a fucking lunatic for all I know. To top it all off, I cannot stop thinking of Clinton. I do not even know who was in the room with me back there, but darn if I did not think it was him! Oh, my God ... his dark skin, his shinny head ... I'm such a bad girl," I said as I crumbled in the chair, feeling like the Wicked Witch of the West, as I began melting down.

"Sweetie, you are not a bad girl – in fact, you are a good girl, a Drama Queen maybe sometimes, but that is just who you are," he replied. "Maybe, just maybe, it is going to take more than one man to satisfy your wish list," he said with an informed look on his face.

Jaxson folded his arms around his chest, mumbling something under his breath. "Get up!" he said, "you have another thing coming."

The dance down the hallway was laced with his hisses, leading me to another room.

"Are you listening?" he asked, snapping his fingers.

His sheer strength was staggering as he placed me down in another chair. Starting with my feet, he began washing each dactyl, taking care of me in a way that I sorely needed. The warm lotion felt so great as it glided up my legs, with his fingers massaging me. The closer his fingers came to my groin, the more excited I became.

As his fingers began to tease in a most unusual way, he glanced his eyes seductively at my eyes and mouth. "This is why I work with Kennedy," he said.

"Kennedy does nails?" I asked as the moans began to escape my lips. "Kennedy does nails?" I repeated, still ever so confused as to what that man really does.

"No, Charlotte, Kennedy does not do nails," said Jaxson before he shook his head and laughed, "but he will make sure you get yours done." He placed my hands in bowls of water and said, "Just relax and let me take care of you."

I slid back into the chair, closed my eyes, and succumbed

to his fingers as they trailed up my thighs. The tease was incredible, and I had to admit, I had never had a pedicure feel like this. As a whimper left my chest, I knew I would book him again. My nails were filed, and before I knew it, they were coated in a deep red that matched my lipstick and toes when I looked back up at Jaxson and said, "Kennedy just makes everything better, doesn't he?"

"Kennedy gives you want you secretly desire; he reads in between the lines and takes things to the level that your soul desires and craves and brings them up to the surface," said Jaxson.

"What else does Kennedy do?" I asked.

"Kennedy manages and directs all manufacturing and distribution of **FooBellas**® natural body care products."

"Now, I want you to go back to the bathroom with that dress and heels and come back out this way, and I want you to make sure when you walk the red carpet that you strut it with confidence and swagger," he said. "I want you to walk back into that room and put yourself together! You got it? Understand?" he continued.

I took a deep breath and said, "I understand," before I picked up the dress and heels and headed to the bathroom. I closed the door, took my robe off, and slipped into the body suit. The beads of gold with sparkling diamonds embellished the bra beneath a sea of white with gold lace. The front leg panels opened at my mid-thighs, like petals of jasmine, as the fabric flowed down to the ground. The sheer shawl, flowing with feathers, reminded me of wings as I slipped my arms into the sleeves. I was amazed at what I saw next.

Sitting on the chair, I adjusted the diamond-studded heels as I propped myself up to the mirror. I could not tell what he was going for, but I went from dirty blonde to platinum, and my makeup was classic with red lipstick. If I did not know any better, I would say I was channeling Marilyn Monroe.

I reached my hand around the knob and as I opened the door. I took a deep breath and told myself to sway like Marilyn and tease like Madonna with my eyes. The way the fabric flowed and opened revealed my smooth legs, and I felt like a goddess inside! My skin sparkled, and it felt like diamonds were emerging from my skin as I transformed more and more into the creature of loveliness that I first envisioned myself to be. With my angel wings protruding from my back, shimmering with pearls and diamonds. As the bright lights shined down, I walked down the hall with confidence this time and back into the room.

Jaxson was sweeping the hair into a corner when he turned to me.

"Honey," he said softly as he walked over, gently running his fingers around my face, "you're an Angel of Love".

As his lips began dancing with mine, I felt the heat come over me as his hands caressed mine. I belted out some silly songs as he did the finishing touches and sprayed my hair down.

"Put these dark glasses back on," he instructed. The white fabric tied together with lace and eyelets still wrapped around my hips as his tongue started to whip me into shape. "You need to learn how to control yourself," he whispered as he made me walk up and down the hall and focus on walking in the heels. I could sense the perimeter of the room and just kept walking, focusing only on the task at hand, when I heard the unmistakable voice of Kennedy McCormick, and I stopped dead in my tracks.

My heart began to beat out of my chest at the thought of what could be happening next when I was led back to what felt like another treatment room and instructed to sit down. I felt my hands begin to get strapped down to the legs of the table.

My legs began trembling as I felt what was surely Kennedy's fingers slowly start to feather my legs. The more excited I became, the more my mind began exploding. My thoughts were racing as I felt the energy change and knew there were two distinctly different sets of hands on me.

I felt like my whole womanhood was going to explode as his hands lithely danced up my thighs. The more I thought about it, the more I realized I had one person holding down my hands, and someone else was on my feet. As the thought went over and over in my head, I succumbed to the sensations as I realized I had two men pleasuring me at the same time.

One set of hands glided up and down my thighs as his fingers teased my lips, feathering ever so lightly. He took his time as his hands ran up my stomach with his fingers barely grazing me, sending spasms right through my body.

The weight of Jaxson's energy was all over me as his nose caressed my jaw line and his tongue glided down my neck. I felt little bites as each wave passed over me until his hands cupped my hidden breast. I could not tell if it was pleasure or torture. In all reality, the torture turned into pleasure as his hands went back to my thighs, dancing so closely to my love canal.

I could swear in my head that I heard Kennedy talking, asking me if I wanted his tongue inside me. "Oh God ... YES," are the only words I could muster as I begged the voice in my head to comply. My legs trembled over and over with just the words in my head. The thought of Kennedy going down on me was something I had been wishing for all along.

I could feel the orgasms start from deep within me and the momentum building up inside as wave after wave of release came over me. Someone re-positioned himself so that his lips were close to my right ear as he began asking me the questions I was begging to hear. His fingers circled around my breast as he made a figure-eight across my chest. My body heaved up towards the ball of white light that was now descending over me.

I heard him ask, "Have you been bad lately?" Oh, the excitement I felt as his hot breath blew in my ear, and I shook my head, hoping this was the response that would seal the deal. My entire body quivered, and the pressure of tiny tremors began to overwhelm me as I lost myself in a state of fantasy.

I heard a slap on the skin, but this time, it was not me being hit, as I heard him say, "You can't touch her like that." In an instant, I felt a second mouth descend on my neck, and I went over the top again, sniffing my own scent as my excitement began to build.

Streams of sweat dripped over me as someone writhed up against my face. His hands roamed over me like he was reading Braille. As his body was hovering over mine, I smelled the testosterone dripping from his glands, hitting my body, with each droplet causing its own explosion within. My strings were still intact, and I felt the head of a shaft as it vibrated up against the eyelets.

My head thrashed, and all I wanted was to scream! I heard Madonna sing *Like a Virgin*, and I still see her in my dreams, on the microphone, begging to be a part of the scene. She is an angel on stage, making love to the whole world. Oh, what a woman!

Just then, it dawned on me who I was really thinking of. Oh! I felt like Marilyn on steroids now, with all these studs around me. My hips rotated to an Aprovechalo beat as the grinding of his pelvis bore down on me. It was way beyond what I could control as I gushed out of my seams, knowing I had three men positioned on me.

I felt a set of hands as the eye hooks opened. His fingers felt like lightning volts coming out of his fingertips, sending me into a further dimension as bolts of lightning electrified my orifice, and I could no longer control the gush of fluids.

"We got a real squirter here, boss," he said in a tone that made me release some more.

Vibrations exploded through the top of my head as I felt

the silky texture of a tie wrap around my eyes. The scent was so reminiscent of Clinton, and I began exploding again. My thoughts were not on anything else but the three men who were taking care of me when I just let go and let it all happen.

I felt like I was on the table of some mad scientist as they kept raising the bar of pleasure. Was it just me, playing damsel in distress, as Gene Wilder and *Frankenstein* came alive in my head? The bar was in my own mind as streams of ribbons came crashing down on me. The "Whips of Ecstasy," my most devilish fantasy, came alive right between my thighs. Oh my God! I knew I was a bad girl now, but I did not care if feeling this much pleasure was bad. I will gladly take the title as I delighted in this game when finally, I let my voice come out and yelled, "Yes, I am a bad girl!"

The torture that some think is pain sent my releases into some other kind of dimension as I liberated my arch-fantasy in the sheets. I felt their breath in both ears this time as a pair of hands hovered over my face. Their fingers were so close to my skin but barely touching. My mind just exploded as I started screaming, "YES! YES! YES!"

I clearly heard Kennedy in my right ear and Jaxson in my left as they encouraged me to say it out loud while I was unable to speak. I could barely even breathe as wave after wave of spasms came over me. Their hands rubbed down my torso in a synchronized spin as they both caressed my chakras open, and my legs begged to feel their hands reach inside of me. Again, I heard Kennedy say, "What's your fantasy?" as I started singing to the gods some half-baked idea, speaking gibberish as I tried to get clear.

"You have to say it out loud if you want it," said Jaxson.

Oh my God! It was like torture either way! "I want Clinton," I screamed wildly from the top of my lungs, "I want Clinton! I want Clinton Tuckerman!" "There, I said it," I panted out loud and reiterated as the words slowed down to a quiet roar. I heard the voice in my head say in the calmest voice that I had ever heard, "I want Clinton Tuckerman."

"As you wish, my queen," Kennedy chimed in my ear, as I felt the sensation I had been aching for come inside me. Each time he pulsed forward, he took my breath away.

"Did he just call me queen?" I wondered in my head. My body repeatedly arched up and down while the flow of gold and white sparks danced around my skin as his vibrating crystal wand reached deep within.

I felt Kennedy rubbing my head and whispering all kinds of delicious notes in my ear as his fingers lightly massaged my face. With each wave of his fingertips, it felt like he was a generator channeling energy from some far-off planet. I felt like Frankenstein's wife as electrical currents strummed in my ears and through my skull. The head vibrated at what seemed like a thousand revolutions per minute as it tried to break through the lace. My body could hardly keep up as he rained more power down upon me.

His whole body channeled the energy like a vibrating flesh machine, and I felt like a nuclear reactor getting ready to explode. As the creamy mask hit my face, I knew that it was not Oil of Olay®. I woke up nestled in the blankets. As I peeled the comforter away, the white gown of feathers was still intact. It was not a dream this time when I got up and looked at my hair and the blonde curls that rounded out my face. I turned to see Jaxson standing in the door frame looking at me when I whispered to him, "Did I get my fantasy, or was this a dream?"

Jaxson laughed under his breath. "Both," he said as he handed me a copy of a tape, "you want to watch?

Letting Go

This is when you know.

You are letting go

Where your fantasy

Is running the show

Your body takes over

Your mind a frenzy state

You have never felt This way.

Intense pleasure

In every way

Voices cheering

As we scream God's name

The owls and wolves

Begging to be let in

The usher of a new era begins.

Where making love is not a sin

You open your arms

Let the love shine in

Accepting his love

With no judgment from within.

The Lead Role

As the object of my eye

Enters in

I see the love

I have hidden for him

I trust him like no other

My twin flames

My lover

My soulmate

My best friend

He calms my seas

With just his words

He can command me

He is my Healer

He is my Magician

He is my Commanding man

He can instantly bring me back again

He is my lead man

My Alpha and Omega

As the ohms leave my lips

As my body begins to rush

I am down for his sacral thrust.

15
Center of Love

With each passing mile, my body remembered heightened sensations until I pulled down the gravel road up to my old Cape, now looking more like a chalet. The construction on the new kitchen overlooking the lake was beginning to take shape as I sat down and went over my next month's itinerary. A commercial was scheduled, and it seemed that every week, I was asked to be the celebrity chef at B&Bs all over the East Coast. The more the calls came in, the more excited I became. I checked the calendar and realized I was booked solid for June and July.

I still have not heard from Clinton, even though I could have sworn that it was him that day, and I figured that I really blew it with him. "That's OK ... his loss, right," I thought. "Were all my fantasies just too much for any one man?" I wondered as I wrote in my journal. Maybe I was not meant to be tied down to anyone. Maybe love just was not for me. I scribbled the last words down and shut the book for now.

Later, I took a drive down to one of the farms in North Turner, where a friend of mine was growing a lot of different strains of cannabis, and I bought several ounces from her fall harvest. Afterward, I noticed lilacs blooming when I pulled out onto Route 219 and headed home.

Soon, I crossed over Route 4 and rounded the bend, where the first glimpses of the water caught my attention. I pulled my car over and stepped out for a bit. A large mountain, with its giant bald spot, took my breath away. I pulled out my road map and realized this was pinpointed Bear Pond. Then, I followed the route lines and found one road that led to the mountain, set the GPS to the spot, started the car, and turned around.

It had been years since I had been here, as Camp Berea took me way back when I was a kid. I kept following the road until I found the spot I was looking for. Then, I laced my shoes up and began the hike up the mountain. The rocky terrain in spots made the climb harder than originally thought when I realized that I should have brought some water. The buds on the trees were just opening, and I kept wondering if I would see a bear, deer, or moose. Then, I wondered what I would do if I did. Finally, I put it out of my head as I continued to press forward.

It was about thirty minutes into the trek when I really wished that I had some water. I stood there for a minute, wondering whether to continue or go back down. I sat down on a rock, thinking if I would just calm down, it might not be that bad.

As I listened to the natural silence, I faintly heard what sounded like water. I got up and started to look around, and just there to my right, was a pipe tapped into a spring with a pool of water in a small basin. Oh, I was so happy! Gratefully, I dropped to my knees and began slurping the water with my cupped hands. I drank for what seemed like an eternity when it occurred to me that I got what I needed. Re-hydrated and reinvigorated, I stood up and decided I would continue my ascent and kept pushing forward. It did not take too much longer to reach the summit.

The more I walked, the more I could see the views from all over. I perched on a large rock that overlooked the side of the mountain, down to Bear Pond and saw how it wrapped around. I laid down on the rock and just stared up at the sky, dozing off for a few minutes as I took all of it in. Then, I walked around and saw some blueberry bushes and thought I should make it a point to come back in July when they would be full of sweet berries.

I started to head back down the mountain. Naturally, the descent went much faster; however, my stomach was growling with hunger, and all I had on me was some pot. I found the perfect spot under a large oak tree and stopped for a cool drink. Within minutes, I was back in my car and looked up a place to eat. The closest place was *Bear Pond Variety*, so I programmed it in, back down the dirt road, and out to Route 219 I went.

As soon as I turned on to Route 4, there it was, on the left side of the road. I pulled in to fill my gas tank gas and ran inside. The ladies at the counter were busily running up and down, filling the orders from the truckers that were lined up all along Route 4. I ordered an Italian sub, grabbed a drink from the coolers, charged it on my Master Card® and headed back out to my car. The day was shaping up, and I put the convertible top down as I drove back to RT 219, past Bear Pond and the mountain I had just conquered. "Not too shabby for fifty," I said to myself. as I continued the drive back to Lovell.

Jaxson and I had been talking on the phone, and we were both excited to take the next step. I saw that my roots needed a touch-up, with all the traveling and book signings. Anyway, I was too busy to worry about my hair.

That is until I realized that I needed to keep up my

appearance. The time was rapidly passing as the weeks flew by and my next class was fast approaching. The last B&B that I just celebrity guested at was in Vermont, and it was a wedding-themed event. Each place I went, I was a big hit, and I was able to sell my cookbooks to damn near every guest I met. It took some negotiating until I was finally back in Jaxson's chair, his fingers running through my hair. We even chatted about opening my own place someday as I hugged him, knowing it was just a few weeks away.

August was fast approaching, as I talked on the phone with Olivianna about when she was coming. I saw from the message board that some of the people from Vegas were coming, and I was excited about this one, for it seemed a lot of my cooking friends were going to be there.

I sat down overlooking the water and watched the carpenters put the finishing touches on my new kitchen. As my cooking show deal with one of the cooking channels was still being negotiated, I began to wonder if it ever was going to happen. I set the oven to 275 degrees F, ground up my recently purchased buds, placed them in an aluminum tray, wrapped it with tin foil, and tried out my new oven for the first time. I set my egg timer for twenty minutes and let my weed de-carb while I sat out on my front porch with my binoculars, intently watching the cars as they made their way down the bend into the long driveway to the *Center of Love Club.*

I saw that Betty and Jane, the two ladies from Virginia, came in. Then, I spied G'anacia, putting her feet in the water and heard her laughter as the wind carried her voice across the lake. There were a few more people I recognized from the gala, Jamestown, or Las Vegas when my timer went off. I ran to the kitchen to pull out my weed. The nutty smell seemingly had transformed the entire kitchen into a cannabis factory.

I headed back out to the chair and looked around to see if anyone else had arrived. I started packing as I got back out of the chair, threw some clothes in a book bag, and placed it by the new deluxe oak and glass front door. I walked into my former kitchen (now turned butler's pantry), pulled my magic butter machine off the shelf, grabbed a bottle of extra virgin coconut oil, headed back to the countertops, and plugged it in. I took full-fat creamery butter, which I obtained from the farmer down the street, out of the fridge and placed the one cup of butter to one cup of coconut oil to one ounce of the decarboxylated weed mixture into the machine. Then, I added a few (no pun intended) cracks of black pepper and some bay leaves to increase potency, placed the lid back down and hit the start button.

I ran upstairs, took a fast shower, and chose what I wanted

to wear before heading back down to the front porch and picking up my binoculars again. I watched as Jaxson arrived in a sleek BMW® as a few other men from the message board continued to roll in. There was a significant difference in age ranges that appeared as funny on the surface but seemed to be the norm for contemporary groups of aspiring entrepreneurs.

I could not help but notice the one Indian man, with his mustache curled up each side, who really had some sex appeal, even from the distance. "Nice package," I thought to myself as I caught a good glimpse of his ass before I let my binoculars slide down.

Then, seemingly out of the blue, a black limousine pulled up, and I jumped out of my chair and pressed next to the glass, straining to see who was getting out of the car. I opened the slider doors that still had the stickers on when my mouth and the binoculars nearly dropped to the ground.

One minute, I was on my porch; the next, I was at his side as Clinton grabbed his luggage out of the driver's hand. He placed it down, turned to me then gave me a warm hug.

"How you been doing?" he asked, noticing the surprised look on my face.

It all happened so fast that I was nearly flabbergasted as I looked back over to my camp, wondering what just happened and how I got here. His hug was way different than what I remembered, as my nose was buried in his chest. Excitedly, I smelled the scent of his cologne and breathed all of him in. As my hands pulled away from his waist, I felt his concealed carry shoulder holster. I could not help that it strangely bothered me today, wondering what he was really packing.

"What are you wearing?" he asked as he looked down at me.

Looking up at him, I laughed. I was wearing my "*Imagination*" t-shirt with the Avatar and a pair of leggings when I pulled on the shirt and said, "It's *Imagination Apparel*®, and I got it off the *Center of Love Club* website.

"It's very telling," he said.

Glancing at the shirt and back up to him, I questioned myself, wondering what I was saying when I sensed the sheer power of his spiritual being, as he is so much more than what he has told me.

"Did you settle in yet?" he asked.

"Nah, I swam over," I replied as I looked over to my left, pointed to my home, and brushed off the question, not wanting him to know I got my wings with Jaxson.

"Seriously," he said, "you are staying here, right?"

"Oh yeah," I said. "I just need to head back over and get my stuff," I explained, nervously chewing on my recently manicured fingernails. Oh my God!

He appeared like a visiting King, with his broad chest snug in the blue dress shirt and beige khakis. His skin seemed lighter to me than what I remembered from being with him that night. The aviator glasses bridged his nose, seeing my reflection as I composed myself. I do not even understand why I cared, but then again, it was Clinton Tuckerman.

I had been trying so hard to get him out of my head, and now, with him this close to me, all the feelings came flooding back. All my fantasies and failures roared in like an avalanche. I wanted so badly to have him touch me again, and yet, I was so scared of him at the same time.

He looked back at me again and asked me if I was OK.

I looked up at him, trying to bury the pain inside my body. I did not want him to think that he had any hold on me whatsoever. I wanted him to think he was just a number, like another order that came through my window – nothing more than just a fleeting ship passing in the night for me. At least, I wanted him to think that anyway as I walked away, looking for

Karissa.

I saw her in the kitchen, talking with Nadia from Vegas, and we hugged. I was so glad to see that some of the people I met before were continuing to work on themselves within the group.

That is when the guy with the heavy Indian accent came over, hugged me, and said, "Hello, my friend, I am Saminder, and I am from India."

I smiled and said, "Imagine that." I hugged him back, and he was genuinely happy that he came all the way from India for this. The more I looked around at all the guests, the more I could see that so many different types of people were there. An Asian man caught my eye, who looked like he was a doctor, when I thought, "Damn, am I stereotyping or what?" as I suddenly took a major step forward in self-awareness.

Walking over to Karissa, I spoke softly and said, "Um, I sort of flew over here ... any chance I could use the car for ten minutes?"

"Yeah, sure, take my car," she said with a perceptive chuckle as she handed me the keys.

I saw G'anacia and Nadia as I was heading back to my house and motioned for them to come with me.

The short drive around the lake gave us a few minutes to catch up on life. I briefly showed them my house before I grabbed my massage table and bags. G'anacia told me that she opened her first soul food restaurant along the Las Vegas Strip, and her pulled pork and baby back ribs were winning awards. I was so beyond excited to hear her say that as we pulled back in.

Nadia told me that she was also working on her culinary skills, concentrating more on vegan soups. As we parked the car, I looked up ahead and saw Olivianna pulling in. According to the new magnetic signs on her car, she opened her own bakery when, lo and behold, one of the next great bakers from *Food Network*® just rolled in from around the bend. Nadia looked over at me and asked if we were at a cooking convention.

"I don't know," said G'anacia, "but it sure does look like it from here," she continued.

"Nah, it can't be. Clinton is from Delaware, and he's no chef," I replied.

One by one, we got our room assignments and unpacked our clothes for the week. The first day was spent just relaxing as we watched Karissa and Kennedy demonstrate a full body massage with a salt scrub on anyone fast enough to get naked and jump on the table. I could not help but get lost in the art form of it all, with all its graceful swaying movement, as opposed to running around a kitchen. My mind was in twenty places at the same time. This place was like a summer camp for adults who never had the "camp feeling." It truly was "A place to unwind from the stresses of life on the line," as the engraved slogan on the brass plaque ran over in my mind.

I synchronized my breath with the group, feeling the energy of the people begin to become one as we all took each other's hands and began chanting Om's. The energy began to intensify as the vibration that was ringing in the cove with each passing minute sent sensations through me I would have never thought I could experience. Then, as if I could not imagine anymore, the beat of the drums came thundering in and rocked my root chakra.

I do not know what everyone else felt, but for me, it was like a collective jolt of electricity going through me. I was spellbound as my body vibrated with an intensity that made me wonder if we had been struck by lightning. I opened my eyes and looked around as several people were spasming and making delicious sounds.

The more I tried to fight the sensation that I knew was welling up into my sacral chakra, the stronger the beats of the drums pounded. Whatever it was, I allowed it to come into me, and there I was, lost in a sea of collective moans, knowing full well we were all having an orgasmic experience together. I blissfully lay there on the beach as the steady beat of the drums awakened something inside of me that I had never experienced before.

Lying on the beach in what appeared to be a pool of emotion, I felt my soul leave my body as I floated up to the sky. I have no idea how long it took this to happen, but long enough to know that it was time for dinner.

The various scents of dinner waft out of the main hall and out to the beach, where picnic tables are set up. Lining the tables were ears of corn, freshly cooked lobsters, steam bags of potatoes, clams, and sausage. Out in the center of the display were all kinds of dipping butter with a description of what each blend was for. One said *High Head,* and the other was labeled *Body Babe.* Grapes, bananas, and oranges were piled on the table, along with bottles of cannabis-infused wine.

The flames of the bonfire lit up the cove as the night sky grew darker. The guests from all over the world had descended on the little compound of six buildings. The hotels from miles around were booked, and I was so glad I had scheduled this one early. Someone said the experience was even better if you were on the beach versus in the hotel rooms for this week's retreat.

Front-row seats cost extra, and I booked mine well in advance. For the most part, we all seemed to get along well with each other, except in the case of one woman, Salem.

There she was, with her seemingly flawless body, loudly chomping on raw carrots and conspicuously turning her nose up at everything else on the table. Her long brown hair graced naturally beyond her shoulders but did overshadow her long, full, and fake eyelashes that glared of cosmetic overkill. Her pouting lips were swollen beyond all reasonable proportions as if she were just stung by a bee. "Must be Botox,®" Nadia said, as she smiled at me.

"Don't pay her any mind," Betty said as Salem put her hands on her hips and marched off, stewing in her own juices at the type of attention she was getting under the chatter.

"Are we all in kindergarten or something?" G'anacia asked rhetorically, shaking her head as we broke into a hearty round of laughter.

The cannabis-infused dessert of chocolate mousse with fresh berries was out of this world as we licked our spoons clean. We gradually made our way back to our camp, whispering to each other which person we secretly wanted. As we stole more glances at the men sitting around the fire pit with Kennedy, Nadia took a jab at me and asked, "Which one do you like, Charlotte?" as the ladies all started laughing.

"I'm not telling," I said, "what are we, seventeen?" I caught myself staring over at Jaxson and Clinton and did not know which one I wanted yet. I did not even know if I was ready to pick, but I felt that I was getting closer as I laid down my spoon, subconsciously knowing damn well who I wanted when I stole a glance at Kennedy.

I looked up to see Saminder staring at me, holding one of my recent cookbooks. He politely asked for my autograph, and a warm rush of love came over me as I sat down and wrote a special note to him. "Well, I'm going to sleep now," I said as I got up to walk away.

"See you in the morning," he said as I made my way to the door. "Excuse me," he said with his accentuated English. "May I talk to you, my friend?" he asked.

"What's up?" I asked. We headed down to the fire pit and talked for an hour as the fire crackled through the night. I could clearly see that he was much younger than me. He was very charming and talked to me about all kinds of foods from India, among other things. He even invited me to come home with him.

Almost taking that as a marriage proposal, I looked back

at him and asked, "Where's my ring?" as I teasingly slapped his legs. "I promise when I go to India, you can give me the grand tour," I said sincerely.

"Ah, thank you very much, my friend," he said softly as he placed his hands in Namaste.

I started to wonder if I really was on a cooking show with all the chefs who were here, and that is when I saw a new guy and wondered how I had missed him. I was overhearing his conversation when I began to wonder if this was some sort of sting operation. He glanced over at me and extended his hand. "Hi, I'm Big Willy from Philly," he said jovially.

"You don't say," I replied, noticing that he was about three inches shorter than me.

He walked up to Clinton and gave him a high five, thanking him for getting him in.

I stepped into my room and wondered. How did Saminder get one of my cookbooks? Did he know me? As I headed into the bathroom to brush my teeth, Salem was taking her makeup off.

"Do you really think you have a chance with Clinton?" she asked bluntly out of the blue.

Irritated by her nosy arrogance, I rolled my eyes as I put my toothbrush in my mouth, totally ignoring her stares and wondered how the hell she managed to get through all the other classes with that attitude. I got into my bed and thought that this was not what this place was about. As I rolled over on my side, I could not help but think back to Clinton. Of course, I wanted another chance with him. All I could think of was to talk to God and ask that he would watch over me. I prayed in the night that if Clinton Tuckerman was my true knight in chocolate armor, then please give me a sign.

The sun seemed to rise much earlier up in these parts as I made my way down to the lake shore, watching a family of loons swim in the early morning mist.

The teacher arrived, and those of us who were already on the beach started the class with breathing exercises.

As he stretched out his arms, I could feel the energy in me come alive. Looking up to my right, I heard water splashing. I saw Clinton, Kennedy and Jaxson running through the water, following behind what appeared to be a veritable herd of men. If I did not know any better, I would think they were on horses. I watched intently as their chests rippled through their shirts, and I thought to myself that it was a blessing just to watch them run to the shore. That is when the 64,000-dollar question occurred to me. Was I really switching back to men?

I headed back to the chairs, where one of the gentlemen from the Vegas retreat came to sit by me.

"I remember watching the women do that years ago; now, I can't even get my legs to bend, let alone run," he said with a laugh, tapping my legs with his cane as he braced himself slowly into the Adirondack chair.

I reached over to him, rubbing his knee. "Yeah ... me too," I replied as I chuckled, wondering what was happening to me. "No different than rubbing a steak," I said, as I let my fingers press into his delicate skin. "Did you play sports when you were young?" I asked.

"Yes," he replied, "among other things."

"Are you looking for love?" I asked.

"No," he replied. "I came to have a week of intense healing for my weary bones, and I have found love, lots of times – just didn't know how to keep it," he elaborated.

"I hear that," I said as I looked up to see the rest of the men running to the lake. "I wonder, how did you pick just one person?" I asked.

"If I knew the answer to that question, I wouldn't be here

now," he said.

"I guess not," I said, playing with my coffee as the staff brought breakfast to the table. I looked at another man who was a real cutie pie. As he fluttered about, I intuitively knew that he pitched for the other team. "Now, that's competition," I thought, watching the men flexing their muscles in front of me as they slowly swayed in the air, stretching and bending.

It reminded me of standing at a vending machine wondering which cookie I wanted to put my money in for when another man came up to me and introduced himself.

"Hi, I'm Allen. Are you enjoying this as much as me?" he asked, smiling back at me.

"Maybe," I said with a wink.

All of them looked so good in their own way, and they seemed to be so oblivious to us drooling women as we assembled on the sand, trying to gain our balance.

Nadia giggled under her breath as she bent her legs into the sand. "I like the man from the clothing company," she said.

"I know, right … I'm so bad … Damn, they all look so good," I replied as we continued to ogle over the men. I was waiting for them to turn around and bend over just to see what their shorts were doing on the back end.

G'anacia plopped down next to us. "Did you get a look at those men just then?" she asked.

Chuckling, we started clapping among ourselves.

Nadia laughed and said, "Now, that guy Clinton is one fine candy bar."

"You had better not lay a finger on him," I said as we rolled in the sand, laughing.

The old man looked at us and hollered out. "I can't believe you ladies comparing men to a candy bar," he said, "times have changed."

"What's your name? I forgot to ask," I said with a laugh. He smiled and looked away, and I thought that he must need hearing aids. As I ate breakfast, I could not help but stare at Kennedy.He carried what looked like a half-moon down to where we had been exchanging energy sessions and began setting it up. My curiosity got the best of me, and I soon found myself staring at the round table while he slid the sheets over the top. "What kind of table is this?" I asked.

Kennedy looked at me with a boyish grin. "It's Karissa's latest invention, and she calls it an energy bed," he said enthusiastically as he pulled out a grid of stones and attached it to the underside.

I knelt on the ground and watched curiously as he adhered the plates of stones underneath and asked what purpose it served.

He showed me one of the grids and began to explain. "This grid is filled with stones that resonate with the sacral chakra, and its purpose is to heighten a massage with sensual energy.

"Does that really work?" I asked as I cast my suspensions out.

"Sure does," he answered as he went for another set of grids. "These stones are for sleep," he elaborated, handing me another grid.

I picked up the grids of stones, ran my hands over them, and then handed them back to him.

"Do you want to try it out?" he asked, already knowing the answer.

My eyes lit up, and I said, "Yes," without any hesitation at all. He soon had me back under his spell as I watched him adjust the table. Karissa came down with more sheets, and the rest of the class assembled around the tables while everyone partnered back up.

Kennedy looked over to me and asked, "Do you want me to demonstrate to you?"

With that, I felt a flush come over my body, blushing as a sly smile escaped my lips, knowing full well I wanted more of him.

I watched the group that had become comfortable with nudity, taking their clothes off and sliding under the sheets. No longer self-conscious about my body, I took my clothes off and slid underneath the fabric. There was something that felt so good about them as my fingers stroked the material when I asked Kennedy, "What is the thread count?"

His voice vibrated in my ear, "It is not the thread count that makes these sheets so good; it is the combination of Delaware Hemp and Virginia Cotton, and the face pillow is filled with herbs and small stones," as he adjusted the levers to perfect angles. I burrowed down into the sheets and asked, "Can I get these sheets for my king-size bed?"

Heaven's gates opened when Kennedy said, "You can order them from our website or pick out a set in the front gift shop,."

I was so happy with that response, and I settled down, knowing I was going to order a set when I got done.

Then that is when Kennedy said, "Take three deep breaths and let's connect." He began to place the oils on my neck and slide down my back, rounding my hips. His fingers grazed my skin as he slowly slid his palms toward my neck. He repeated his descent, each time moving further down my spine until his hands were on my buttocks. I relaxed even further with each breath I took as his hands lingered down on my thighs. Eventually, he spanned from the tips of my fingers to the souls of my feet, taking away the tension that had been accumulating for years. "This is called effleurage," he said as he pushed it out of my body in long, gliding strokes.

I have been wanting this moment for years now, and as his hands continued to peruse my flesh, I slowly descended into the magical realm of Kennedy McCormick. Slipping back and forth between both worlds, I was acutely aware of Karissa walking around the tables, describing the process she was guided to create. Her voice lulled me in a seductive tone that had me slipping further into her world as her hands hovered over my heart chakra.

Karissa's voice flowed as if she were speaking on the clouds that were floating by. "It is very well-documented that cannabis alters our perceptions, so it only makes sense that it would heighten a sensual energy exchange. Naturally, we wanted to make sure that you were all good and high before we started today's energy sessions," she said.

My thoughts began to wander to what I ate with cannabis today, and then, as I remembered the Lemon Poppy Seed Mini Muffin, I began to float away.

"To prepare the mind, body, and soul to make love incorporating the elements of energy, plant therapy and massage. That is what we coined *Maschakra*," she said as her fingers ran the length of my body. "The very first thing is deciding that nothing else matters – no clients, no kids, no what is for dinner, no appointments – nothing. Nothing else matters but to show love to your partner," she emphasized.

With her words, I began to swoon in an ecstatic vision of Kennedy making love to me. I was lost in a vivid dreamlike escapade as his hands ran along my body.

"Is anyone not feeling high right now?" she mused over the beach of people lying face down on the massage tables.

Everyone giggled as waves of laughter echoed out over the water. As my spirit continued to fade in and out, all I remembered was being on some celestial plane. I took a deep breath and could smell the scent of peppermint as the blend called Muscle Ease® began to envelope my body. I became acutely aware of how my body began to vibrate with so intense an energy stream.

"That's the crystal bed that you are feeling," Kennedy said. "Do you like it?"

I could not even respond to his question, for I was already all the way in. The chuckles began to mellow out as we each settled into our space. Even though I was the one receiving, I was aware of what Karissa was teaching and could see it all in my mind as she instructed the givers to put their bodies into position.

"With your legs at a ten and two position as on a clock, bend your knees slightly and take three deep breaths, connecting the giver and the receiver," she instructed.

I listened as I took each breath. On the first one, my head was traveling faster than the speed of sound, and I saw flashes of my youth as my age went winding down.

Gently, with her whole hand caressed my face, using her fingertips to massage in small circles around my jawline, flowing up to my ears towards my temples, down around my eyes and then flowing past my nose, around my lips then back down to my jawline. Repeating the sequence on my face, I began to relax even further. Then, I felt my breath grow shallow as I slipped further into another realm.

Her hands continued to wrap around my shoulders and neck with a sweeping back and forth motion, rotating from the right to the left side while Kennedy's hands cascaded up and down my legs, using what Karissa called an **Energy Massage Bar**, a blend of stones and essential oils in a block form. The sensation of both male and female energies working on me had a balancing effect on my body while the smooth stone massage sensation.

My eyes were still closed when I felt the "energy bar" being placed up against my skin. The oils released their scent as the bar slowly melted on my skin. I felt the smooth sensation of the tumbled stones as they glided around my body. Kennedy's right hand hovered over my throat as my body arched up to the sky, vibrating at an incredible velocity. He placed his left hand on the sacral chakra and held it for three minutes.

It has been months since I had sex. With so many men surrounding me, my body veritably screamed for pollination as the melted bar of aromatic oils and smooth crystals lingered over my solar plexus. I felt my sacral start to spin, and before I knew it, my whole body began heaving into a sexual vortex that

I never thought could happen. While my pelvic floor was pulsing right out of my skin, my breath began to pulse faster. When I heard the sounds around the cove, shrieks of delight rang out. An orchestra of yeses, as each person was releasing, having astral orgasms without physical sex.

I felt his right hand slowly descending to the Root Chakra, and he hovered over my love canal. As Kennedy held his hand in position, holding the space, my legs began to shake as my root chakra began to quake.

"Oh My God," I murmured as he climbed on top of the table right between my thighs! He gave full hand pressure to each leg as he slid his hands from my toes, past my knees, then in between my thighs. My whole body convulsed out of control when, at that very moment, I felt my soul succumb to him.

16

As the Pot Thickens

After the first massage was over, we took a small break and went to the water for an energy session with a group of masters. Floating in the water, I began to feel my body vibrate and tingle as the energy wrapped around me. The gentle sway of the water engulfed my ears. Now thoroughly suspended by the hands holding me up, the pent-up memories of my past began escaping from my fingertips. I would get a brief glimpse of some distant memory, and my body would flicker as I let it go.

I soon felt the need to be free and began swimming along the bottom of the lake. A sunfish stared back at me, seemingly welcoming me to his family. I swam as far as I could go, with each wave of my arm commanding the strength inside of me to push myself just a little bit farther. I was far out into the lake when I saw the staff bring the lunch out to the tables and made my way back in.

By the time I got to shore, I thought I was going to die from exhaustion as my legs and arms trembled from exertion. I had just enough energy to plop down at the table when Nadia asked Kennedy, "How did you learn to release a woman the way you do?"

The iced tea that I was guzzling down my throat nearly blew all over the table when I looked around. I grabbed a napkin and tried to clean myself up when Kennedy answered her question.

"Well," he said in his Ronald Reagan voice, "when I was eighteen years old, I went to trade school to become an auto mechanic and turning wrenches, working to bring old cars back to life, was my dream."

"I could see it all so clearly in my mind, the bruised and battered ladies as they rolled into my life. My hands massaging the warm, soapy water over their hood, lovingly revealing their beauty. It took a few years before I could get the cars to where they would purr for me. I had only one woman, one goddess of the night. I was only ten years old when my dad brought her home."

I could not believe what he was talking about and could

not believe that anyone would even ask. I tried to act nonchalant when, in all reality, I was hanging on every word as he continued to spurt.

"She was my dream, with her claws razor sharp, as she raced down the highway. To take me to my most hidden desires and then bring me back all in one piece. A few more years went by before I realized that I was not going to reach my dreams of financial success turning wrenches. I was going to have to make a change of careers, and I enrolled in a finance class with my eyes on Wall Street."

He took a deep breath, pausing for a moment. "As my career was fast-tracking, my interest in making love to the cars dwindled as the lure of making my first million was on my mind. I was wildly driven and loved to set goals and accomplish them. I was in my mid-thirties before my career took off, and I was successful," he summed up.

"We both were," Clinton interrupted Kennedy.

I looked over at Clinton and asked him what else he did.

He smiled back and said, "I've done a lot over the years. Jack of all trades, master of none," as he winked back at me.

I looked back at Kennedy as he continued, "One night, the woman of my dreams walked into my living room. I met her when I hired her to come to my home and massage me". "My marriage was not in the best of shape, and I knew hers was in the same spot. I tried to convince her that I could save her from her brokenness. I set out to win her, and I enrolled myself in a program to learn how to massage her. I wanted to give her what she was giving me. I thought if I impressed her with my massage skills, I would have her lapping out of my hands. No matter how many times I offered, she declined my request. Part of me liked it, and part of me was mad over that. I knew she just needed to be tamed. Teaching her the lesson of who runs this game," he said.

My eyes got all wide when I heard him refer to her as if she were a horse on a farm. "What an asshole," I thought for a second.

"If I could just harness that energy, I knew that she could really go places," he continued. "I remember the night I spanked her over the settee. Of course, I was not really spanking her, but I did put the smack down, so to speak and let her know who was in charge."

His eyebrows went and did some funky up and down motion as he looked straight over at me. "From then on out, I knew I had her, and she would do anything I asked."

"There was something about the way she would massage

my feet that always made me feel loved. I always wore my black dress socks for my massage, and she always put my socks back on my feet when she was done. I knew when she massaged me down on her knee, she was, in a small way, paying homage to me. I did not understand it at the time, but deep inside, I rather liked the feeling. I guess you could say she made me feel like I was a King."

I blushed for a moment, and my mind went back to the day in Vegas when I was massaging the old Hollywood legend, and I remembered the black sock. Somehow, I was able to relate to it all.

"The tension at home was at a breaking point, and I seemed to lash out at everyone. I knew I needed a change of life. I was building a home in the nearby county and filed for divorce all in the same year. I just needed to feel love, and I wanted the temptress that would massage me to yield to me. Frustrated with her denial, I cast my sites on another option and broke out the massage table that I had bought and began to advertise my services, massaging women. Quietly, you see, I really was only doing it for myself. It was a way I could touch a woman and pour my soul into loving someone. I had always wanted to do this. If I am honest, it's why I love to wash my cars myself. There is something about using my hands to do something that has such meaning. I never understood that until

I started to massage someone, it had a deeper meaning for me," he narrated.

"Route 52 was the gateway to the lovely woman of the county. I began this little – shall we say – 'side' business. While their husbands were tucked safely in town managing empires, I was nestled between their wives' legs. I was affectionately referred to as "The Fingler" as he giggled as if my fingers sparked gold ... Ah, the tales these fingers could tell," he said.

I closed my eyes once again as the thoughts of his fingers gliding over my skin were driving me insane.

"The goal was never to take them for myself as he stood up and walked around the table. I had no desire to have a wife; my goal was merely to help appease other women, while I satisfied my own longings for release," he said.

I closed my eyes and imagined what it would feel like to have him deep inside me, shuddering as the energy engulfed me, trying to pull myself out of the trance I had so willingly gotten myself into.

"They say if you love what you are doing, you will never work a day in your life," he proclaimed as he squirted some oil into his hands and began rubbing the neck of the woman who was sitting in front of him. "I had amassed a loyal list of clients over the next couple of years as my fingers' reputation developed. My high-pressure job of trading was lucrative, but the stress was unreal, and I longed to focus more time on giving and receiving pleasure. I never really broke too many rules with my friends. I had a promise myself to never have sex with another man's wife," he said.

"I adopted the 'Presidential Philosophy' to what defines sex. I had a fantastic time in life. To the outside world, it looked as if I was running the stock market and I merely had two appointments each day. I worked eight hours in total and amassed over ten thousand dollars each month. This was the easiest money I had ever made, and to say that I enjoyed going to work was an understatement," he continued.

"In one way or another, I loved all my woman. From the tall and frail to the short and plump, each had a quality that endeared me to them. However, only one stood out from the crowd, her red hair piled high, revealing a crown of beauty. Those soft hazel eyes would truly light up when she saw me. The woman who used to massage me every week – pressing in as hard as she could in some areas and then as gently as can be in others.

Some nights, I could swear the way she massaged my neck, it was as if she were breathing with me – like I felt her release the tension with me. I felt connected in a way I had never felt before and felt safe in her arms. For whatever reason it was, I knew that I could trust her, and I missed her. She could do things to make pain go away in my body, unlike anyone else I had ever known before. There was something different about how she worked — something magical or mystical. She just had a way about her that I cannot describe. I had so many times wanted to reach out to her but, for one reason or another, I did not".

"As I made love with my lips upon many a woman's legs, it was Karissa's body that was always in my mind, her naval I was always kissing and her soul I was longing for," he shared, as Karissa moved closer to him. "Each woman I loved as if they were her," he said. Then, he looked up at Karissa and said, "I'm so sorry, my love."

"I knew who you were," she said with a grin as she rubbed his shoulders.

"I always brought my new loves chocolate to charm them to me. Most sessions lasted for hours, and it was all about the dance of making love with massage. As I prepared my table with sheets and aromatic scents, I would instruct them to disrobe. I would sage the room and open the windows to take in the air. I would light candles all around the room and adjust the music to encourage the heaving of the soul," he revealed.

We sat around the table as he continued to talk, and my eyes were glued to his mouth and what he was saying. The second wave of cannabis infusion had hit me. The lobster with a cannabis butter toasted roll kept the buzz in my body lingering as we broke from dinner and began exchanging once again.

As the sun made its way down into the water, we began the energy massage. I had yet to trade with Jaxson, and I felt like I could hear him calling me in my head. We kept glancing at each other through the glowing embers of the fire as we massaged under the setting sun.

The moonlight also subtlety called me as it cascaded down over the lake. I could no longer ignore its calls as Kennedy and Karissa ended for the night. Watching them walk hand in hand to their camp from across the lake, I could see the glow of the lights from my own camp as I motioned to Jaxson, asking if he wanted to go for a swim. I have been swimming the passage for the last few weeks, trying to build up my own endurance. I found a sand bar out in the middle of the lake, where I stopped for a while and took a break.

Running into our sleeping quarters, I reached for my bathing suit and yelled, "I'm going for a swim. Anyone want to join me?"

G'anacia started chasing after me, yelling, "Girl, are you doing what I think you are?" she asked.

"Why yes, I am ... Care to join me?" I responded as I ran back out the door into the water.

I could see a few other couples out in the water, already frolicking, as I made my way towards my own camp. As I approached the dock where Jaxson was waiting, we embraced for the first time in weeks. The excitement must have been too much for both of us. Before I knew it, our wings had opened, and we were flying over the Maine sky in a combustion storm of colors.

Flying to Bear Mountain in what felt like minutes, we swooped up to the Canadian Border, where the temperatures felt almost twenty degrees cooler as we watched the moose scavenging for food under the canopy of stars. Making our way back to Lake Kezar, we touched down right in front of the Center just as the fire had died down to an ember. I crept back into the room and slinked into bed, hoping to catch a few winks before the sun came up.

"How was he?" G'anacia whispered.

"Magical," was all I could reply as I drifted off to sleep.

Morning came sooner than I had expected as I made my way down to the beach. Today's breakfast was all types of fresh fruits swirled together for smoothies. I went over to the chairs that were fashioned into a big circle.

Karissa stood in the center of the ring as she began to guide us. "The intention is to take you to your special place, so picture yourself right now walking down a stretch of beach. Put your mind there right now. Take a few deep breaths and relax," she said.

Guided Meditation to Invoke the Goddess Within

Looking out into the water

Massive rocks tower

over the waves

Swim out

climb on top

The Millions of years

that the ocean has beaten

this rock

have nestled

a bed into its center

A cocoon envelope you

as the sun begins to set

tranquil blue-green water

beating against the rock

a reminder the strength

and power the ocean has

As the tide rolls in

feel the spray mist your skin

tiny drops of dew

are now covering me and you

allow your hands to caress

the salty moisture into your skin

As the mind gets engulfed

by the current of waves

intense electricity

begins to build

the sun going down

the wildflowers

releasing their scent

Breathe the smell

of Jasmine that grows

A heady perfume

mixed with the salty air

proving to be a love spell

you are in love

with everything right now

in an oasis of sensations

your mind is calculating

all the senses

you taste salty

on your skin

you smell perfume in the air

and most of all you

feel the power of the waves

as they begin to crash

furiously against you

the massive rock

you are protected in

you become entranced

and succumb to the call

to be free with yourself

As the waves crash

spraying you with mist

you tap into

the sexual energy

of the ocean within

to feel the power in the waves

as you begin to chant

feel the magic of spirit

come into your chest

It began with a small pool

of water hitting your flesh

as the water reminds you

pearls from the ocean

offered as gifts

A large wave

comes crashing down

against the rock

splashing

sending a ripple shock

from your genitals

through the top of your head

a massive tidal wave

of colors

exploding in you

your love spilling

into the ocean blue

as you release

let your fingers guide you.

17
Kennedy's Declaration

The scent of baked oatmeal was clinging to the breeze, lulling me out of the blissful meditation I was in. I saw two young men carrying plates of fresh fruit, trays of muffins and platters of breakfast meats. Looking over at Kennedy, I asked him, "How is it that you ended up here?"

"Karissa always wanted to have a B&B. When we spoke with a broker who specialized in B&Bs, they said, 'Location, location, location.' The more we traveled the country trying to figure out where we wanted to live, the more we realized we did not want to settle on one place, and that is when the dream of the *Center of Love* was born."

"Is that what makes this place so different? That instead of these being vacation destinations, they can be a full-time residence, if you want them to be?" I inquired.

"Yes, if you want. Some locations are not set up for year-round living, but as we grow, we continue to expand our real estate portfolio. We add more properties that bring the dream of our all-inclusive cannabis-themed healing destinations into a lifestyle community for the open-minded," he said.

Nadia spoke up and asked, "Are there options to migrate from town to town like a vacation club does?"

"Well, yes, we have communities like that, too. It is like a co-operative, so to speak, so lots of people live on the property – you could call it a share – whatever, you really need to see it to understand. Either way, some people have been here for a few years, others stay for a season, and some just use it as a vacation resort."

"Damn, like we can all be in the dream?" asked G'anacia.

"We all can be," said Kennedy.

"Wow, how do I sign up for this?" she said.

Clinton spoke up, pointing to Kennedy, "And, how many places we got now?" he asked rhetorically.

Kennedy counted out loud and with his fingers: "Jamestown, Rhode Island; Bath County, Virginia; Lowell, Maine; Las Vegas, Nevada, and Natchez, Mississippi – We've got five Clinton and a few more on the way," he said with a laugh. He rubbed his belly as he made his way to the table to fill his plate. "Oh, damn ... I meant six ... we got six; I forgot about *Camp Werthefukrwe* that's in Odis Field, Maine," he added, as he slapped his hands on his forehead.

I reached deep down and asked, "What made you want to help people with sex?"

"I didn't think of myself that way at all," he replied, as he began to make all kinds of car and tool impressions, blowing air out of his mouth.

The baked muffin was calling my attention, and I began fumbling with the wrapper, "So, Kennedy, do you have any stories to go along with this washing lesson for today?" I asked.

Karissa laughed and said, "Oh yes, he does ... want to tell it like it is, Kennedy?"

Rubbing his fingers over his face, he looked over at everyone and asked, "You guys really want to hear about this?"

As the ears perked up and the chairs moved closer, we all agreed, "Yes, tell us a story."

Karissa grabbed the muffin tray, offering some more to everyone else. "Eat up, you guys ... The story is always better when you're high," she said.

"Thanks, dear," Kennedy mused before he began to tell the version of his life before Karissa. "It all happened one day out of the blue, the phone call that would change my life forever. In less than thirty minutes, she would be at my door. My hands were so nervous, running around, making sure none of the chicken was still in my teeth when I heard her car enter the driveway and the door shut.

I stood there, nervous as can be, as her hands wrapped against the wood grain of the old wooden doorway. With my hands on the knob, I took a deep breath and opened it. Standing there, a woman wearing a mini skirt, with her red blouse unbuttoned low enough to see her breasts busting through the top of her 44 Triple D-cups. I tried to hide my excitement as I led her into my home and to my office around the bend. I had just graduated from massage school, and this was the first woman outside of class I had ever worked on. My hands began to sweat even more. I looked her up and down. I wasn't expecting a woman to be this hot, as everyone in school wore medical scrubs," he said.

"I had her fill out a client information form and then instructed her how I wanted her to lay on the table. My hands were fumbling as I walked out of the room. I closed the door to the powder room behind me and began to wash my hands, slapping cold water on my face. This woman was incredibly good-looking with her long blonde hair, and I could feel my penis begin to fill out the space. Horrified, I tried beating it back down, as I kept on telling him, "No! No! No! Not now," he continued.

"My hands were dripping with water when I looked and saw a few wet spots on my pants right at my zipper, and my underarms were perspiring. 'How the hell am I going to massage her now,' I asked myself, as I looked like I had already busted a load in my pants. I struggled to get it together as I stared into the mirror and looked myself in the eye, pointing my finger at myself, saying, 'You had better not screw this up for me, buddy. I am a professional!"

"The hall seemed so much longer than what I remember it being as I took each step towards the room. I kept on going over it all in my mind. Did I tell her to get undressed? Did I tell her to get under the sheets, take her bra off and keep her underwear on? 'Oh God, help me,' I prayed as I held on to the handle and knocked on the door."

"A voice from the other side announced that it was OK for me to enter, and I peeked around the corner to find her sitting in the chair with a sheet wrapped around her. Her long blonde hair was pinned up on top of her head, with wisps of curls framing her face. It was all I could do now not to take the sheet off herself and rip her underwear off with my teeth, but, at the last second, I forced myself to get a grip."

"I quickly turned my head and asked her to hop up onto the table. With my eyes closed, I tried to help her get the sheet all the way up her body. I saw her red lace bra was still up against her chest. I came around to the front of her head. I was so nervous that I could not remember her name, and I was quickly becoming unglued in my head. I got up, feigning that I forgot my oil, and I glanced down at the sign-in sheet for her name."

"OK, Carla, I want you to take three deep breaths with me," I said, clearing my throat. "I am going to place my hand on your stomach so that I can connect to your energy. From there, I will go back to the front of your head, and we will start. Are you OK with that?" I asked.

Carla looked up at me with her beautiful blue eyes and nodded her head.

I took a few more breaths and squirted some oil in my hand. The scent of lavender and geranium filled the room as my hands began to caress her neck. I knew that I was going to ruin her bra if she did not take it off. Softly, I whispered in her ear, 'Are you sure that you want to keep your bra on? ... The oils could ruin it'," he said.

"I could tell she was just as embarrassed as I was. As she sat up to take her bra off, I could see her underwear was red lace, too. Her fingers fumbled with the latch, and she was having trouble getting her hands to work right. Then, she spoke the words every man wants to hear: 'Can you help me take my bra off?' With my hands already full of oil, I quickly rubbed the side of the table to oblige her request."

"As my hands grabbed both clasps, I started to breathe even harder. It was as if my penis had started running the show. I could almost hear it scream, 'Let me do it.' As I simultaneously dealt with the bra clasp and my penis in my head, I silently told them both to shut up. When I finally managed to get the clasp undone, I could swear that it was almost like my penis had suddenly developed hands of its own and was trying to pull the zipper down from the inside. My hands were gripped tightly to the table as I breathed harder and harder, telling it to 'stand down'. My heat-seeking precision-guided missile acted like Tattoo from *Fantasy Island,* trying to get my attention. "Look boss, an egg, an egg," it virtually nagged me on," Kennedy embellished.

"There I was, just standing there, looking down at my penis, "Yes, I know, buddy, I can see the egg, too. I don't know what to tell you," I thought. My bad boy shrank back down, defeated, at least for the moment. As my hands settled back down and I planted my butt on the seat, I took the oil into my hands again and began to caress her face and neck. My hands rounded her shoulder and under the back of her neck, I could see that her nipples were erect through the sheets, protruding through the thin fabric like twin missiles on a launching pad. I didn't want to look, but I could not help but see her dark brown areolae through the sheets," he said.

"This is how it all started. I did not mean for it to happen this way. I tried everything in me for people to take me seriously. The harder I tried to be professional and do the right thing, the fewer and fewer people called me. In the end, I had no other choice. Faced with mounting bills and the real thoughts of losing my home, I did the unthinkable," he concluded.

18
Kennedy's Quest

Kennedy continued his story. "Firstly, I don't know what kind of S.O.A.P. notes there are for what happened that day with my client. Secondly, if there are notes for this, I surely will be going to jail. I am sure I have now breached whatever ethical or moral code there is. Today, the lady I have been massaging asked me to pleasure her. I must have looked so stupid when she asked me if this was my first time. I had no idea that a woman would even do something like pay a man to release her, but that is what happened. It all seemed to happen so fast. It was like a different person suddenly emerging from the uncharted depths of my personality.

All I can remember is that I was standing by her right leg with both of my hands on her inner thigh. My touch was light as I was strumming my fingers from about midway up her thigh all the way to the top of her hips. Each time my fingers went towards her, it was as if her flower was opening her petals to me. I could smell her scent of vanilla bean and musk, like a cookie, waiting for me if I just allowed my nose to go deeper and take her all in. The sheet was covering up her privates, but I could see the red lace panties she was wearing. Each time I let my fingers trace her skin, the sheet would edge back a little more open until I finally had a good view of her pink lips.

Her underwear was like dental floss, which hardly covered her vulva. I could tell she was hairless, and the wild thoughts of letting my fingers massage her clitoris consumed my mind. I did not know how many times my hands went up and down her thighs, but each time I did, she would open her legs even further to me. Her breathing was so heavy now. She was thrashing her head back and forth, whimpering "Oh God," over and over, on the verge of having an orgasm.

The more she called out to God, the harder it was for me to resist. She started to buck her hips all around the table. My all-beef frank was so freaking hard. I just wanted to climb up on the table and stick my throbbing wiener in, but instead, my fingers slid in. As soon as my second and third fingers were inserted, it sent a spasm that heaved her whole pelvic floor. Her honey hit the ceiling as it gushed out of her, splashing the table, and I knew I had a gusher. I had never seen anything like this before, her back arched up to the ceiling, and she pulled away the sheets, revealing her whole lotus blossom to me.

The warm, wet flesh started to release, and I felt waves of spasms that seemed to engulf my own arm as I went in deeper. The more she thrashed, the more it made my arm shake, and the more she convulsed.

I was so excited that it happened just like magic. I felt an overwhelming sensation come over me like a waterfall of light – like something out of Paradise. There were no thoughts at all – just pure passion and instinctive reaction. All I knew was that my mouth went over her clitoris like white on rice.

My tongue lapped her like an ice-cream cone on a ninety-eight-degree day. My right fingers pumped her so hard as my left hand pinched her clitoris. It was like watching a volcano getting ready to erupt as her legs shook wildly to the beat of her passionate moans.

"In an instant, I was on the table, nestled between her legs. The sloshing sound her body was making as each time I plunged my fist in her vagina drove me utterly wild. The whole thing was driving me crazy, and I longed to slide my own beef stick in. It was like she was a juice box, and each time I squeezed her nipple, she would splash my face with her golden elixir. I felt like a homeless boy starving on the streets who had not had a meal in weeks as I savored the taste of her sweet sauce. I inserted my right index finger all the way in until I found her pink jewel. Then, I massaged her g-spot until she was screaming for me to eat her out again."

"It seemed like hours went by as I brought her over and over to climax. I was exhausted and excited all at the same time. Her swollen pink lips pulsed with her heartbeat as she began to slow down. Her whimpers were all in some other language as I lovingly massaged her lips and slowly brought her back. She just laid there on the table as she continued to spasm."

"I asked her how she was doing. All she did was smile and shake her head up and down, reassuring me that she was very well indeed. I must have really pleased her because she re-booked for next week and left three one-hundred-dollar bills on the table," he regaled.

My legs were in convulsion, and I cringed inside my head as I squirmed in my chair. I glanced over at Clinton as he cut a look at me. I put my head back down and started to breathe as Kennedy continued to torture me with the next round of lurid details.

"I remember this woman. Her husband was married to make money. No matter how many hours dangled over his head, it was never enough. He worked tirelessly to enhance his private portfolio and amass an empire worth well over ten million dollars."

"It was what he was neglecting at home that caught my interest, and I set out to introduce myself to her. Her long, curly brown hair caught my attention at the club. I watched her from across the room as she fiddled with her wine glass. The men were hitting the gold balls over the range as the night progressed. The room was a smorgasbord of lonely ladies. As business deals were being negotiated on the greens, I staked my claim on this lovely long-legged creature. My eyes finally met her gaze, and I motioned for her to go to the bar. Staring ahead while I nursed a three-fingered Johnny Walker straight, I slid my business card down on the polished wood and left."

"I loved the slow dance of reeling a woman in. It reminded me of when I was younger, going crabbing with my grandparents, lying on my belly as my fingers listened to the string. The bait put them into my trap as I slowly wrapped the string around my fingers, bringing those tasty crustaceans to the surface. Women engaged and paid me handsomely to please them by unlocking what was hidden deep within, and I amassed a reputation that delivered on that promise," he continued.

Nadia asked, "Can all women be multi-orgasmic?"

"Yes, I believe they can be. At least, that has been my

experience," Jaxson expertly chimed in.

Kennedy began to elaborate again, "Truth be told, a little bit of cannabis always seems to help. In fact, I remember it like it was yesterday as my Mercedes® pulled up around the long brick-paved entrance. She opened the front door and invited me in. I found out that when you consume a cannabis editable if the strain was geared to have a sexual response, ones such as the Purple Kush, that the body opened to the experience much easier. I had contracted a friend of mine who had been secretly making confections to supply me with some hard candies, and that was when my experiments with cannabis and sexual massage therapy began to start. I had begun to add other services to my menu, and today was all about "the wash."

"I took a bar of soap that was made with Geranium, Lavender and Cannabis named **Spirit** and placed a basin of warm water nearby. As I got on the table, I placed the sheet over her body and allowed my hands to slowly slide around her shoulders and around her neck. I felt her breath rise, and a chill comes over us both. With my hands placed firmly on her head, I took a few breaths with her, connecting our energy."

"I placed my hands in the warm bowl of water and began massaging the soap in between my hands. Slowly, I let my hands run down her face, my fingers grazing her cheeks and down the length of her body, making my way to her feet. Her manicured toes were in a rich, smoky red. I took my hands and again ran the soapy water through, creating a rich lather, massaging the milky water, starting with her toes. Allowing my hands to caress her leg, circling around her knees, I then cupped my hands in the water and let the aromatic bubbles glide up her inner thighs. I ran my hands ever so slowly up and down, encouraging her to breathe in deeply with me. Each time I began to get closer to her, I could see her body twitching as I teased her," he said.

The more I listened to him speak, the more it felt like it was all happening to me as I felt my abdomen contract and release.

"Using the small hand towel, moistened with warm water, I slid it up and down her legs. The warmth of the towels gave a sensation all over her body as she was now getting my full attention. I brought the towel around her feet, massaging each toe. Taking my time, I ran the towel in between each of her digits. Running my finger in between her toes delicately, I moved over to the next leg and began my slow descent. Her excitement took over, and she started to shake."

"The warm water cupped from my hands as it glided over her skin. I allowed my fingers to graze her lips and smiled inside, knowing that I was getting to her. Her body was writhing on my table, and her hips were gyrating in a circular motion. Her breath became more and more labored as tiny fissures began to engulf her. Her anticipation of wanting me inside her was mounting as the warm towel glided down her legs. I placed the sheet over her legs and began pulling the fabric from her chest all the way down to her torso, revealing her quivering mountains."

As I watched Nadia at the table, it was clear that just talking about what he did was getting to her. I could see it as her body was beginning to shake, and I knew she was already there.

"OK", said Kennedy, "For the sake of everyone in the room, I'm going to stop with the story for now," he stated.

The entire cove was filled with moans, and people were seriously waiting for the rest of the story. Looking over at Kennedy, I could tell he was worried about continuing. Everyone started chiming in. begging him to continue.

He looked around at all of us, pausing for a few seconds. "You guys really want to hear the rest of the story?" he asked rhetorically. A chorus of yeses resounded around the cove, and Kennedy continued.

"Moving to the top of her head, I filled my hands again with the warm, soapy, aromatic bath. As I ran my hands past her shoulders,around her breasts and down her navel, I added more water, slowly making my way down to her well. With one more long, slow stroke and my hands encasing her lips, my fingers ever so gently fanned the top of her mound. My fingers slid up and down her rib cage, and my hands cupped her breasts. Her chest heaved up to me, wanting my mouth to nurse her. Each time my hands come close to her yoni, her legs open, revealing more of her perfume."

"I placed warm, wet towels over her breasts and abdomen, giving myself time to pay extra attention to the ever-growing mound of her womanhood that was thrusting up towards the skylights. Adding more warm water, I diluted the soapy mixture as I massaged her love canal."

The cove was filled with clearly audible moans coming from all directions. Kennedy continued to delight us with his version of events.

"My fingers paid close attention to every splendid detail. Her chamber was one of the most beautiful ones that I had ever seen, with extraordinarily little hair and all but a mass of curls at the entrance. I really did not have the heart to tease her anymore. As I wiped away the soapy water, I allowed her to guide my fingers deep inside of her and, with a come-hither move, I easily brought her to a most joyous state of arousal," he continued.

That was all it took for Nadia, and she was rapidly in full-body spasms. Watching her writhe on the table was so provocative. She was so ready, so primed. I could feel the heat and pressure in her rising, and I knew she was going to be flooding the table soon, and I could understand why. That is when I noticed the moans escaping around the cove and how many people were now feeling each other up.

As Kennedy's voice started again, I heard him say, "I usually like to wait until further into the wash to have them explode, but this one was ready to go. Taking the towels off her breasts and abdomen, I wiped away all the soap. Removing the sheet from her, I climbed up onto the table in between her legs, nesting in her space. As I spread her legs open, revealing her blossoming rosebud, I began to tease her with my tongue when she started grinding her hips for me. I wanted her to be fully released, the floodgates to open, and to taste her elixir of love. Using my left hand, I eased my ring and middle fingers and reached deep inside her, feeling her spongy nugget of gold swell. With my mouth firmly suckling down on her jewel, she opened the floodgates, spurting out her milk and honey in torrents," he relayed.

With that, Nadia jumped off the table, grabbing Allen's

hands. Off to the woods, they ran as we all looked around, wondering which one of us would be next.

The thoughts of me being washed like that excited me to no end, and I could not help but look at Clinton. I wanted to wash his body so badly like that and be washed in turn when Kennedy dismissed us for a small break.

I walked over to Clinton and asked him if he would allow me to wash him for the next session.

"I'd like that," he said.

I was so excited that I fell out of my sheets. Running back to the bathroom, I could not help but rub on my own clit. I was going to explode if I did not at least get off one little bit. I flung my fingers deep inside of me, grinding my back up against the wall. Somewhat satisfied with my release, I ran back outside, grabbed a bowl of water and a bar of soap, and got my station all setup.

Clinton climbed on the table facing down and pulled the sheet up to his waist. I paid close attention to every choice word that Kennedy uttered as I let his sage words guide me.

The more he spoke, the more my own body heaved under his spell. Echoes of delirious languages filled the cove as waves of sensations came over my body. The sun seemed to grow brighter as full spectra of brilliant lights came over me.

"I began again with her legs," said Kennedy. "This time, I suckled on each toe, taking my time, as my mouth tongued each red tip," he continued.

In my mind, I could not tell if it was in my head or it was really happening. Either way, I did not care, as I totally succumbed to the literary offering and began to wash Clinton's feet with the same attention, carefully kissing each of his toes. The warm, sudsy water sprinkled from his toes all the way to his buttocks. I felt like we were in a dream world under a canopy of cocoa and coffee trees. I had somehow been transformed to an exotic location, where birds were singing and rare flowers were blooming. As his body writhed up against the table, it felt like we were on a secluded tropical beach in Mexico.

Kennedy built up to the crescendo of his recitation. "I helped to stand her up, bending her over the table with her heart-shaped ass begging for me. I wanted so badly to mount her. It was all I could do to keep my pulsing plunger in my pants. With my left hand massaging her lower back, I used my right hand to reach back inside of her. I inserted myself inside her channel and began to flutter my fingers like I was playing a violin. I hit pay dirt as her river quickly opened up and flooded my hands with her warm elixir," he said.

"Oh my God," I thought. This was driving me crazy, as I held tight to my own self, determined not to explode in front of everyone. The moans from deep within the woods were much more audible by now as I began to fantasize about Clinton touching me down in my g-spot while my hands ran the length of his body. The energy of everything happening all around me made it harder for me to control myself. As the couple next to us began making love, the task of keeping myself from exploding was proving to be impossible. I could not help but think of buttercream frosting, and for some reason, I kept looking at cakes as I rounded my hands around his hips and up his back. I was so excited as my breath continued to labor, and my hands trembled, thinking of the time I had him down in Long Neck, Delaware, as I glanced over at Olivianna.

When Kennedy concluded, "I whispered into her ear, 'Would you like to schedule lesson number two?'"

"Wow!" exclaimed Sharon, "I would never have guessed that of you."

"Well, you asked me how I made the kind of money I made. This was just one of the ways. The second way happened when I had inexpertly turned the corner, and there she was, the woman of my dreams, as Kennedy looked over to Karissa.

"I had just pulled into the area coffee shop when I happened to notice Karissa walking down the steps of a local spa. She was holding onto a box as she walked to her car. I decided the coffee could wait for now. I could tell she was going through something when I walked up to her and asked, 'Are you alright?' That was when the tears began to roll down her cheeks, and I knew I had my chance. I took the box out of her hand, looking at the contents. I saw bottles of massage oil, soaps, and jars of sea salt scrubs when I asked, "Where do you get these from?".

"Rubbing the tears off her face, she half smiled when she said, 'I make them.'"

"Why are they in this box?" I asked.

"'Because I just quit the spa I was working at, and I am packing everything up," she muttered as if she was not telling me the whole story.

"I stood there for a moment while the sun shone through the strawberry waves and asked her, 'Karissa, would you like to get a cup of coffee?'"

"It turned out she had become successful with massage and had her days filled with exploring and making all kinds of body products. What I found out was that she really liked to cook with cannabis. She had been toiling away at her craft, exploring all kinds of aphrodisiacs. I sat and listened to her tell me about all the effects that her products had on her. Over the next few times we talked, I would get lost in her voice as she would read to me what she wrote. I even remembered having to pull the car over one day when I had her on speaker so that I could pay full attention to her voice and her plans."

"I knew she was just exploring this newfound version of herself. She even told me of the special chocolates she made — the kind infused with the extractions of the Purple Kush Cannabis plant. 'One peanut butter ball is all it took to open up the Sacral Chakra, right Karissa?'" I asked.

"'Yes, you are right,' she said.

"I had confided in her about what my extra-curricular activities had been and asked if she could create a product for me — a natural body scrub using Jasmine and Lavender with Gold shimmer for females, with Sandalwood and Geranium with Platinum shimmer for males. I wanted sweetness to be on my lips, as we enjoyed tasting and exfoliating, so I instructed the base to be made with sugar and honey. As I waited for the products to come my way, I accepted a sample product that she had been working on and began to imagine how I could elevate her," Kennedy continued.

I heard a container open under my nose and smelled the emulsion. The blend of lavender and honey caught me. With that, we started to come to the table and take a break. Sitting down again by the chairs. I felt like I could explode. All the talk of sex was getting to me, and it was all I could do not to run into my room and take care of the need that was screaming to be released. I held my legs tights as I longed to have Clinton touch me like that.

I watched as Karissa brought down containers of products and placed them around the tables, "Body scrubs are next, pick a partner," she said with a smile.

Kennedy's narrative unfolded further. "At first, I was upset that I was paid to please a woman. That is until the calls and the money began to pour in. I loved knowing I was making women happy by giving them something they needed."

"Karissa dropped off a new box of sample massage bars with a note asking if I wanted to learn how to give sensual energy healing. I was a bit perplexed by the note. I knew her products were good, and she was expanding her business. I decided to call her, and, to my surprise, she was going to give me a session! The exact time and day were arranged, and I anxiously awaited the appointment."

"As I pulled up to the three-story brick frame townhouse,

I was surprised by its appearance. The last time I was here, it was shrouded by a big flowering tree. As she led me into her office, the scent of sage was still in the air with hints of ylang ylang".

"She instructed me to lie on my back as she adjusted the sheets so that my whole body was exposed. She placed a small hand towel over my midsection. Naturally, I was a bit disappointed as I really wanted her to see me buck naked, but I respected her wishes and kept the towel over my throbbing penis. She had carefully arranged various kinds of stones and crystals in a row on a towel beside the table. Red Jasper, Orange Calcite, Citrine, Jade, Lapis, Amethyst and White Quartz were laid out in piles of different shapes. She began by instructing me to take several deep breaths. Her lips were so close to my ears that I could hear her own breath as she matched her breathing to mine. She virtually danced around my body as she placed her hands on my shoulders. Her sensuous touch enticed me. Oh my god! I could not believe the sexual energy that she had, and for the sake of my wife, I will leave it at that and talk to you about Bermuda instead," he said.

"This woman, I will call her Madison, had been a client of mine for several years. An awfully bad breakup just two weeks before led her to call me. This was the first time that we would be spending this much time together. I must say that I always found her chocolate skin so alluring. She was a more robust woman, yet greatly confident in who she was as a spiritual and sexual being, not to mention that she owns half of the world's sneakers stocks."

"In all our sessions, we just seemed to dance at the thought of going deeper. In all the years I worked on her, we stayed strictly on massages. I was very curious as to what this vacation of sorts was going to be. I packed my assortment of products for the trip and headed to the Port of Baltimore."

"Within two days, our cruise liner docked in Bermuda, and we eagerly headed out to explore the island. The next day, Madison decided to take a day by the beach by herself. As the night approached, I grabbed a beach blanket and some massage oil and decided to see if I could find her. I knew that the large rocks would make an excellent place to delight her."

"As I rounded the corner, I placed the blanket down on the rocks, gathered some wood and started to make a fire."

"I could see that Madison had perched herself onto one of the rocks out in the water. I made my way towards her when, out of the corner of my eye, I saw her clinging to a rock. The surf had become unexpectedly rough, and I knew she was having trouble. One large wave came over her, and in an instant, she was gone. I saw the color of her swimsuit suit, and fortunately, I had her in my arms on the first dive. I brought her to the shore, carried her over to the blanket, and I laid her down. Luckily, she had only been scratched and startled. As I held her and talked to her, she said that she was going to be alright."

"As we lay on the beach, cocooned between the wall of rocks, I used my iPhone® to open the app to Pandora® radio and programmed the Enigma® station. As I turned and started to kiss her on the lips, I said that I had something for her. She flipped over, lying face down on the sugar-fine sand and relaxed, listening to the surf and the music. Her dark skin and curvy figure gave me a good canvas to work with. The heat of my hands warmed the oils, and I began to squeeze an oil called **The Goddess Within.** I massaged it all over her body, using the setting sun as the backdrop to invigorate her skin."

"I first began to kiss her ass cheeks, slowly making my way down her leg behind her knee, starting with little baby kisses. Then, I reached down, firmly holding her foot, as I began sending my healing Chakra energy into her, beginning with red and continuing in my head, successively imagining orange, yellow, green, blue, indigo, and violet. Then, I poured a small scoop of the honey-infused aromatic blend in my hand and began to gently rub the body scrub in a slow circular motion."

"Nestling my body in between her legs, I started to infuse the scrub into her skin. The scent of jasmine fused with her own scent enticed and intoxicated me. I leaned my long arms back as both hands wrapped around her feet," Kennedy elaborated.

With that, the class began to partner up, and I soon found myself on the table. I could now feel the products on my legs as Clinton followed suit, putting the same scrub on me. It felt like the ultimate back scratch, as the products were rubbed into my flesh while Kennedy's voice continued to lull me.

Kennedy continued, "I slid ever so slowly up her legs and circled around her firm cheeks, making my way up her back. Her long, black, wavy hair was rigidly attached to her head as I ran the oils up through her hair, giving it just a little tug. The darkness of the night veiled her moist pink flesh. Her swimsuit, with strings to the side, gave me a golden opportunity to let my fingers linger as the aromatic oil caught the bright orange glow of the burning wood. As my right hand began to massage her right buttock, I could not help myself but tap her ass with a little slap."

"I needed to see how I would be scrubbing the scented infusion into her, as some women like it gentle, while others like it rough. She did not make a sound, and as I was having trouble figuring out how she liked it, I began to massage her deeper, gradually pressing more of my body weight into her. She let out a guttural moan that let me know that I was on the right track. I tickled her neck and whispered, 'You like it rough, Madison?'. She relaxed quietly as her head motioned, YES."

"I scooped some of the shimmering emulsion, working in long gliding strokes, as I vigorously massaged it into her smooth dark flesh, running up and down her body, being careful not to be too rough, but just enough. Once her back and arms were done, I asked her to roll over. Her large breasts in no way were confined to her bikini top. Using a bottle of water to rinse my hands, I moved to the top of her head. My legs straddled over her face as my hands glided the oil from her neck down to her abdomen."

"I felt her hands as she reached up my swim trunks to grab me. My growing missile longed to be encapsulated by those pearly white teeth. I allowed her to slide my suit off, fully revealing me. Her hands firmly grasped for me as I made my way with the oil down to her toes."

"In response, I could not contain myself any longer. As the fluid started leaking out of me, I gripped my legs tighter," he intimated.

As I listened to Kennedy with rapt attention, I began to

squirm as he vividly described her advanced oral skills.

"How she did it, I will never know, but her mouth took me to another word. The taste of sugar and honey infused with jasmine enhanced the relaxing effects of the lavender, helping her to open as our bodies began to writhe while the ocean steadily beat the shore."

"The moon danced between the clouds, giving me a beam of light to watch as she gushed with delight. She was the sweetest surprise, and I drank all day to quench my thirst. I felt her fingers as she began to make her way up my back. In all the years of doing this kind of work, this was the first time I went over the line. I looked up at the night sky and suddenly realized that I violated my own code of conduct as I mounted her."

"Just then, I watched as a star jetted across the sky. A passion came over me like thunder, and I began to make love to her. As the night lingered on, the water came closer to our bodies. The fragrance of Lavender and Jasmine began to fill the night sky, as the ocean reached our entangled limbs while the moon beamed down upon us in the darkness. The sugar-fine sand created a lovely floor upon which to heal, and the ocean washed away any reminders as we stood in the water. Nothing was left but the shimmer on our bodies as we made our way back to our blanket."

"It was a night to remember, for it was almost too hard to let it go. As we walked back to where our cruise ship's berth was, I knew that I had played my part. I also knew that I would never be able to see this lovely lady again. A week was way too much time to spend with a woman making love with no other woman to break up the flow. I could see where my income could be greatly affected. My job was to act like her boyfriend – not be her boyfriend," Kennedy concluded.

Within minutes, the staff was bringing down the dinner, where a salad with coconut shrimp was waiting along with a Mango Puree with ginger and lime finish. Some sliced tomatoes with fresh basil rounded out the picnic table. The more I listened to Kennedy talk, the more I realized how close he and Clinton were. Their personalities felt so close to each other, and I got the sense that they must have known each other for a long time. We began to pair back up again, and this time, Nadia and I were exchanging. It felt good to just relax for a bit and not worry about who Clinton was or who he was.

Charlotte's Cry

Hear me cry out Lord to you

Bring the abundance for me to use

Heal your people I will do

Lead me Lord into something new

I have built every step of the way

Listened as Mary paves my way

Healing products was on the list

The wash sequence goes like this

Diamonds on my little sheets

Offering of people at my feet

Take me Lord to your land

Bathe in the lake is the command

I have a fire inside of me

Burning desire to help humanity

This is what was built in me

This is what you have been guiding me

Lord, I Release this petty shift

All the diplomatic bullshit

Hear me cry out to save this land

Hear me try as best as I can

Hear me universe, I command

The 6 stations at my hand

Calling out the wind to you

What you built me to do

Rise above and set me free

No more bullies harassing me

I have declared that I am free

Confessions

Last night, I got the call

I felt the spanking

As I sat on the couch

I did not realize

You are something else

crawling down on my knees

I am excited for this

You must first begin

With a kiss.

I am the cello

With my wide hips

I want you to rosin

Your bow and whips

I am a bit kinky

If you did not already know

Mutual is a part of this show

Before you can have me

I have just one thing left to do

I have been wanting another show

I cannot seem to get him off my mind

His staff is amazing one hard time

I need a good sucker sometimes

And just like that, in a flash

I am lying on my back

fingers shaking

as Jaxson attacks.

19
The Queen of Love Enters

The sun began to set as we gathered around the fireplace by the roar of the flames. Clinton came over to me and pulled his chair closer to mine. Looking over at him, I asked him if he wanted a back scratch.

"I'd really like that," he stated. "Wait a minute," he said as he jogged up to his camp. He quickly came back with a blanket and laid it down on the beach. Taking off his shirt, he got down on his stomach. "Come, sit next to me," he said.

Kennedy was getting ready to tell us how he knew Karissa was his perfect partner when he first met her.

"I've heard this story a million times," said Clinton as he settled down on the cool sand.

Kennedy began, "I arrived home to find a package waiting

on my steps with a note from Karissa. Inside was a sample kit of her latest massage products with an invitation to try a session with her. The note explained that she was studying energy healing and that she had been working on healing herself. I kept her letter on my desk for a few weeks."

"One day, while I was relaxing in the bathtub, I decided to take the bar of soap out of its wrapper. The blend had a flowery smell of Neroli and was referred to as the *Heart Blend.* I was rubbing the bar of soap over my body as if she were in the tub with me. I virtually felt that my body was resting up against hers and imagined that she was in her tub miles away, doing the same thing, wanting me to join her. I let my mind go there for hours in the middle of the night while I called out her name. There was something about being spiritually connected to someone that I was just beginning to realize that when someone was in my dreams, I was in their dreams as well."

"What could I frankly not tell, was if I was calling her, or she was calling me? Did the little lines I said to her over the years sink in? No way was this girl playing me, as I was the master. I firmly made the decision, just like all the other ones before. I would have bet money on it. She was calling out to me, and I decided to take her up on her offer."

"As she approached my front door, I could tell she was

being reserved. It had been some time since we saw each other. I especially noticed the way her eyes flickered when she reached out to hug me when I thought that a simple handshake would do."

"It seemed like she breathed more of me into her with each breath she took as we embraced. By the time she took her third breath, I was in a different place. I felt something in me move, and for a second, my body swayed. I showed her around the house and took her to the spare apartment, off the main house, where I had my massage table set up."

"She walked around the room, sniffing the air as if searching for something. She had a much more feathery or lighter feeling about her from the last time she worked on me. Then, she opened a bag, which I assumed was just her purse, and it contained a bowl of sage in a conch shell, a handful of crystals, and a rose quartz crystal on a string."

"As we began talking, she told me about how, after twenty years of massaging, she was ready to venture into new areas. She talked more about the cannabis products she made – not that I had not done cannabis in college – but, in my line of work over the years, cannabis just did not fit in."

"She laughed when I said that for her, it was the opposite. Then, she went into prayer mode and instructed me to change into a bathing suit. We went into the pool, where she gave me an energy session. I was a bit caught off guard with this approach but remained open and curious about what she was doing."

"At first, it seemed to me that I was just lying in her arms, but within a few minutes, I noticed that my body was reacting in unfamiliar ways. As the session continued and her soothing words flowed from her mouth, I could feel negative emotions and anxiety immediately leave my body. I would just sigh or belch, or my body would jerk as memory was leaving it. Over the next week, the sessions really began to work on me."

"Some would have gone back to points in my life. As the night weaved its magic, it seemed like every desire I had for my life would be played out for me in my dreams, like a check list in the night, reminding me of promises I had made in jest. I began to realize that what I wrote down for my desires was beginning to come true."

"This time, as she approached the house, I saw a more seductive side to her that I had yet to encounter. I could tell that she was working herself up to do something different, and she was thoroughly turning me on. I remembered that she spoke few words as she approached, and I gazed at her silently, as our eyes locked on each other."

"She placed a unique dessert in my mouth, and I intuitively knew that she had laced the chocolates with cannabis. As I sat back on the couch, she began to just touch my head, and I felt her warm hands as they rolled down the side of my neck and slowly worked their way back up."

"I instantly felt like I was a gemsbok, and she was a tigress coming in for a feast. The sensation of being hunted was both delightful and overpowering as I trembled in anticipation. Oh my God! I could feel the flood of sexual energy in her. I closed my eyes and just allowed myself to experience everything that was unfolding."

"As I felt more relaxed, she led me to the living room and began a wash sequence on me before a huge bowl of warm water. I wondered what she was going to do, as I was still sitting in my work clothes, but all she did was take my shoes and socks off. What happened next was indescribable but not overtly sexual. If it was, I do not think it was her main intention, although it felt very sexual, as I underwent a series of internal explosions that seemed to take me to other places."

"If I did not know the Bible any better, I would have thought I had Mary herself at my feet. I felt again like a king, not even aware that I was a king. I relived it in my mind over and over, remembered entering a room feeling like I had entered a chamber or cave of some sort. The walls were dim, and the only glow was of the candles placed all around. The scent of jasmine filled the air. A large blanket and a pillow were spread on the floor next to a bowl of water and a crock pot of towels. I stood there as she took all my clothes off, kissing the corresponding area of my body as she removed each article."

"As I closed my eyes again, I breathed in as her first kiss landed on my hand. Her lips grazed up my arm, and I began to feel my whole-body tremble. As her fingers traced my chest, I began to feel deep releases as tremors came over me. She was blowing my mind and matching what I was giving."

"I closed my eyes closed again, feeling aroused, as her hands rounded my waist. Shortly thereafter, I felt her soft lips again as she began to kiss my feet. Her hands circled around my knees as her lips danced over my skin, and I trembled with excitement."

"I looked to my left and saw a bowl of fruit and a glass of wine. I closed my eyes as I allowed her to make love to me. Her soapy hands electrified my soul as they massaged their way up my legs. The touch of her hair against my skin sent a tingly sensation that reached deep inside me, and I knew that she was luring me into her. As she nestled her body in between my legs, I felt her hands glide from my feet all the way up my legs."

"When she came to my solar plexus, in the center of my torso, I felt shifts in my abdominal walls. She cupped the water into her hands as she poured it over my abdomen. The sensation of the energized water flowing on my skin felt like lightning bolts shooting into me. My body convulsed rhythmically, and I felt deep waves of energy bursting up to the ceiling, shooting through my entire nervous system, as her hands continued to glide over my body. I felt further shivers down my spine as her hair continued grazing my skin. As she washed my entire body, I felt myself shift into a new dimension."

"I suddenly found myself sitting in the garden, where soon, her naked body was underneath me. As her legs ran up against mine, she massaged me with her most luscious body. I inhaled the scent of lavender and jasmine and knew the irresistible power of the blend all too well. The product's emulsion of gold shimmered on my body in the candlelight as her hands slid down my neck. The hot water was almost up to my chest as she worked her will in the flickering candlelight," Kennedy expounded.

As I scratched Clinton's back, I was still lost in the way Kennedy's words hung in the air and fell into a trance as I laid down on the blanket. Looking up at the stars, I succumbed to the next meditation:

"**Nine**, I want you to imagine a giant ball of red-light hovering about your legs, just at your pelvic floor or base of the buttocks

Eight, in this light of the orange fire, is the ability to stabilize all your power

Seven, you are rooted and use all the energy in your legs to harness this experience

Six, Bringing it from deep within the ground up through the base of your spine

Five, Feel the energy begin to swell

Four, as we reach, feel the expansion of light burst through you

Three, releasing the energy like an explosion of Love

Two, your mind blowing again into a sea of spasm

One, heaven's expansion ... KABOOM!" the sequence unfolded.

With that, I felt my soul leave my body, and it seemed like I was scanning the lake and the regions around the mountains. As the wave of moans cried out, the releases of emotions echoed in the woods, and I succumbed to the overwhelming spirit of the moment.

20
Beam Me Up

I slept like a baby, for not a noise did I hear – not even the rumble of the passing storms that happened in the night. I did not even remotely recall coming into my room, and the last thing I remembered was gazing up into the night sky. I headed into the shower, excited about today's lesson. This is the one that combines the energy with massage techniques, called Maschakra.

I walked down to the picnic table, where I saw Salem talking to Clinton. She gave me a look that let me know she was challenging me as she walked away from him. I walked up to Olivianna and asked if she wanted to pair up.

"Sweet," she said. "I've been wanting to pair up with you," she continued, winking at me. She slipped under the blankets, lying face up, staring into the bright blue sky as Karissa began explaining where to place our hands.

I felt the *Energy Massage Bar* being applied as the oils melted under the heat of her hands. I opened her to the universe by placing my hands on her head, with my pink fingers resting on her ears, feeling the amethyst come in. I placed my hand over the forehead and let it rest as Karissa continued to guide us.

"Placing your hands next to the top of the throat and gently put pressure in. Feel the surge of power coming into your throat chakra. Feel it as it begins to spin open. Allowing you to speak your truths to the universe in a sharp and clear voice. Let your wishes be heard! Shout out to the Gods and the Universe! What do you say when I ask, "What's your fantasy?"" she instructed.

It was slow and quiet at first, but then, the Spirit of the Universe came into me and gave me a taste of her. I felt my body spasm from the top of my head all the way to the soles of my feet. In that instant, I felt like one. I wondered if I would be able to be self-pollinating before long. Would my body be able to repair and let me house babies again? Could I get a new womb? I wanted it all.

Olivianna shouted joyously when her soul began to blossom as her wings expanded and spread green and gold stardust. I saw her spirit as it floated in the air, blowing kisses as she manifested, "I want love and a family, a few material things and some money!"

"Imagine now, your partner's hands directly over your heart space located in the center of the chest, in between your breasts. The Heart Chakra is the home of our love, where we receive and give healthy sex. Take a few deep breathes and imagine a current of energy flowing through you."

"Now, imagine your partner's hands on your heart, sending you massive amounts of love and healing from past traumas, breakups, abandonment, or death. For a few minutes, just receive and feel the energy between your partner's hands and your own heart space," she said.

I knew this was exactly what Olivianna needed today, as it did not work out with her boyfriend, and she was looking for a new man. "What about that cop working on Francis?" I whispered in her ear. "What's his name?" I asked.

She turned her head to me and said, "The Italian one."

"Yeah," I said.

"I'm sure it's Francis Nicholas," she said.

Karissa's voice trailed in again, "Using your right hand, about six inches away from the base of your spine or Root

Chakra, I want you to imagine sending energy in. Using the left-hand, hold on to the top of the head or Crown Chakra and hold the space here for about three minutes as your partner breathes and sends energy up and down your spine."

"The Root Chakra centers around our core needs for survival, security and livelihood, while the Crown Chakra influences our deeper understanding of ourselves beyond the physical or material. As that energy moves, you and your partner are connecting to the Earth, pulling the energy from the ground below and harnessing the energy from the heavens above to move through both bodies. The energy will begin to flow as you both breathe in deeply the elements of air and water and send its waves through the body," she explained.

"Your partner's right hand now glides up from the base of your spine or the Root Chakra to your lower abdomen or Sacral Chakra. The left hand now slides from the top of your head to between your eyes, or the Third Eye Chakra. That energy starts to create a current of electricity from the Sacral Chakra to the Third Eye Chakra."

"Your Sacral Chakra is the home of your reproductive organs and influences your creativity, artistic expression, and sensuality. The Third Eye controls our common senses, spirituality, wisdom, memory retention and intuition. Imagine, if you will, that as the energy flows at this moment, you are connecting. Be confident that you effectively communicate what you are seeing in your mind's eye," she said.

"Imagine for a moment that your intuition and your sexual desires are now communicating with your partner exclusively on an energy level. Holding the space and encouraging each other to breathe together is an excellent way to connect your energy. I encourage you to allow for three minutes of hand placement on each Chakra, however, your own intuition as to how much time you spend is what is best before you move on," instructed Karissa.

Olivianna giggled and said, "I'd like Francis Nick to spend some time on my Sacral Chakra."

I snickered girlishly and took a few deep breaths as I imagined Clinton being in my Root Chakra. He was lying face down with Salem, rubbing him, and it appeared that she had no idea of what she was doing.

"I've been rubbing pork tenderloins for years. I can really take care of him," I thought to myself. I watched him for a few minutes as I listened to Karissa and tried to imagine what she was saying.

"Now, your partner's right hand is sliding from the Sacral

Chakra or lower abdomen up towards the navel, about two inches into the space of the Solar Plexus. This is where your identity and self-worth are housed and your power is located. Hold the space for a few moments and just breathe. Next, move the left hand from in between your eyes down the front of your face and settle right at the Throat Chakra. It is responsible for effective communication of our desires, thoughts, opinions, and feelings," she continued.

In an automatic hold of breath, I felt the energy intensify as if a beam of blue light were penetrating me. My body began to convulse as I looked up to see Jaxson by my side, with his hands resting on my chest. Our eyes locked as he encouraged me to just breathe through the release. I continued to focus on my breath as Karissa continued to guide us.

"Next, place both hands at the heart by sliding from the Solar Plexus and Throat Chakras and meeting at the Heart Chakra, located in the center of the chest. The heart is the most important chakra to work with when we are engaging with our partners to connect to them in a very deep way. It has the responsibility of giving and receiving love in a healthy way, to cope with sadness due to traumas in the past, loss of loved ones, abandonment, and death," she said.

"When you are satisfied that you are ready, flip your

partner over. Your body should be firmly placed in the center of their body. With your legs spread and knees slightly bent, you will glide up and down the body," she specified.

"Now, place your hands around the toes and run the bar from toes, feet, back of the leg, up the thigh, around the buttock, up the back, around the shoulder and then down the arm to the fingers," she continued.

The sensations were blowing my mind, and it felt like bubbles inside my throat were popping like it was freshly opened®. As each bubble burst, I saw glimpses of childhood memories. I remember standing in the driveway and being in the dining room. It was like I had a movie camera in my mind and was inspecting each frame when I heard her voice again.

"Moving to the top of the head or crown chakra, place the massage bar in your hands at the back of the neck and just breathe in. Hold it there for three minutes. Begin with massaging the neck, using the sway of the music to guide you, run your hands around the shoulder, then down to the back, in the pattern of an upside-down heart. The lower back is the point of the heart. The shoulders are the arches or 'angel wings' of the heart. Let your hands glide down the back until your hands reach each other, forming the point of the heart," she communicated.

My mind was lost again as his hands glided down my skin, with his skilled fingers so large and strong. Then, I felt my chest rising. At first, it felt like it was just my lungs filling with air. Then, the more air I took in, the more it felt like I was a hot air balloon and could float away!

I almost thought I was dying for a second when Clinton whispered in my ear, "Relax and let your body fly."

I closed my eyes again and continued to focus on my breath when I felt myself going back in time. At first, it was just my childhood and then, I saw more things from pasts unknown. I just continued to float to each experience and beheld each one that unfolded before me. It was as if I was watching myself starring in my own TV show. I virtually went deep into hyper-dimensional realms as I drifted back even further through space-time in a transcendent bubble.

I began to wonder again if I was dead and thought that, even if I was, it was peaceful, and I worried no longer. I continued to explore enthusiastically as the sound of the Paste Symphonic Gong elevated me to a higher level. The vibration coming off the 30-inch bronze and mixed alloy base was taking me even further along the path of revelation. I must have levitated off the table when I felt hands on my feet and arms. I knew my body was bending back, but I had no control over it.

It was as if the Mother Ship was above me with its spinning lights and lotus flower opening, beckoning me to come aboard.

The beam was so strong, and I wanted to just go into it, having felt it many times before. As its energy called me in, I felt its warmth and magnetism again, but this time, it was much stronger, and it simply did not matter anymore if I was dying. I was ready for it. I was not scared. "I had a good life," I thought to myself.

I stood there in the landing pad as babies so small walked all around me, in their green oval skeletons with white and green skin that shimmered like billions of diamonds and emeralds. Their eyes were like a marquise-cut black diamond of at least three karats. Collectively, via telepathy, they asked me how it had been. I beheld the looks on their faces as one child came up to my face. The little girl appeared to be about twelve years of age, and that is when it hit me. She was the daughter I gave away. I looked her right in the eye and said, "I promise you that I did all this to give you a better life; I will always come back for you," as I blew her a kiss goodbye.

I watched as I floated back out of the white lights as the lotus slowly closed. The red and blue began to flash on and off intermittently at first and then in a pattern reminiscent of the flashing light games I played when I was seven. I watched as the orbs continued to spin until a purple ring appeared, progressively fading as it continued to draw me out. Suddenly, I was in fields of lavender and lilacs and was breathing simply fine, then danced in the water with Clinton by my side.

I awakened feeling rather refreshed, still feeling the ship from many light years away. I looked up at Clinton and said, "You're never going to believe this."

"You wanna bet," he replied.

21
The Darker Side

By the time my soul had fully returned to my body, it was dark out, and I heard the voices of everyone else down as I strode towards the lake. Looking up, I saw Clinton's smiling face as he threw a robe around me, and his radiance shined upon me. Locked into his gaze, I knew I was in good hands as we walked to the fire pit. When, suddenly it hit me, I tried to head back to my camp, but no way it was happening. That is when I made a split decision, pee on myself in front of everyone or jump into the lake, where no one would know a damn thing!

It is days like this that make me laugh. "I might look like I'm crazy," I thought to myself. "But at least I didn't pee on myself in public." That is when I heard a voice from behind, whispering in my ear.

"It must be all that detoxing tea we've been drinking," intimated Nadia.

I tried to pretend that it was just a warm spot in the lake but did not think that she was buying it. Considering I was laughing so hard, I was peeing again and openly cackled all over with laughter. "Okay, you got me … I was peeing," I admitted quietly.

"Me too," she exclaimed, pointing back to me as we high-fived and hugged each other warmly. We walked hand in hand, laughing as when we were kids. It is funny when you make new friends – even when you are fifty years old – it is funny how everything looks.

I continued to laugh so hard that my bladder's incontinence got the best of me again. "Boy, how I wish they made Depends® for the water," I thought in the liquidity of the moment. I got on a plastic air mattress and just breathed for a moment, feeling more relaxed, as I floated on the lake. Soon, I drifted off into some magical realm as I spiritually connected deeply with the water. I felt like I was a little fish canvassing, darting to and from, looking for a new home or some treasure hidden in the lake bottom debris.

22

In A Nut Shell

Kennedy threw another log on the fire and said, "Funny ... the woman who made all my love potions and boxed my chocolates had lured me into her own trap. Karissa and I developed a curriculum that incorporated Universal Energy Healing, sexual healing, Massage, Body Wraps, and Facials enhanced with infusions of cannabis. Paired with my abilities to please the ladies, we formulated an ingenious way to teach couples how to expand their language and practice of love. Not only did we turn our massages into mending, but we have also turned our energy sessions into sexual healing."

"We have been restoring love from every situation we encountered and have become each other's comfort. We taught each other and fused our modalities to create what we refer to as the *Center of Love Club*, where you now find yourselves. From the outside looking in, no one would ever know what went on behind closed doors. For people choosing to evolve, this is one of the places you can come to save your marriage, find your life partner or soulmate, learn what life or past loves had not taught you, and learn what very few people know how to do: to experience energetic lovemaking.

I thought for a few moments about where I was a year ago with my own sexual self and where I am now. The one thing that came to my mind is that I felt more open about it, like I had come out of hiding and did not realize I was even there. I guessed it must be working as I looked over to Clinton and asked, "Hey, can we talk for a minute?"

"Sure," he said as he got up.

As we began to walk away from the group, he took my hand, and I thought it was a bit odd at first, but something inside made me smile, and I held on tightly. I cleared my throat and asked, "Do you ever notice how in nature there are so many things that remind us of our sexuality?".

"I'm not sure what you mean. Can you explain?" he asked, somewhat perplexed.

"Yeah, you bet. Take the fig, for instance, if you peel the skin off, it takes on the appearance of a man's testicles. If you open the ripe fruit with your two thumbs, it reminds me of what a women's vagina looks like. As I look at a fig, I see it as a representation of both the divine male and the divine female in one. I have been secretly making my own line of cannabis-infused products. It has tremendous capability to create arousal, and I named it *The Naughty Fig,*" I replied.

"Wow, I never thought of the fig like that. We have several figs on the property in Mississippi, so we might just have to do something with them," he said.

"Oh, I'll make a spicy fig jelly when I can get my hands on them next time. I have some figs, and I'll make it for you so that you can taste it for yourself," I said, with a sparkle in my eyes.

"The Naughty Fig," he giggled, "What's that? A sexual product you can eat, like chocolate covered penis on a stick?" he asked sarcastically.

"Not far off-base," I said with a laugh, "it's a line of editable sexual massage products created to increase sensitivities during sex, and I want to talk to you about bringing my line to **FooBellas®** Skin Care."

"We have been wanting to tap into that market, to bring a whole chocolate massage line in that is made with cannabis extracts of CBD as well as THC. So, what you are saying to me is that you have your line already in development," he said as he crossed his arms, looking rather curiously at me.

"Yes, that is essentially what I am saying. The whole thing is edible while still in product development ... mind you, we need to do some more testing," I said with a wide grin.

In my mind, I began to imagine coating chocolate mousse all over his body. I smiled and said, "I make a fantastic Chocolate Ganache; maybe I could frost you with that."

He wrapped his arms around me and started kissing my neck. "How soon can you make that for me?" he asked.

"Whenever you like," I said as I lured him back into my own carefully designed honey trap.

I was virtually lost as I felt his kisses all over my body. It was about all I could do not to take the few extra steps over the lake and break into my new bed. Already, I felt my clothes coming off as he continued to whisper in my ear.

"In essence, we incorporate massage, reiki energy, stone therapy and cannabis into our sessions, harnessing the Kundalini Energy that is inside of us," he said, as his wings began to expand. "It is in the spirit of healing that we created The *Center of Love Club Sexual Healing Retreat*," he elaborated.

I looked up at him, surprised when he said that. "What do you mean?" I asked.

Clinton pulled himself together and said that he knew something had happened to him when he came to Maine a few years ago to stay with Karissa and Kennedy for one of their first retreats. "I was going through a bad divorce, and they took me in with no questions asked. It was a time of deep reflection and healing in my life. Eventually, I moved on from the pain of a wrecked marriage when Kennedy and I met for lunch one day. They helped me a lot with how I was looking at women, and I decided I wanted to join them," he said.

"As a matter of fact, and I am not mistaken, I believe I was already at that point on the night that you fell into my arms. I signed the papers and began investing with them. I've taken their operation from two to seven in less than two years all over the United States, and I am not done with the expansion," he explained as he kissed my hand.

The night had a very somber feeling as I helped Karissa carry the trays of food into the main center. "I don't mean to pry, but didn't it bother you that Kennedy did what he did for a living before?" I asked.

"No, I knew who he was when I reached out to him – as a matter of fact, it was the reason I went after him the way I did," she answered.

"How so?" I inquired.

"Well, you see, I had a lot of emotional issues when it came to sex, and I had an exceedingly difficult time with the whole process. I had several female clients who told me about him. I knew him, as he was a client of mine, for a few years. The more stories I heard about what he did, the more I felt it was close to what I needed, so I reached out to him. I did not realize he was in love with me until he told me his stories. By that time, I already knew I was in love with him. It just seemed like we had something that we could build with each other, you know what I mean?" she said.

"Yeah, I think I do ... It's like there's no room for jealousy in my mind," I said. "So, hey, what about this whole Angel thing?" I asked.

"Well dear," she said, as she put her arms around me, "that is what I teach people to see, to unlock the hidden side of them and liberate the divine being within," she explained.

"What do you mean?" I asked, rather perplexed at her response.

"I teach people how to make medicine with cannabis and herbs. Then, I systematically show them how they can take that knowledge and help others in their own special way," she replied. "Really, that is cool; I like that," I said.

"Think of it as a pot of chicken soup. It has got lots of ingredients in medicine. I wanted to make infusions that would have a multi-layering effect, to help someone to relax and be more open to what they were experiencing in the energetic and metaphysical realms," she explained.

"The woods here are filled with all the natural ingredients I need to make my natural medicine. I do not mind what Kennedy did to help other people, for what he did opened a whole new world for me. He saved me when I was broken. How could I have the right to tell him he needed to give up what he did for a living?" she revealed.

"I guess I can see it that way, but do you do what he does with men?" I asked inquisitively.

"Not like what he does. I have my own way, and I prefer to teach the angels and plant-based medicine stuff. I just let him be the sexual guru, and I benefit from it," she said with a grin. "So, what do you think so far of the retreat?" she asked.

"I'm loving it so far … Why?" I replied.

"We have a few very special clients this weekend, and they are checking out what we do here," she said.

"Oh," I responded as I looked back out, scanning the shore.

"I don't know which one it is. What Kennedy told me is that he's got some plan up his sleeve, and I won't know anything until October when he closes the retreat for the season," said Karissa.

"It doesn't bother you that he is not telling you?" I inquired.

"Oh, heck no, he thinks I don't know what's going on, but, in truth, I am way more psychic than he is, and I've got a good handle on what's going on so, I just like to let him think he's the boss," she responded with a laugh.

"It keeps him happy thinking he is in charge, so I let him," she explained.

"So, where do you grow all your cannabis?" I asked, dying to know the source.

"Oh, down the road at *Camp Werthefukrwe*," she responded with a straight face.

I started to laugh again at the very sound of the place.

"Yeah, that's the place, and I'm surprised you never heard of it before yesterday ... I mean, with all that you have been doing this past year," she responded. "We have another plant in Delaware that makes some of our products. Another location is in Las Vegas. Our cannabis production is done here in Maine, where it's legal," she added. Pointing over to a large box, she said, "That's the cannabis detox body wrap, and we're going to be doing those tomorrow," as she walked out the door.

I headed back down to the water, where Nadia and G'anacia were talking. "Guess what? Body wraps tomorrow, ladies," I said with a smile. I placed my hands together as I glanced over at Clinton and bowed in Namaste. His eyes looked back at mine as I came back into position. I could not break my stare this time as I walked over to him. "Have you ever had one before?" I asked him.

"Oh yes, I'm an expert with this stuff," he said, shaking his head.

"Today was a lot to take in," I said as we walked along the beach. "It gives me some hope that someday I will get to where I want my life to be ... you know what I mean?" I inquired.

"What's your biggest dream," he asked as we walked further down the shoreline in the opposite direction from last time, picking up some rocks and skipping them across the lake.

"My dream ... Oh, my dream is to own a destination

wedding theme B&B, and I feel that I am so close to it," I answered. "I've noticed a lot more confidence in myself since I started taking these classes and the crazy thing is, I feel like things that once bothered me are drifting away. I'm still focused on my career and all, but I really like meeting people this way," I went on.

"Have you ever been married?" he asked as I looked up at him when he took my hand and rubbed my fingers, a strange feeling crept inside me.

"No, not yet," I said.

"Have you ever thought about it?" he asked, picking up more rocks and throwing them into the lake.

"Sure, I've thought about it, and that's why I am here, but I just can't seem to make any lasting connections, and at any rate, I'm not ready to make any major decisions yet," I replied, as I picked up some rocks and tried to skip them.

"What if any of the men or woman here this weekend asked you?" he inquired. "What if a shiny brand-new ring meant just for you suddenly popped up? What would you do then? Would you just leap in and do it," he interrogated in rapid succession.

"What should I do, leap in blindly and marry a man I had

never met before?" I responded. "I don't know about that, and I thought that what I did with you on the first night we met was crazy … you think this is Vegas?" I laughed.

He chuckled and said, "Imagine this: we could put wedding chapels all over the place," as if he were a magician, spreading his hands out, flicking his magic wand where a hotel would suddenly appear.

I looked at him more attentively as I became enamored by his magnitude. My hands began to shake, and my heart began to flutter. My eyes closed as I felt his lips get closer to mine. Soon, I was lost in his warm embrace as his skin touched mine. The sky glowed with stars that seemed to be shooting all around, and I totally let go of myself as I reached around his waist and kissed him back with the most passion I had ever felt for a man.

We walked back to the Club just as the staff was bringing out some late snacks. If there is one thing I know for sure, it is that the buffet sure looked good. We converged on G'anacia and Nadia as we all came back to the table.

"It sure looks good, girl," said Nadia as she began to put some food on her plate.

"What about Jarod?" I asked G'anacia.

"I had an energy exchange with him yesterday that was very good," she said as she picked at the food on the table.

I laughed and said, "You really should get his private one."

"Oh my god ... did you guys have sex?" she asked excitedly.

"No," I protested, "but you know, it was the strangest feeling; it was like sex without the sex." I also kept asking myself the biggest questions on my mind: Do I need to have a man? Do I just feel like I am supposed to, or do I need more than one?

"I know what you're talking about," said G'anacia. "There's a lot to consider when it is not just you. Looking out at everyone, I cannot help but feel like something is missing for me. It is like I have this deep, dark secret of myself that I am just so frustrated with getting out. How is it that I am an angel underneath all this skin, yet I have these fantasies that would seem not angelic?" she said.

"Maybe we have it all wrong," I said as I looked out at the three men that have captured all my awareness.

As I headed back to the room for the night, Jaxson caught my eye, and I motioned for him to talk.

What is up?" he asked.

"Jaxson, can I talk to you about the night at your place a few months ago?" I asked.

"Sure ... what's going on?" he replied.

"Remember when you asked me about my fantasy? Well, my problem is I have had lots of fantasies over the years, and I am having a really difficult time dealing with who I thought I was and who I am. I am questioning everything about myself and what I wanted out of life," I elaborated.

"What did you want out of life?" he asked.

"Well, for starters, I have been working awfully hard on a cool restaurant idea for years, but somehow, I'm just not feeling it anymore. It's like I have two people inside of me, and I don't know which one I want to entertain more," I said.

"Charlotte, I tried to tell you this before. Sometimes, you just must let things purge themselves from your spiritual being. It does not mean that this is who you are forever. In fact, you do not have to accept that you are an angel or anything. These are your conceptions of what your reality is. You are just having trouble facing that you are an energy being having a human experience. You came here to learn about life – not to be judged for your choices," he explained.

He sat me down and continued, "I think you're forgetting

you're at a place to deal with your sexual emotions. There is nothing wrong with you for having fantasies. We all have fantasies, and there is nothing wrong with finding out who you are and what you like," he imparted. Waving his blonde hair, he changed his stance and said, "Look, you're here with a bunch of single people trying to find out who is going to be the best match for you, and the cool thing is that you don't need to find it out now. This is my second time coming up here. I have been working with them for years, but even I do not know if I've met my match yet," he said, as he gazed up at Karissa. "Some secrets are buried very deep. Give," he explained as we walked back to the camp for the night. "You are dealing with a lot. Let things settle," he concluded.

23
Chocolate Cream Dreams

What are your Top 20 fantasies?" was the reply to that text I made in my bathtub on that fateful night almost a year ago. I had contacted Kennedy McCormick, thinking I was hiring him to dominate me to make me stronger. Instead, I hired him to find me the perfect partner who could help me to reach my desires.

It took me almost a year to answer all those fantasy questions in full. As I lay in the bedroom of the *Center of Love Club*, I began to realize that my fantasies had been coming true. Everything was happening, all in its perfect timing.

Staring up at the ceiling, I began dreaming about Clinton, with his ebony eyes staring down at me and his brown skin glistening with beads of perspiration as the tiny drops hit my flesh. I envisioned his facial hair cut closely to his face, his defined pectorals and biceps flexing, pulling me tighter to his heart. His protective sheath was so safe that I could unzip his armor, climb into his chest, and then zip myself back in.

I kept dreaming about him but did not know he thought the same way about me. He seemed to know me better than I knew myself. He handled me way differently from any man I have ever experienced – confidently in charge and strong enough to back anything up. His powerful, commanding presence in a room could overtake any woman's rational thoughts.

I have been reliving that glorious night in my house in my mind. What keeps stopping me from going where I want to go, both in my career and in my own personal life? The words I kept on hearing in my head were the biggest four-letter word I ever heard spoken. I felt it gong like a ball of black hate – like the judgment and condemnation all rolled into the faces of the two-faced people who smile at me when, deep down, they hold nothing but resentment for me.

The word I am so scared of is 'FEAR.' Unable to sleep, I started talking to the Angel Metatron, standing in a hue of purple light next to my bed. I watched as he placed his divine hands over my eyelids. In my mind, I headed to the water and saw a figure walking along the shoreline towards me. The closer

I walked to the image, the more I felt that I was being led. With each step I took, I walked further into a wall of lights, where tiny filaments of colors engulfed me until I stood in front of a broad figure. I heard his deep voice tell me to lie down on the beach and close my eyes.

I obeyed his command and rested on the warm sandy earth, with my legs fully outstretched, pointing to the lake, as my arms came together above my head. My whole body arched up as my solar plexus reached for the night sky, leaving only my heels and head on the sandy surface. I felt the warm glow of his presence as his soul entered mine, burning like a fire inside my body. I saw a trail of red lights hovering over me as I went further into the recesses of my mind.

Rainbows of colors began cascading down from the sky, like a waterfall flowing into my spirit, pouring love into me. I knew this energy, as I felt it before and, in truth, I wanted it again. I felt his touch come back inside me as I reveled the night in front of my fireplace. It was the special way he cradled me in his arms, carrying me down the steps. His legs never struggled as he knelt on the floor, showering his love upon me.

I awoke from my blissful sleep, knowing I needed a much deeper session this time. I anxiously awaited the body wraps that were scheduled for today. Reaching for my phone and going through my emails, I saw a message from my agent. My fingers shook as my eyes scanned the e-mail. My book sales were looking good, and I expected an increase. I closed my eyes again and envisioned walking down the long hall of red carpet with my wings fully splayed. The closer I got to the room, the brighter the walls became.

As I entered the room, I felt my hands suspended in the air, as if some invisible magic strings were holding them up, whirling me like a ballerina, as bursts of light fell like stars shooting past me. The more I swirled in the orbs, the more I felt love surround me. The love was like gold, pouring out from the heavens as I floated blissfully in the Sea of Tranquility itself. I felt the soft touch of hands as they glided up and down my skin, sending shivers through my spine.

In an instant, I was deep in the woods, lying on a plush blanket of green moss, upon which the spongy earth comforted me as the sun peaked through the canopy of trees. Surrounded by exotic flowers, as the chirping birds called out. Then, I heard a waterfall, and as its essence rained down on me, I was transported to some new world.

Hovering above my body was a white-winged creature, his hands gliding up my legs. The closer my spirit descended to him, the more I felt it was Clinton. From my vantage point, I could only vaguely see his outline. His cocoa skin kept confirming in my mind as his fingers trailed up my thighs. I saw myself writhing against the Earth as his hands lingered over my chakras. The birds and deer were talking to him in a language I was just beginning to learn, watching my body tremble under his fingertips as sparks of gold showered down. He placed his hands on my head and navel as he breathed new life into me.

Suddenly, a most joyous feeling of peace and serenity came over me, and I felt my own wings open even wider as I flew around the lake in my dreams. I could not help myself anymore, as I fell in love with him. Then, I heard my name being called until my eyes fluttered open, whereupon I saw G'anacia and Karissa staring down at me.

"Are you feeling alright?" asked Karissa. Salem also looked down on me as her eyes rolled to her right.

"Yes," I said. "I'm not sure, but I think I just left my body," I explained.

"It's possible," said Karissa, "Do you feel like you had a seizure?" she asked.

"I don't think so. I am not sore or anything, and my jaw feels fine," I responded, sitting up in bed.

"Here, to be on the safe side, take this cannabis gummy I

have been working on. This one is for you, and it has been genetically strained to target epilepsy. With the body wraps today, if a seizure is brewing, it should help with any muscle spasms," she said.

As I sat there and thought about it, I had not had a seizure in quite a while now. I got up from my bed, still in my pajamas and robe, and headed down to the picnic table. Today's breakfast was little cake balls called Abelskivers, with a triple berry compote and maple syrup to dip them in. Pitchers of green tea dotted the tables with sprigs of oregano, mint, and lemon to help detox the body from the inside out.

The sun broke through the trees, beaming a ray of light on one of the massage tables that called me like nothing I ever felt before. I wondered if this was another energy table, with solar blankets lined with a large sheet of plastic placed on the table that extended down the sides.

Clinton approached me and asked if we could pair up for the day.

I was so excited that I unwrapped my robe and ripped off my pajamas as fast as I could. I hopped on the table facing the ground as I watched the ants crawling around. The warm oil slathered my skin as his hands glided over as he expertly massaged the detox wrap into my muscles. The rest of the guests gathered around and watched as Clinton described to the group what he was doing.

He took his time as he concentrated on my legs, pushing upwards from my toes to my hips, then running his fingers back down, spreading the emulsions of cannabis, lemon, and oregano that made up the blend. The more his forearms slid up my hips and back down my legs, the more I felt a rush of energy come out. The vibration of his breath in my ear sent a ripple of goose pimples down my flesh.

"Flip over and slide down on the table," he said, starting again with my toes. His fingers danced as he ran the scented healing blend up my legs between my inner thighs and left my body practically screaming for him.

I felt the oil over my abdomen as his palms spread the blend in a clockwise fashion. I concentrated on my breathing as his hands engulfed my shoulders and arms, down to my hands. When the plastic wrap enveloped my body, I felt like a mummy when the heavy blanket cocooned me.

Clinton instructed me to close my eyes and take three deep breathes. He whispered in my ear as I felt his fingers trace my face. "Rise," he instructed me to repeat to myself.

"Rise ... Rise ... Rise," I said, licking my lips as I repeated the words out loud. I sensed his hands as they hovered over my heart, pulling all the muck out of me.

"Repeat after me: 'I love myself,'" he said as I took a deep breath.

"I love myself ... I love myself ... I love myself," I declared as I uttered out the words.

He instructed me to repeat it again.

"I love myself … I love myself ... I love myself," I repeated.

"Good", he said. "I love you, too," he declared.

I nearly froze at his utterance.

"Now, I want you to go deeper – deeper than you ever thought possible," he said.

"How can I go deeper when the man of my dreams just said, 'I love you'," I thought to myself. "Oh my God," I began to chant as the idea ran on in my head. Did he mean what he just said? Or was he just saying it? My heart was nearly beating out of my chest as the thoughts and visions that he loved me danced in my head like the Bolshoi Ballet.

"I want you to say, 'I love my body' ... say it out loud," Clinton said, as the depth of his voice increased.

"I love my body! I love my body!" I exclaimed, with all the life force within me.

"Good", he said, as little kisses touched down my face. He continued coaching me and said, "I want you to say it louder."

I closed my eyes and shouted out loud, "I love my body! I love my body!".

"Good," he said. "Now, I want you to go deeper. I want you to go further back. I want you to go back to when you were a little girl. Do you remember what you looked like back then? Do you remember who you were?" he asked.

I felt his fingers touching my neck as he cradled my head in his palms.

"Now, I want you to repeat this to me and say out loud: 'I am the master of my own destiny'," he said.

I began to feel a surge in the center of my body as I repeated, "I am the Master of my Destiny ... I am the Master of my Destiny ... I am the Master of my Destiny."

"I am so proud of you," he said. "Now let me ask you something: Could you love me?" he inquired.

I was shaking so hard in my plastic wrap with my arms bound up, and all I could do move was my neck. I looked at him with tears in my eyes and revealed, "I've loved you since we first met. I didn't want to seem too vigorous and was afraid to look desperate."

"YES!" he shouted out louder.

I felt his hands on my Brow Chakra.

"I want you to repeat after me, Clinton voiced: "I love my fat."

As the words "my fat" rattled through my head, I thought of every word I ever said. I was teased so much for being skinny as a kid. All I wanted was to be fat; my body was so thin when I was young, I was nothing but a rail. I looked up at Clinton with his eyes full of tears as he held the top of my head. I could see his body shaking as the words flowed out as I whispered.

"I was so excited when I had a baby growing in me. I had gained weight and did not look so frail. I did not mean for it to happen and did not think it ever would. I suddenly fell down a flight of stairs, and that was all it took. With a compound fracture in my leg, I lost so much blood. Not until I was doubled over in pain did my uterus feel like it was falling out of me. I started crying, and I knew I was losing it. Despite an emergency cesarean section, it was too late. When they opened me up, it was not just a baby they saw. There was a large tumor growing inside of me as well. Everything was gone within a matter of minutes. It was the only thing they could do to save me. I wailed out in pain as the spasms came over me again. I lost my baby that day. The scar on my skin is all that reminds me of what I was willing to do to keep him safe. I felt Clinton's hands as they rested on my Sacral Chakra.

"It was just not meant to be," he said, "It is not realistic for you to not have battle scars. It is proof that you earned your stripes with each stretch mark on your skin and each line across your flesh. Each wrinkle on your face is you receiving amazing grace," he said softly.

I felt a smile come over my face and the warmth inside my heart space began to grow and spread to different regions within.

"You are glorious, and I love how you shine and how you can make my heart sing," he said sweetly. As the words came from his lips, the tears in his eyes said everything as he bent down and kissed the scars on my forehead.

The darkness of that tumor was still attached to me before he released the fetal soul still clinging to me. My baby's spirit had stayed with me, making sure I would be OK. Now, I felt he had handed me over to Clinton in some very strange way.

I clearly heard the beat of the drums as Kennedy walked around the beach. Upon releasing all our memories, I said to Clinton, "It is OK. I understood why he died that day. It was my boyfriend who pushed me down the steps, and it happened when I was twenty-seven. I see now that it was the only way to get me away from him, and I would have died had my baby not sacrificed his life for mine. The tumor was growing very rapidly in me. That is why I have been so afraid of men. However, I finally understand why it happened," I said in clear revelation.

"You're safe now," he said comfortingly as I felt his head rest up against mine.

I could sense his hands over my Root Chakra as I floated out to the water. Off in the distance, a large sailboat was waiting for me. The closer I got to the vessel, the clearer I could see an image of a man standing on the bow. I climbed the knotted rope ladder dangling over the edge until I was up on its deck. Flabbergasted by his appearance, I shouted, "Jesus!"

The thin figure pointed his fingers off in the distance. In a blink, I was there in the water with him. Tiny rocks lined the shore. I heard a voice say, "Cradle him in your arms today." I could see the wounds on his feet as my hands reached out to touch him. Each scar seemed to disappear as my tears washed away each pain. I saw the sun beaming down on his legs as his feet reached up to the light.

My body began tingling as I felt the gold shimmers raining down my face. Now, I could see in my mind how I could help him. I could see the food come into his body, and I could see that what I do matters. As the dragonflies danced around my head, I felt my body recharge. I saw the veins in my arm pump harder and regenerate as my wings sprouted from my back. In an instant, I was on the boat, commanded by the best captain Lake Kezar ever had.

The Shaman beat his drums alongside Kennedy. His round-lens glasses reminded me of the bygone John Lennon days. Standing in the boat with him were several other men and women. The commander of the kitchen scene, the sous chef of my whole dream. Um, um, what is his name? Is it Jessie Thomas James? A fleet of men was underneath him.

I felt my soul drift back as Clinton softly called me. Back to the shore, I floated as he counted backward, starting with ten. I awakened to see him looking down at me. "Welcome back, Charlotte," he said with a tender kiss on my cheek. Wanting to escape the confines of the plastic cocoon, I squirmed to break free.

"Let me help you," he whispered as I felt his fingers trace my face. The blanket quickly came off me, followed by the plastic wrap. The air was a most welcome feeling as it hit my skin, alleviating the unbearable wet heat and shedding toxins. His hands pushed down on my legs as he worked the oil back into me. The way his fingers massaged my inner thighs sent chills through me.

I felt the warm stones as he placed each and began to chant in my ear. His voice was like a wave of notes I could ride in my mind as I came closer to his heart. I felt his core as each one of my energy centers began to ignite, firing off in sequence, as my body released memories buried deep in the recesses of my brain. As soon as I would see a fleeting image, my body flickered, and out it went!

"How do you feel?" he asked as he kissed my cheeks.

Looking up at him, I fumbled, desperately trying my hardest to get the words out. "I floated out of my body," I stammered. I was sitting on a boat with a man who reeked of liquor. I could not see his face, but I knew who he was just the same. I saw that it was killing his liver. I took him across the lake where I did a healing session and felt the spirit go right through him and me," I elaborated.

"You must have had a vision," he said as his hands rested on my solar plexus. I felt like he was sending his healing energy right through me. I felt drained and energized all at the same time as I put my robe back on.

Clinton wrapped his arm around me as we headed down to the lakeside tables for lunch. Halibut with mangoes, peaches, and buckets of Middle Neck clams with basil and garlic opened before our eyes, with cannabis-infused butter and pineapple gracing the table.

24

Put Your Hands on The Rock and Hold On!

I took my plate of food and sat down in the Adirondack chair overlooking the water. The chunky white flesh of the halibut was so clean tasting, with its simple butter and herb seasoning. Accompanied by wild rice, walnuts, and raisins, my mouth was a symphony of flavors. Looking over at the plastic raft floating in the water, I thought about taking my lunch and just relaxing for a while when, off in the distance, I heard the cackle of the voice that insisted on attacking me.

"Clinton, can I go for a ride on your boat?" said Salem as she glanced at me, cutting her eyes while adjusting her perfect breasts and plastic ass as she wiggled up against him.

Clinton looked up from the Jetboat® at Salem, then me when he reached out his hand and said, "Charlotte, do you want to take a ride on my vessel instead of that float?"

I bit my upper lip as my other set began to tingle. "I would like that very much," I replied as I took his hand and climbed on board, glancing back at Salem. "You're no match for me," I thought as I waved to her goodbye while she threw a hissy fit, stomping in our wake as Clinton gunned the motor and we flew across the lake. Coming into the cove not far from my own camp, the engine decelerated as the boat leveled out and slowed to a drift.

The hot afternoon sun was beating down on me, and I opened my robe to cool off. The orange life preservers made a nice bed as I gazed up into the white fluffy clouds, stealing glimpses of Clinton as I watched him look off into the distance. "Damn, that man looks good in those shades," I hollered out. "What are you thinking?" I asked.

"You want the truth?" he asked, looking back.

"The truth would be nice, as I'm getting tired of lies," I said as I sat up, paying closer attention.

Laughing at me, he said, "The truth is lunch was good. However, something was missing from it."

"Really, what was missing?" I asked as I sat up with my back to the engine. My robe slid off my shoulders as the sun baked my skin. Then, as I watched him come closer to me, it was as if time itself had slowed down. Lying down next to me, like a camera in slow motion, his body hovered so close to mine. The touch of his forefingers electrified me as it skimmed from my navel all the way up my chest until they reached my lips. His deep brown eyes embedded into mine as they investigated my soul.

"Your love," he said as he opened himself to me. The fireball of explosions flashed as our wings protruded from our backs. His chest muscles, in their brilliant hues, made it easy to see that he already knew. Hard as steel, he pressed his whole body into mine. "Come, swim with me," he said. His wings retracted as he got up and flexed his leg muscles. I almost heard blood pumping through his veins.

He balanced his weight when he threw the anchor overboard and jumped into the lake. I watched as he swam off for a bit. Looking over at him, that man is all that and a bag of chips! I looked around to see if anyone was looking. I doffed my robe and jumped into the water. It felt so refreshing on my hot skin as the oils still clung to me, and I swam closer to him.

"Do you know how hard it was to not make love to you back there?" he whispered in my ear. His naked body was now up against mine in the water as I felt his fish up against me. His hands ran down in between my breasts as his lips danced on my neck.

"I've been dreaming of making love to you in the water ever since I met you," he confessed. The vibration of his vocal cords so close to my ears sent shivers down my body. As my legs drew near, we embraced in a slow dance that created its own wake.

"May I ask you something," he said.

"Sure," I answered.

"Why did you want me to beat you?" he asked.

"It's all I ever knew," I answered, taking a deep breath as I uttered the words.

"I'll never hurt you, but only if you want me too, and I know you're a bit kinky," he said.

"I guess you do know me then," I laughed.

"I do," he replied. "I will ride you hard, have no doubt of that, harder than you ever thought you could take. I have a lot of plans for you if you can attack back. You are a better chef than any of them, you just needed to grow into your skin. You needed to learn how to fight your way up and figure out what it is that you want. Then, fight like a champ in the center of a boxing ring," he continued.

"Who are you? ... Evander Holyfield?" I asked with a laugh.

He laughed back and said, "You never know who I am, and I can be anything I want to be. The sensation of his lips on my cheeks felt comforting as his tongue danced back in front of me. "Cook for me," he whispered in my ears.

"Cook for you. Is that your final proposal," I asked.

"Do you have any idea how good your food is?" he replied, with his eyebrow glaring down at me.

"No, I don't ... tell me," I said, looking back at him as a smile came over my face.

Clinton started to lick his lips as he began to think of what to say. "It tastes like you pour your whole essence into what you cook. I have never had anyone like you before. You are like an *epi pen*® for my allergies, and I feel your soul calling me," he said softly. He spun me back around with my back up against his chest, wrapping his right hand around a lock of my hair as he pulled me tightly to him. "Cook for me, and I'll make all your wildest fantasies come true," he said as his left hand spanned in front of me.

I could not even begin to describe my feelings, but I clearly remembered the smile on my face. The direction of the sun, what shade of blue the sky was, and seeing his wings fully unfolded. The sun blinded me for a moment, and when I glanced up into his milk chocolate eyes, I was virtually in a trance. He asked me about my wildest fantasies as I began to rub his head.

I stammered for a few seconds, knowing my wildest fantasy I did not dare to utter when he brought his lips to mine. "Do not worry, love, I already know what it is," he whispered as his arms pulled me back into his embrace, "I'll take care of you if you take care of me."

I could not help myself as I shuddered in his presence, grateful that I was in the water as my fluids spurt out on him. "My deepest desire is well hidden, my King, deep enough that I don't even know if you could recover it," I told him.

He wrapped his arms around his chest as his eyes glared down at me and said, "Do you want to wager a bet on that?"

As he spun me back around, my hands reached out, trying desperately to obey his command, when he said, "Come follow me." He took off, swimming to a large boulder, jutting out from the water.

"Put your hands on the rock and hold on," he said, with

his lips up against my ear.

My breath resonated with the vibration of his voice, and my fingers trembled as I ran my hands along the rock, wondering if I could handle this much. His sheer strength encapsulated me as his chest melded into my back. Taking my arms from the rock, he placed my hands on his hips. His right hand slowly twirled my locks, pulling my head to his chest. "Tell me what I want to hear," he said as he opened me wider, and I felt his hard bolt of dash.

My eyes rolled behind my head as I saw the round blue carpet of the Oval Office flash before my eyes. I saw the tropical flowers, little huts, the rivers, and a scenic gorge. Fluttering in a lake of fantasy, all I could think of was, "I ll cook for you."

"Damn right, you will," he affirmed, as he spun me back around, wrapping my legs around his waist, as his circumference engulfed me again. I looked around and saw not a soul on the lake, and I let myself go, lost in talent, as his massiveness felt like it was in my chest. "You like what I have, Charlotte," he said confidently.

I blushed in utter embarrassment as I loudly squealed with delight. I could not help myself as I called out to God and rode him like he was a bull on the Vegas strip. I did not even care that my breasts were hanging out. All I wanted was to stay firmly planted on the rock and ride the waves of erotic pleasure that ensued from his cock.

"Wait," I hollered, "Before you go any further, I have a confession to make. I didn't finish culinary school, and I don't have a degree," I stated frankly.

Smiling, he looked back down at me, pulling his right hand tightly to the back of my head. "That's what makes you the very best. You learned the hard way ... life was your test," he said as he kissed me again.

I swooned in his arms as I felt him thrust back in me again. His chest muscles protruded as they rippled underneath his skin.

"I've got something I want to give you," he said.

"I thought you already were," I replied, as I started to tremble again, fully feeling the penetrating force of his expansion.

"When I asked you to put your hands on the rock, I was trying to get you to feel it all the way up," he said.

Looking at him, all confused, I exclaimed, "I'm trying to, Clinton, but it's a lot to take!"

"Relax, I already know everything I need to know about you. I have been doing a lot of studying up on you. I tried your one-wing dish, and I knew I could exploit you. The trouble is that I fell in love with you," he said.

He lifted me up onto the large boulder and told me to reach into a crevice at the top. His hands entered me from behind as I felt the coolness of the moss-covered rock that I was sliding up against. My fingers reached inside the opening of the large stone, and I latched onto a loop. I looked down, pulling a ring of metal out of the mass.

"Do you like it?" he asked, looking me directly in the eyes.

It had the largest stone I had ever seen, set in solid platinum and encrusted with diamonds around the shank.

He placed the ring on my finger and asked, "Will you marry me?"

"I thought you were offering me the job of my dreams, and you were an executive of some large production scheme," I stammered.

"Oh, I am ... and a whole lot more," he said, as his mighty hands squeezed my cheeks, driving himself deeper inside of me, giving a whole new twist to mixing business with pleasure.

"I am really the man behind the production plan – just not the one you might be thinking I am. My name is Tuckerman, Clinton J. Tuckerman. I got teased like crazy as a kid. You can imagine, with a name like Tuckerman, the things I was taunted with. Every day in the cafeteria, I heard, 'Hey, Clint! ... you wanna fuck this?' It was unrelenting. One day, I started working out, and over time the bigger I got. It only took one punch to knock old Sammy Grout out. It took me years to realize how he helped me and how I learned to defend myself and put others at ease. Take your time," he said, "you got a lot to think about."

My heart was still pounding as he lifted me back into the boat. "What do you want me to cook?" I asked as we roared across the lake, the mist spraying my face.

"EVERYTHING," he resounded as he put his arm around me, kissing the top of my forehead.

"This is going to take me a long time," I said as I looked back up to him.

"That is the plan," he said as he pulled the boat back into the *Center of Love Club* dock.

I tucked the ring into the pocket of my robe, letting it slide up and down on my finger, asking, "How could it be that he picked me?" We made our way back to the massage table, and my ring finger tried to get used to the feeling of the diamonds. "I need to get dressed and compose myself before I can massage you," I said to him. My legs felt like rubber as I ran back to the room and put my black underwear on. Tucking the ring into my cleavage, I ran back out to see Clinton.

As the oil warmed up in my hands, I found myself engulfed in his flesh. My hair lingered up his legs as the cannabis-infused *Muscle Ease* penetrated his skin. Wrapping the plastic sheet, I took out my pendulum and began checking his chakras. Each one spun large and wide as I made my way up to each energy center. In my mind, I was in a far-off place, with blue water surrounding me. I placed my hands at his Root Chakra and felt the energy rising from the souls of my feet. I closed my eyes again as flashes of light came in.

Clinton looked up at me and said, "That's why it is so important to not think of sad things, so when you see something that looks bad, imagine God's love surrounding it. That is one thing you can do to protect them. Second, you can always manifest good for them by wrapping your love around them. Show them that they matter, no matter what they say. However, love them anyway. Forgive the people that have wounded your soul and release yourself from the bondage only you hold."

I let his words roll around my head and when I found the words, I wanted to say: "For anyone who has ever wished me harm, I thank them for building me to be strong. Thank you to all the men and women that have helped me on my quest. I knew on a spiritual level that this was an incredible test, but could the planet learn to heal?"

"Revenge is not something we do out of love. Revenge is not what this world was made of. Just imagine if the word "Revenge" did not exist. No definition inside any disk, a little microorganism that causes a paradigm shift or a mutation if you wish. Just imagine the new blood coming in Charlotte, the Purple Blood of a spiritual revolution, free from bondage and original sin!" he continued.

"Now, that would be a book for *Harlequin*," I replied, as I gazed into his eyes, "doing everything wisely with the intention of doing no harm, that all your endeavors will land jobs to rise across this land, and to be the best President the world has ever seen," I said. "Damn, is that what I see?" I asked myself silently.

"Who is Clinton Tuckerman?" I asked as I stared back at him. Was I blowing into the future President, or what? As I looked across the water, I could see it as plain as day. The lights were flashing before our eyes as the bulletins came whizzing by.

"Oh my God, is he going to be the President?" I asked

myself. My eyes sent my senses into another realm, wherein I saw myself suddenly surrounded by seafood, fruits, and vegetables, virtually dancing in front of me. I saw shrimp scampi with spinach over a bed of fresh pasta in a white wine butter sauce in a large, well-appointed dining room with ornate chandeliers and yours truly, standing before cameras and lights flashing all around, dressed in an elegant white long gown.

I envisioned ravioli with a roasted red pepper and chunks of lobster in a champagne cream bath. I beheld diver scallops in a brown butter garlic infusion, sitting on a plate of grilled asparagus as it was handed to the chief of staff as I looked over at Jaxson. The more my hands lingered over his body, the more I saw crab meat stuffed inside a piece of sockeye salmon garnished with lemons and dill. My mouth was starting to water as I saw jumbo gulf shrimp and scallops over a bed of carrots and zucchini, as my signature Parmesan cream sauce was drizzled over the fresh tortellini, topped with a hint of Old Bay® and Cayenne pepper to taste.

As the wrap came off his body, the desert round took place. My hands massaged the oils into his heated flesh. I got up on the table and crouched in between his legs. My arms ran from his toes to the tip of his head as I danced around his soul, breathing all of him in, massaging his muscles, thoroughly aiming to please him. Then, I closed my eyes and whispered, "I will cook for you, my King."

I saw the chocolate mousse nestled into a bag, fashioned out of a blend of white and dark chocolate in a mound of whipped creme with a strawberry glaze wrapped around the plate. I saw a bottle of Johnny Walker Blue® poured into the cast iron pan, caramelized with butter and brown sugar with a hint of black pepper. The banana stood erect over a mound of vanilla bean ice cream beside a yellow sponge cake with a mango puree in a butter cream frosting garnished with fresh pansies. Are you seeing what I am seeing? I watched as the champagne poured into our flutes, with bubbles brimming up around the edges. The sweetness on his lips as I tasted the Purple Revolution Malt®, with barley and hops and a hint of cannabis bottled in Delaware.

The more I massaged him, the more food I cooked as I rolled my fingers down his back. My hands circled around his hips as I envisioned his meat in my culinary tryst. The more I massaged him, the more I felt drawn to the kitchen to create all the meals that were dancing in my head.

It was almost dusk as we finished our massages under the golden sunset as dinner made its way to the picnic table. The crackled skin of the honey-roasted quail made everyone moan in delight. Pearl onions, celery, and cranberries nestled in cornbread overflowed from the bird, covered with a savory herb-infused gravy as it slowly dripped down the roasted Navy potatoes with garlic, chives, and parsley. The fresh green beans with butter and heavy cream took me back to when I was cooking on Bean Street.

Away again to my memories of a child, wanting so badly to come back to camp again. I was a little nerdy girl who was in Camp Berra on Bear Pond as we walked back down the beach, his hand in mine. I began telling him about my upbringing.

"I would shuck peas with my great-grandparents along the side of the lake. There was this boy from *Camp Wekeela*. Man, how I remembered him! It is strange how I still remember this one dream. I was only about ten, and I dreamed that I swam from one side of the lake to the other. Right before the lilies. Right in front of where the mountain sits. I remembered seeing diamonds, rubies, emeralds, and pearls wrapped in shell shaped covering – almost like a wasp nest or like a beehive, but much smaller. Sometimes, it even reminds me of a shell I found walking along the ocean," I began.

"My grandparents lived in North Turner, Maine, just around the bend. I got to go to the Christian camp one summer with one of my friends. The lake used to have a nice park with paddle boats all about, called Bear Pond Amusement Park. It was my favorite place to be, with go-karts, a moon bounce, a water slide, and all kinds of games inside," I continued.

"That sounds nice," he said. "It sounds like the future site of my *Spiritual Retreat for Children*. You see, I had no children of my own, so I had to adopt a lot of kids, so I had a legacy to pass on," he continued. "Please know all past and future friends as he commanded the heaven with his hands; your children will always be in safe hands when you journey in my lands," he recited.

Looking up at him, I fully internalized that he was the man of my dreams. With tears falling down my face, I asked him what else he knew about me.

"I know that your mom died when you were eleven, and your father was an alcoholic who beat you a lot. If purple blood continues to run through my veins, "I will never let anything harm you again," he declared.

This is exactly what I heard as I blew my life force into his chest. I understood everything as I got down on my knees and kissed his feet. "I understand your legacy," I said as I looked up to him. "Who are you?" I asked.

"I am the future," he said as he looked up at the mountains in front of us. "I am the revolution of the mind, the new post-political paradigm shift, the leader of The Purple Party," he answered.

"What's that?" I asked, not even remotely understanding his answer.

"The Purple Party is about individual freedom and popular empowerment in the greater public interest," he said as he lifted me back up to him. "Once the American People fully realize how the two major parties are screwing us by selling us out to corporations, banks, special interests, fringe groups and foreign powers, they will flock to our ranks and drain the swamp at the headwaters, leaving them in the dust and relegating them to the dung heap of history without firing a single shot! It will happen when they discover their greatest latent political power – **the Power of Withdrawal.**

That is how they will finally break their chains and become the sovereign masters of their own destiny. They will be liberated by breaking their collective *authority addiction*." he concluded.

"Wouldn't that be something? It's definitely time for a real change – not the garbage the corrupt and inept establishment politicians serve up every two years," I said as I took his hand. "Woker than woke," I added, in the spirit of the moment.

"Precisely," he said, "Can you imagine a country no longer divided against itself, where we all get along?" he asked rhetorically.

"Oh man, can I," I replied, as I clung to his waist, "I would love to see that. It would be amazing," I said.

"You will, my dear, I promise you that," he said as he kissed the top of my head, "together, we shall usher in a new era of Freedom and Prosperity unparalleled in Human History."

"Priceless!" I replied, "sometimes I feel so foolish. I thought you were already the President when I breathed into your chest," I said.

"Ah ha, you can foresee future events, he said. Excellent! I knew I picked the right woman," he said as he twirled me around. "I promise that you won't regret it," he added as he put me down.

I saw a thousand tears in his eyes as he kissed my hand and hollered to Jaxson to drive the boat, as he strapped on the life jacket and put on a pair of water skis just as dessert was being spread out.

The fire pit was alive with Kennedy's stories as he thumped the drums of his chest through the night. Karissa came up to me while I was standing in the wake, watching Clinton as he skied across the lake.

"I have a request. I know this is your retreat, and we are supposed to be cooking for you, but I have a feeling I need to ask this," she said.

"What's up?" I asked, with a puzzled look on my face.

"You are being requested to be in the kitchen tomorrow. Kennedy just told me to give the sous chef the day off with pay and that you're up at bat," she informed me.

"It's Clinton, isn't it?" I said, looking up at her.

"I believe so," she said, looking over at Kennedy. "I wonder what these men are up to?" she asked as she watched Clinton doing tricks on the lake.

I looked over at Karissa and said, "If I don't cook tomorrow, I think it will be the biggest mistake of my career."

"I think your right," she replied.

We sat down over a cup of tea and began planning the menu with passion and intensity. Something told me that I had better cook like I had never cooked before. I headed off to the dorm room, where G'anacia and Nadia came up to me and asked what was going on.

"All I know is that I am being asked to cook tomorrow with Karissa," I replied. "Other than that, I have no idea what is happening. All I know is I better bring everything I've got," I said joyously.

Free Fall

Captain of the Free

How you risked it all for me

How loving was easy

Hiding behind jealousy

How did Neptune

Get to me

How did his staff

Penetrate me

How did the captain

Again find me

Hiding behind

A mulberry tree

Then, all of a sudden

In a blinding rage

You steered the vessel

Deep within my cave

Exploding deep inside of me

Flooding me with your mercy

Guiding me to safety

You take the wheel

One more time

You handle me from behind

Sending bolts of electricity

Penetrating with intensity

Thrusting your rod ferociously

Oh, how Clinton has captured me.

25

Feast Fit for A King

The aroma of the coffee was lingering through the morning mist with the bird songs in the air, and the cock-a-doodle-do call of the rooster clearly indicated that it was time to rise and shine. "Let's go!" Karissa exclaimed as she grabbed the keys to her Escalade® and hit the remote control.

I felt the black leather against my back with heat and cool options with a flick of a switch. "Damn! This one is hot," I said, relished in his seat. The sun had fully risen when we pulled into the driveway of a large white house. Around the back were fields of vegetable and cannabis plants, with tacks of beehives in between the limbs off in the distance. We watched as the workers harvested bushels of apples, plums, and peaches.

"This was like a dream," I thought as I went through the

rows of plants, seeing what was ready to be picked. I found several zucchinis and squash. Radishes were popping out of the earth's crust, and rows of flowers bordered all the crops.

"So, is this where all the people in recovery work?" I asked.

"Yes, it is," said Karissa, "We also have people who suffer from mental disabilities. They all work in different facilities. Therefore, cannabis was so important to our revolution," she continued.

"Wow, Karissa, I had no idea you guys do all of this," I said, "now, I understand what you are all doing." As the asparagus was still hiding in the rhubarb bush, I cut some, knowing that I was going to grill them. We bagged up our crops and headed back to *The Center of Love Club*.

The temperature for today was expected to reach 86 degrees, and for Maine, that is hot, let alone the humidity, when I happened to notice several black trucks parked around the back of the club and wondered what type of delivery they were expecting. I thought long and hard about what kind of impression I wanted to give and how I impishly knew that I would be a bad girl as the savory rolled out. Nothing, however, could have prepared me for what I was about to face as I walked into the kitchen and saw Salem standing at the sink. I look over to Karissa with an incredulous look on my face when she says, "it's not a competition without some heat." I look back at Karissa with a half-smile coming out of my mouth. Cake walk is all I thought when I began to lay my plans down. For now, breakfast is where I will make my start, with a drizzle of some fresh blueberry syrup for the pancakes and slices of ham in a maple glaze. I would like those "bud spuds" placed on a plate with farm-fresh eggs in an omelet with spinach, cooked in a buttery cannabis finish. I poured some warm water into a large silver bowl and sprinkled it with some sugar and yeast when I could not help but notice the offering that Salem had mounted on the plate. Seemingly from out of nowhere maple-infused sausage sizzled on the plate, a stack of 6 golden pancakes with fresh whipped butter sheepishly drizzled down her sides, nestled was a generous heaping of Aroostook County Potato Shreds with 6 slices of bacon hanging over the plate. Placed on top, not to be outdone, was pan-seared over medium duck eggs, and all I could imagine was dipping that bacon in her yoke when I realized Salem was not to be overlooked.

Twitching in my Jacket, intently reading with winking eyes, I refreshed the mugs and listened closely to the voice inside. I hear the buzzer go off for the sausage and egg bread. My eyes scanned every face as I walked back down the steps.

Clinton put my bread bloomer to the taste test. I noticed a hint of approval on his face as he and Kennedy talked about the next phase. The look in Clinton's eyes was intense when he put my bread up to his nose and said, "You got a lot to do if you want to win this race."

Away I turned as I climbed up the steps through the kitchen, where the next batch of dough was rising. I added more water, olive oil, and a sprinkling of salt. I chopped up some garlic, and rosemary and added it to the aromatic pot, along with the slurry of liquids in the silver bowl under my nose. I went to the refrigerator, found Orinoco Ramona, Parmesan Reggiano and grated a pile of it up. Tossing it into the emulsion along with some flour, adding more as I stirred the mound of sticky dough when I looked back up to what Salem had cooked up. On the counter was a batch of bubbling bread, and I knew it was sour dough that was dancing in her head.

The more I kneaded the bread, the more I envisioned my future ahead. I could now seriously picture myself in my own B&B. I could even see couples lining up to get married as they overlooked the scenery. The more my hands rolled in the dough, the more I could see the brides along the beach, with their veils blowing in the breeze.

I could see the line of little angels with flowers in their hair as they danced around the tables, sprinkling petals from the garden over the isle runner leading up to the stars. I could see one child with long, golden blond hair. Her smile shined radiantly as she tilted her head to the right, holding onto her bouquet with her eyes glancing upward with delight. Little wings fluttered in front of me as she danced away to her mommy. The bride was not quite ready to bloom as she looked from the window seat. The sounds of laughter as the boys and girls were beaming about, picking the flowers that bordered all the crops, when the clash of the frying pans brought me back to the center as I watched Salem add ricotta to a bowl, and that's when it hit me, she was copycatting each recipe I was cooking!

I poured more olive oil into the bowl and let the doughy ball of love rest. The towel was placed over it so that it stayed protected until fully risen, for about an hour or so in this kitchen. Then, I put the bowl under the window, where the morning sun was raising my grains. In my mind, I pictured the dough doubling in size before I took it out for a beating. Letting the green goddess of olive oil drip between my fingers.

I rolled the dough back and forth between my hands and slathered on more olive oil before rolling it out into a rectangular metal pan. Lovingly, I pressed my fingers through the outstretched dough, put it in the oven, and let it rise again, free from drafts about an hour or so once again.

If you would like to sprinkle a little more course sea salt – or better yet – pink Himalayan, please do so. (The little bee just landed on my keyboard to tell that to you.) I was so beyond pleased with what I made that I beamed my light on my dough for a few more gazes and sent my bread another dose of love as it was rising. In another hour, I will bake it in a preheated oven at 475 degrees Fahrenheit for 20 to 25 minutes. "Oh yeah, baby," I thought lovingly as I shut the oven door.

As I watched the guests receiving the day, the food I prepared was on the way. Lunch is where this girl starts to play. Did you think I was not aiming for your belly? All this is prepared for you my King, the one who has started this whole thing. The lunch of grilled cheese reminded me of lunch at my grandmother's place. However, I must do my own little twists; making grilled cheese fancy is one of my trysts.

The zucchini and squash were grilled to perfection and layered with fresh Mozzarella and pesto emulsion. Nestled in between that was Focaccia bread, pressed down in a panini press. The fresh tomatoes and garlic roasted on the hot fire, swirled together with some hot cream for the ride, laced with a basil sprig, and toasted Parmesan ring! Now that is grilled cheese and tomato soup to make the crowds sing. Or so I thought when Salem whizzed past me, her sourdough buns on the tray along with Ground Moose and Stag infused with garlic and caramelized onions with a side of potato wedges cocked in tallow, and I knew this girl was holding on as she gave Kennedy a wink.

It seems that Kennedy was high on my list. How did I manage to fall in love with him, Clinton, and Jaxson all in the same time frame? There is something about them all that has me wanting to please. I love a self-made man. In my mind, it is easy to see why the men I need are calling me.

Vivid thoughts of me massaging all of them at the same time flooded back in. My fingers reminded me of the love I will make as they raked the lake. They are all the objects of my eyes, and how I smiled when they caught me staring at them. This is where Clinton came in, his dark skin glowing around the lake and the water from the speed boat churning as I stood in his wake. Releasing the rope as his skis glide across the water, I have been longing for his eyes to gaze at me again, to touch him one more time, and to run my hands along his neck, wondering to myself, did I really impress him?

My arms opened, waiting to embrace him as he came right up to me. His kisses nearly drowned me as his body fell into me, igniting Salem's jealousy along the beach. I could feel Salem's eyes piercing through me as Clinton's kisses once again danced upon my yearning lips. Again, I was in another world as we walked up to the camp to get dressed, and the impending implications all danced in my head, knowing full well that Salem wanted my head.

"I know you are doing your very best," Clinton said as he helped me to get undressed.

It was all I could do not to succumb right there. His gentleness was enchanting as he toweled dried my hair. The way he slid the zipper up made me shudder, knowing he was going to fill my cup. To think of the political implications of what could be next was enough to keep my eyes on the prize as I got dressed.

A crack of his hand sent a shiver of tingles down my back as he smacked my ass. "You know, you like it like that," he said.

It was all I could do to not rip his bathing suit off and throw the future President on the bed. My legs shivered and shook as I knelt to put my black nylons and slinky dress on.

"Take three deep breaths," he told me, looking me directly in the eyes, "I know you are going to get this."

He must have heard my sighs and panting as my voice started to shake. With the laser look in his eyes, I knew what was next as he rapidly marched me to the kitchen, hollering, "Sign her up for the Write INN."

Gold Rush

As each explosion
Erupts in me
Flooding my bed
In liquid gold seas
Teasing me
With hopes of thee
This is what
It is all about
Learning how
To release
Without loosening
your belt
So buckle up
Your saddle
Things are
Bout to be told
How Glorious sex
Can be

When you get old

You learn that a man

Is a delicate Ming

That being hard

Is no big thing

It is the temptation

That brings me

Erupting on you

Teasing me

Not knowing what

He will do

My body exploding

With each little thrust

Tempting me with

Your sacral thrust

Alas,

I have rocked as much as I could

My body is limber

And it feels good

If these young

Knew what we did

The planet would have

A few less kids.

26
The Conductor in Me

Driving you into my glorious plan, I wrote all my best recipes in. I will cook a feast fit for Kings and Queens, princes, and princesses as I look out at the gathering crowds, knowing I am going to win this.

I am not Barbie with a skinny waist and will not starve you to make corporations look great on Wall Street. Love is defined when you are amassing grace. Lo, the Rose! The language of Love blossoms forth when you notice her making love as the moonflower ignites.

As I fluttered about the kitchen, it was the ravioli that kept calling for my attention. The Rosemary sang as it rose in the oven. A bowl of Ricotta and Parmesan cheese was begging me to whip them with some parsley. Add a pinch of salt and, "Oh my," as the eggs get a good whipping! "Put me in the fridge and let me sit for a bit. You have got some more thinking if you wanna win this."

The dilemma is, as my mind wants to taste that I feel traditional is good, but I am in the Lobster State. I will make a compromise to you instead, as Jaxson took me and said, "How about a naked tail on the bed?"

"I will sauté for you the spinach I picked. I have some red peppers that I can grill up," I said as I took the spatula out of his hand. "I will deliver a deal for you, my chief of staff," I continued as I rubbed his pork tenderloin down.

"How do you make food such a sexual lure?" asked Jaxson as I beat the flour some more.

"You see, my pretty, this is my last shot. Take it or leave it. I am busting up Salem's plot."

For the farm fresh eggs I gathered today, four eggs at a time are a good way, with a sprinkle of salt as I beat it with a fork. I sprinkled 1/2 cup of flour each time, and then I beat it some more. (I added enough flour until the dough forms a ball, about four cups of flour in all). I kept kneading my dough with all the love that I have, and I want you to taste the years I have.

Recalling this one from my grandmother and placing the crustaceans in the pot, I set the timer for 15 minutes, boiled, and let them cool for a few minutes. Peel away the shell, with a crack of its back. (Sorry, we do not mean to do you like that.) Slide down the little flap and discard the trails in the center of its tail. Break its claws with a cracker and pull out the meat in chunky size bites, as we are not trying to starve you tonight. The pasta dough is ready at last, so pull a chunk off about as big as your hand. Roll it around in your palms and dust some more flour on the *Center of Love Club* Island.

Flatten it out with your fingers while you dream of the plan. Smiling as I grab the rolling pin. Roll each ball in your hand from tip to tail as the wood of the pin stretches to make the dough trail.

Pliability is the key each time you flip. Soon, as you have it less than 1/8 of an inch thick, dollop in a spoonful of the sweet ricotta mix dotted along the seam in an egg wash dream, pinching the edges to keep them from opening. Boil in water for a couple of minutes, then spoon the lobster bisque over for the finish.

"Do not forget the Chief of Staff is gluten intolerant," Karissa reminded me as she handed me a plate to finish.

A grilled portabella sat in the center of the dish while my fingers trembled, knowing I was cooking dinner for the future President! Ladling a pinch of sautéed spinach, I placed the naked lobster tail in the center and finished it with a purple orchid as I blew him some kisses, a potful for the POTUS.

There she comes as she walks down the steps, Salem holding a plate with butternut ravioli with pan-seared scallops in a brown butter reduction as she placed it down in front of Clinton, glancing back at me as her left lip curled up as she toyed with me. I stood there listening as the crowd moaned over her dish and knew in my heart there was no way I was going to win this. I did my best to get her out of my head. As I made my way back to the kitchen, I overheard Karissa scolding Kennedy. "You need to watch your numbers, your diabetic darling, and I do not want you spiking," said Karissa, as she caught him sneaking a cannabis-infused cookie off the tray. I took another deep breath as I wrapped my hands around the stove, knowing this was my last attempt at beating Salem, when I opened the jar labeled maple syrup and placed it on a low-heat burner.

The maple (my God, your bad little boy) was asking me to tap your tree some more. Boil your syrup until it gets an amber pale and drizzle with caramelized cannabis infused walnuts, if you dare. Let the cream and maple simmer on the stove until the vanilla pod is ready to explode. Lace it all with some Pineapple Fields Purple Kush inside a maple pecan butter cookie. This is the goodness that will get your feathers fluffed

– the maple vanilla bean ice cream dream with a rush! Finally, sprinkled some cannabis candied walnuts on top when I glanced over at Salem's plating a chocolate sponge cake with whipped cream and raspberries, and it was at that moment that I knew I still had a chance.

All of this was being prepared as we rushed around the floor, pouring our hearts out to the judges once more. Of all the things we love to do, cooking for you is nothing new I have given you everything I have. This is the real me, holding nothing back as I make my way out to the picnic table, gleaming with pride as homegrown love is nestled inside.

This is what I am sending, the plate of love I am making for you. I placed it down in front of Clinton's face, waiting for his approval as he started to taste. I watched closely as his fork went down, paying particular attention as his jaw churned around. Just then, you could hear lids and pans clanking and hollering coming out of the kitchen as Karissa's voice bellowed out, "Salem, what are you doing?"

"This is good," Clinton said, looking up into my eyes.

"I know, I made it," I replied, smiling back as I bit my lip.

"Damn, woman, how do you do it?" he asked with a smile, "come on over here and sit on my lap; I want to feed you some of that."

Savoring the moment, I walked over to Clinton as he opened his legs to me, motioning for me to sit down on his lap while I watched Salem run out of the kitchen, figuring she was infuriated with my win! I felt his arm wrap around my waist as he whispered inquisitively in my ear, "Did you do all of this for me?".

I laughed, "You could read me like that? I am not done with you yet," as my fingers began to massage his neck, "I've got more for you." I whispered into his ear, "You haven't seen anything yet!"

"You got more?" he asked.

"Of course, I got more," I replied, as I looked into his eyes. "I hope you feel the love I have put inside, and I can't wait to go on to the next phase, as I have a big plan and it took a lot for this to bake," I stated.

For a moment, I envisioned that the men started falling to their knees, with diamond rings flashing before me, all yelling "Pick me, pick me!"

I eyed Clinton up and down and asked, "Are you satisfied with that, Mr. Investor, I presume?"

"You cannot top that" as he winked at me.

"You wanna bet?" I replied. I pulled the ring out of my breast, letting it sit in my hand, still thinking about it, as I gave him a wink. Karissa brought Salem down to the crowd in front of the judges and asked, "who won?" The tension was so thick that I could feel my heart beat out of my chest when Clinton turned to Karissa and said Charlotte Bennett. Thank Goodness for that, I just caught Salem cheating, that's what all those black trucks were here for, she didn't cook a thing, she hired a caterer and tried to pass it all off as her own! You mean I won fair and square as the votes came in and the tally was done. Clinton took my hand and said, not only did you beat Salem, but you also beat the catering company she hired to rob you of the win. I looked back over to Salem as her green eyes burned with rage, "Thank you for putting me up to the test, I forgive you for everything you did to take me down, you were one heck of a threat, but I really got you on this," I said, as I walked away, blowing her a kiss. Taking Clintons hand as we danced on the beach. I knew you could beat her Charlotte, if you were given half the chance.

27
The Secret to A Woman's Heart

Kennedy walked out to the barn with a bucket of warm water in hand, to where his "mistress" was waiting for him. He pulled back the linen, revealing her tresses as he pulled her slip down. Through his eyes, I could see her headlights pointing up at me, beckoning me to wash her with him, and I virtually felt that I was there.

It was as if I was hiding inside him, looking at her through his eyes, like a thief in the night, bending towards the light, I was all the way in Kennedy's body this time. Throwing her dress on the shelf, we competed for who would command the hand. We compromised and put both our fingers in, running over her Gold Crown shining in the dim light of the barn, as our hands lingered upon the cool metal of her back.

She was more than ready for us as Kennedy slid in,

buckling up for the ride. Her high beams were blinding, fingers fluttering like a feather duster on hemp oil racing, bending down for the tasting. The further the hood came up into the air, the more I saw her true brilliance. Her chrome valve covers screamed for me to look at them and give them a good polishing.

Reaching down, I slipped my right index finger in a come-hither motion and stuck my digit in all the way in. Pulling the long rod out, I ran my fingers up and down its shaft, rubbing the sticky oil in between my fingertips. Excited that the oil was looking good, I poked the dipstick one more time and pulled it back out, wiping it with my hand before I slid it back in again.

Kennedy stood there massaging his head, wondering if he should take her down to Charlotte or to the back shed. The snowflake wheels with the Firebird® symbol beckoned me to take her for a spin.

"No, a car is like a woman. She might look like a classic — and trust me, she is, but deep down, she has the desire to shed that classic rating and go for the bad girl title once again. The 1979 Trans Am® begged me to bring her back to life. She was tired of Sunday drives and runs for ice cream and needed a party that she could really sink her teeth into. With her legacy once so strong when she raced the countryside for the

American People, delivering Coors® Beer to the dry counties, the same adventurous girl clamored to get her slicks back on the open road again.

Taking a leather pelt and beating it against her fender, making it soft, I dropped it in the bucket, swirling the soapy water into a nice lather. I hated like hell to squirt her with cold water from the hose, but I loved how her headlights shined when I did. Starting at the roof, I gently let the water flow over her. In my mind, she was like my own wife, standing under the shower as the water washed over her headlamps down to the ground. I took my clothes and began washing her mound. The more my hands rolled over her body, the more she shined.

Her legs and arms transformed into wheels as they shook under my touch. The warm soapy water in the bucket was a gift, massaging the lather into her veneer. Taking time to make sure I did not waste a drop. I took the chamois out of the tube and ran her down. The water soaked up as it wicked into the material. As I wiped her back end, I could not help but slap the hide up against her. I pulled the wax off the shelf and dabbed a bit into my fingers, working it into her flesh. Inch by inch, I rubbed the *Cannabis Wonder Lube* into her until she was fully wet.

I ran my hands along her flesh and really put some muscle

into it. The shine came through as the overhead light beamed down on her. The more I used my arms to polish, sliding back and forth, the happier she was, and I heard her roaring. The more I saw her potential, the more her beauty shined forth. I worked for hours, pumping her good and hard with my hands making her purr. My reflection was caught in the mirror as I bounced off her glistening hood. I kissed her emblem one last time, running my tongue down the arrow for good luck and could not wait to hit her rosebud.

I got the can of window cleaner out, spraying her glass. Reveling in her interior, her engine roaring on my head! Oh, the golden Firebird® as it strives to come back to life, begging me to put my keys in her ignition, and fire her up, just to taste her emissions.

Opening her up, I slipped into her seat. Her flesh was warm against my skin. I sprayed my sweet creamy *Rub Away*® cannabis-based cleaner on her. Her dashboard reminded me of the wrinkles and stretch marks of my wife. The reminder of the war that her body went through to give me everything I liked.

I went back to the drawing table and mixed the materials together until I had a nice gel between my fingers. Using the entire contents of the blue bottle, I spread my lubricant into her cracks. As the emulsion was absorbed in her flesh, I saw the lines clearing up. As I massaged my love into her, she was a lot smoother, I thought to myself as I wiped the rest of the emulsions off.

I took out the vinyl conditioner and sprayed my sheath first. A natural spray-on lubricant that acts as a barrier before I rubbed her back seats down. Sitting behind her bucket seat, I rubbed my hands along her sides as I reached around to the front seat, pulling on her knob. I went back to her rear, running my hands over her spoiler, until I felt her rose bud and twisted the cap off. It turned me on as I sniffed her rear end one more time. With the smell of the hemp blend, my motor has never been happier.

"Oh yeah, you gotta check her from behind before you slam her into gear," I heard a voice bellow through the barn. I crouched down, not realizing someone else was in there. I watched from the ground as his leather boots walked towards the back. All I could see was the dark jeans as he walked closer to me.

"You might need to add a mileage blast to that ass," I heard his voice again. I jumped to my feet to see a man standing out in front of me in his Wrangler® jeans, still as slim now as they were back then. With his hat on his head, he made his way in.

His fingers ran along her sides as he eyed her up and down.

"Is she ready?" he asked.

I tossed him the keys and said, "Fire her up." I poured the fresh hemp blend down her fuel port and locked the gas cap. I open the door of the passenger seat as my dream comes to life.

He rubbed the wheel with his hands and began purring to her. I was a bit jealous as I watched how his fingers caressed her. I could feel it as he pumped the gas and turned on the ignition, ramming her good and hard.

"Come on, baby, I know you can do it," he cooed. He continued turning the ignition over with his right hand as exhaust sputtered out her back end.

This time, she fired up without hesitation as the Golden Phoenix screamed back to life. The engine shook the whole carriage as her gasses ran through the tailpipe. I almost exploded in my jeans as the legend looked over at me and asked, "You think you got what it takes to do this?"

I looked over at him and asked, "You feel like getting some chowder?" Our eyes grew wild with fire as he slammed her into gear. She roared back to life, dual exhaust blasting with the petal to the floor, leaving nothing but clouds of smoke in her wake.

As the Golden Goddess came tearing out of the barn with her end swaying in the breeze, I saw my beautiful wife walking out the back door with a large bag of goodies. The 1979 Trans Am® screaming around the bend, my strawberry temptress tossing me her hard candy cannabis infusions. Looking over at the racing legend to my left, I said, "South Carolina's not legal yet, wanna do a Cannabis Run?" The legend hit the gas, leaving nothing but clouds of smoke in the rear-view mirror!

28
Let the Games Begin

I have never eaten a piece of candy like that before, but by just looking at his face, you can tell he would be the most delicious thing you will ever eat. He is the appetizer, Insalata, Zuppa, Intermezzo, Entrée course kind of man. You know all of this before he even brings his selection of desserts for you to sample. But it's the sound of the crack of the spoon as it hits the doughnut that has your cream leaking out of the bag long before he even begins to top you with his whipped cream dream. It is like nothing you have ever seen…until I caught myself in the reflection. My long curly locks framed down my shoulders as gold rained down on my flesh.

The scent of Jasmine and lavender permeates my skin. My body glowing as the fire encapsulates my soul. The Roar of the Phoenix comes to life. Wings of Fire burst through my back, exploding in a million different directions. Black Feathers cascading down the edges of sheer panels of crimson and gold. Red Talons firmly clasped around The Crooked Spoon as a sly smile escapes. Ever so slowly, biting my bottom lip as I look him up and down. With a twinkle of my eye, smiling, I say, "Turn around, and bend over." It was the sound of the Crooked Spoon whirling through the air, the first gasp that nearly made me collapse as the excitement welled I mouthed, "Not so fast." Grabbing the bull by the horns, I threw the President on the bed. The music "Wrapped Around Your Finger" by the Police rang out in my head. I massaged his head as I pulled off his tie. "I'm the Queen of this castle, and I'll lay my money down, you think you can win me with this six karat crown? If you think you can overrun me, I will wager one last bet. I venture my bottom dollar I'm the best Dominant you've ever met."

"Dancing up your legs, as the ropes come tangling down, tie you up, I will, take you round and round. Think this is exciting, as my rhinestones dig into you? I will show you, my darling, a thing or two. I can play, too, been tested, taught by the best. Nailing you to my poster bed in my black lace best. You think you can handle my ass yet?" As the whipped cream from my Banana Foster dream licks you up and down, sending a shiver straight to your crown. My hands lingered down as I reached for the nuts. How I watched you shake with glee. I see how you want me, licking your lips as the cannabis honey wine drips down your chin. Your staff rockets up to orbit, sending waves of electric currents. How have you been teasing me inside my sheets? A flurry of wishes blew over me. How about a cannabis chocolate ganache? You wanted a mask for your rocket ship that would cause a blast. I lathered my cocoa all over his mast, wagering my own bet. The dandelion is good for you. It is bitter, no doubt, so disguise her in an endive dress, crisp bacon, and some sugar beets. That is how you will get your love to meet. I will teach you how to make the men crawl, show you how to make love to them all. Slurping out of your cup, they will, as everyone loves a good meal. Just like that, he was down on his knee, "Marry me, Charlotte," as he slipped on the ring. I will marry this man as I watched him dance around the stove. "Pack your bags. You're coming with me." as his tongue slid down my left index finger. Pounding his meat into my flour until I screamed, "Yes! Yes! Yes!" The decision was instantaneously made as we leaped to wed, grabbing his phone, making the call to fire up the jet. Now, I saw clearly that my dream was reality as I pulled his ham hock out of the collard greens. His craft now dangling his plantation in front of me. Oh my God, who could this be? How did this man get hold of me? Charming me with his southern hospitality? I watched as he took command, firing off orders as Jaxson emerged from the back of the plane. "Who was that pilot?" I asked as his aviator shades reflected on me.

"That is Captain WilKatta. We call him 'The Wild Kat.'" My jaw dropped as I looked into his eyes, "Welcome to The Center of Love Club, Charlotte Bennett, are you ready for the time of your life?

The Master's Plan

There is healing in the tonic

As her elixir comes flowing In

Shuddering as each Spasm

Releases from within

I never believed

I could have

Such a feeling

Calling me open

Cannabis is Healing

A gateway to release

Of Infinite possibility

I cannot help but tell

What your leaves did for me

Giving me my life back

Healing me from me

You see it was my mind

Clouded with the lies

Unable to tell the difference

Between truth and lies

Now I see how your rivers flow

Felt it in me as the energy arose

The Spirit that swells in me

To free you of the myth of Sin

I would not have ever known

Had I not taken the chance to win

What a gift I was given

In that dance

Now, wonder they prohibited it

The Cannabis Plants.

THE END

Is Only

The Beginning

Proudly Made in Delaware!

About The Authors

Kathy DeMatteis spent her career as a massage therapist and esthetician. Over the years of her practice, she began to make the massage oils and soaps that have adorned the pages above. Her desire to see her products manufactured in a way that served the special needs of the community is something that drove her to write this story.

It was not about the money -- it was about the meaningful jobs that could be created. Knowing full well that her visions of a cannabis-infused alternative healing resort were in the future, she felt the best way to tell the story and generate awareness was through a book story. Plagued with her own emotional issues she crafted her story to not only heal herself of her insecurities but to share it in a way that could benefit any other reader by helping them to identify with the character, which is why she is writing from the first-person singular point of view. She wanted you to feel empowered as you journey with her. She wanted you to release your emotions in a safe way from the comfort of your own bed.

Her burning desire to help the world heal is something she backed up when she ran for Governor of Delaware as an Independent in the spring of 2020 during the pandemic as an innovative alternative to closed-loop special interest politics as usual in the First State. Her desire to implement alternative healing modalities in conjunction with medical modalities is at the crux of all she does. Having spent her career studying plants and their health benefits, the use of mindful meditation and positive affirmations, she has focused her life on service to Humanity.

Kathy wrote this book with the help of her husband, Conrad DeMatteis.

In her own words:

"For without him, there would be no *Center of Love*. The *Center of Love* we created for ourselves to have the life that we wanted to live. We have found that what we did has created a bond between the both of us that has made us stronger as a couple. Without these modalities, I doubt we would have survived the last few years that were spent creating, marketing, and advertising our way of life. We have been able to withstand the rigors of homelessness as we traveled the country, bringing awareness to our brand. Many couples, when faced with a mid-life crisis, often walk away from marriages. I knew I was changing. The love I have for my husband was something I knew was fragile. To try and keep my marriage and move forward with him was something I spent a great deal of time working on. I came from a failed marriage, and in no way did I want another one. Especially to find myself.

At the time of this printing, this is the third and final edition of *The Stimulus Package*. So much of what I wrote came true that it overwhelmed me. If, for some reason, ALL the plans that I have tucked inside this book never come true, at least I know that I healed myself enough to have the courage to see it through as of right now, much of what I wrote has come true. In fact, so much was true that I took the book out of print; it blew my own mind. Most of you will only see this as a story, and that's the best way, for it is way too complicated to try and explain to each person the relevance inside. I know as well the many people who I unknowingly delivered messages too. For me, this book proved to me my abilities as a psychic medium.

Time can only tell what will happen. I have done the best I could with what I have had to work with. The rest is up to God."